ETERNAL RIVER

For James + Vickie Long, family + friends,
Remembering All of the good
in our lives with gratitude —
Very best,
Thomas G. Young

THOMAS G. YOUNG

Middleton, WI
March 11, 2018

ISBN: 1466356855
ISBN-13: 9781466356856
Printed by CreateSpace, an Amazon.com company

For Lynne

CHAPTER ONE

My glass is full, and now my glass is run,
And now I live, and now my life is done.

-Chidiock Tichborne

"It looks like a drinker's walk to me," said Hefty, who loomed in the front doorway of his rustic tavern. A jovial smile creased his broad face as he welcomed the first Friday afternoon customers.

"Come on in, boys. What'll it be?"

"Beers all around, on me," said James. "Right, guys? And we aren't boys, Hefty. Save that for the college kids." No one contradicted him.

The Riverton tavern was dark as a cave, and the three young men sat blinking as their eyes adjusted. Hefty, now a man of action, promptly served up three foaming mugs of cold beer. The men drank quietly, finishing nearly half of their beers before James got around to paying for them.

"Damn if that first one don't go down good," said the tall one. "Don't they always taste better on Friday after work?" They raised their mugs in unison, and nodded their agreement.

"It's going to be a short session for me tonight," said James, feeling a tinge of guilt. "That's why I'm buying the first round. My girlfriend is having a little party for me. I promised I'd be home by six."

"What's the occasion?" Hefty raised a quizzical eyebrow while sorting change into the register.

"Birthday," said James, evading Hefty's curious gaze.

"No kidding? Yours?"

"You got it."

His fellow workers laughed. "Don't push him on it, Hefty. He's finally legal in here. Number eighteen. Eighteen big ones, right Jamie boy?"

"James to you, big mouth. Big deal. So I'm the last guy here to join the club. At least I'm not gray or fat like a few people I know."

Hefty winced and brought over a shot of brandy, which he deftly slid up against James's mug of beer. "Have a legal drink on the house."

To the cheers of his two factory friends, James threw back his head and downed the brandy chaser in one gulp.

• • •

Suppertime had come and gone. James found himself reluctantly following the river path he could walk with his eyes closed, drunk or sober. He wished it were some other guy's birthday, and that he could have stayed for a few more rounds. When he came around the bend to the apartment building, James saw a familiar figure. His first apprehensive thought was to tell her how attractive she looked, with her brown hair blowing in the wind.

Her best dress, too, he thought. The periwinkle blue one. He tried to read what was in her eyes.

"Where've you been, James? I've been waiting with our food for over an hour. Your parents and brother stopped by, and finally left. What was I supposed to tell them?"

He tried to grin, and said something about a pipe breaking at the plant.

"I checked at the plant with Doris," she said without smiling. "Anyway, happy birthday, Jamie."

"I had to leave to check on some parts." Then James turned away from her face to hide his alcohol breath. "Sorry to keep you waiting, Bethany. I really am. Hey, c'mon. Let's get to the food."

They walked to a picnic table not far from the wide river, which ran close to their apartment building. James squeezed

Bethany around the waist, pulled her into a half embrace, and kissed her partly on the lips, mainly on her cheek.

She pushed away. "How many beers, James? You promised."

"Ah, honey, just a couple with the guys. I mean, it's my birthday, isn't it?" He grinned at her, and Bethany returned a half smile.

"I've already put the cake and stuff on the table, but I'm afraid it's gotten too windy. If only you'd made it at six, or even six-thirty."

She pouted attractively through a slight overbite, and he gave her a playful swat.

"Stop that. Let's get to the table, if you can still walk a straight line."

James stiffened with anger. His reaction was as predictable as sunset. He went quiet. Even after she sang "Happy Birthday" his sullen silence remained unbroken. He realized they were at it again. He turned to face Bethany, who was cutting the cake. Their angry words broke forth like thunder.

An impulse flashed to throw the cake, but he checked that idea. He thought, That's what my dad did once, when my brother and I were kids. He threw mom's cake over the fence to the chickens. I'm not my old man. Still, he and Bethany glared at one another, and he felt as useless to change things as when his folks fought. I love her, but she sure doesn't understand me, he thought. He stalked away to keep from fighting with her. James glanced back to see her walking toward the apartment building with their picnic basket. He sighed a deep sigh, and headed back to the tavern.

• • •

He felt dejected and alone at the bar that had pulled him in again like a magnet. He poured down beers followed by shots of brandy. A wayward strand of dark hair hung across his forehead, while he stared into the bottomless schooner of beer.

James heard Hefty yell, "Hey!" at him from down the counter, and James stared back as the bar manager mopped up nameless spills. "Birthday party over already?"

James continued to glare at him. Hefty shrugged, picking up an oversized glass for a refill. When he returned, James had drifted once again, shaking his head at nothing and no one, fingering the small brandy glass. He usually drank beer without the chaser, but tonight it tasted mellow.

"Eighteen isn't the end of the world, you know. I didn't start getting the right view or really enjoying myself until I hit eighteen," said Hefty. "Why you might say that's when childhood gives way to manhood. Know what I mean?"

"Tell me about it. My girlfriend is pissed at me. I hate my stinking job. She wants a house of her own someday, and I couldn't get close to a down payment, even if we got married. We can't afford crap. If you think ten years in this town is childhood, you're—"

"Nah. I know. I don't mean it that way. I just mean in your teens you get a notion of what you can and can't do in this world. It's time to explore. So you find out what you don't want or what you can't have. You find out life's no bed of roses. But that doesn't mean things can't change for the better. Here, James. Have one on me."

· · ·

An hour before closing time, James pestered Hefty for a final pitcher of beer to take outside, which was against house rules.

"If you weren't the birthday boy," said Hefty, "I'd already have bounced you out the front door."

A muscular, tan-faced fellow worker staggered up to James. "Where's that good-looking little gal of yours? If I had me someone put together that good I'd be with her right now, not sitting here getting smashed."

James struck him in the stomach so quickly that the man collapsed more from surprise than force.

"Get your foul mouth away from me!" said James. "You keep that creep away from me, Hefty, or I'll bash his head!"

"Boy, some guys can't hold their drinks," said the dazed man, getting up from the floor. "See if I buy you a round again."

As he backed away and turned to leave, James threw a bottle after him that splattered against a light fixture.

"Hey, that's about enough, fellow. James, you hear me? That's it. Drink up."

"Ah, c'mon Hefty. That bastard's been asking for it all night. Like what he just said about Bethany. Did you hear him? Tell you what. Give me that pitcher. Fix me up that pitcher and I'll take off."

"Negative. Drink up and sleep it off." The normally affable Hefty turned grim.

"I gotta pee."

"Be my guest. Think you can find your way to the can?"

Inside the men's room ten minutes later, James was leaning against the sink and talking to himself when he glimpsed Hefty's reflection in the mirror above the sink. James looked at his own reflected image and said for Hefty's benefit, "What the hell are you doing this for? Why? What's the sense? You stupid jerk!" he said looking at himself in the mirror. He paused, forgetting for a moment that Hefty was behind him. "Someone ought to bust your face," said James, searching the reflection of his own troubled eyes. James turned and once again saw Hefty's angry face.

"That's it," said Hefty. "Get out!"

"One beer for the road?"

"Negative." Hefty was in no mood to negotiate. He firmly escorted James to the front door. As Hefty glanced back at the bar, James grabbed a nearly full pitcher of beer from an unoccupied table. Hefty yelled as James tucked it under his arm, clumsily trying to keep it from the bar manager's sight. James failed to hide it, but he won the race through the front door.

"Sleep it off!" he bellowed after James, probably hating to lose a regular customer. "Sleep it off before you get into real trouble!" James and Hefty stood some thirty feet apart, silently staring at one another. Then James heard the big man sputtering as he shut the door and went back to work. Only then did he feel a twinge of remorse for having stolen the pitcher. But, he mused to himself, Hefty would have just poured it out, and I can always take back the empty or buy him a new one.

• • •

5

James paused a ways up the street from Hefty's tavern, swaying in the cool night air. Now he laughed at his light-fingered larceny. Taking a deep swallow of slightly warm brew he staggered, then headed for the river. As fuzzy-headed as he was, James still knew the exact place he would finish it off—the old swimming hole downstream from Riverton's bridge.

When he finally lurched onto the deserted beach, his pitcher was nearly empty. The boats. Gotta get me a boat. Where's my shoe? Crawling across the damp sand, he dimly realized both shoes were gone. Where's me boat?

A misty evening fog had come up the river, and James rubbed his eyes to see better. He stumbled and banged his shin against a small fishing vessel that was beached for the night. The pitcher dropped and James swore. He watched through glazed eyes as the last drops of golden liquid trickled into thirsty sand. James hurled the empty pitcher as far out into the river as he could. A muted splash reached his ears.

"Bad night, lad?" a voice asked from upstream shadows.

James wheeled abruptly as a small figure came out from the shallows. Rubbing his eyes again, James beheld the ghostly white face of a middle-aged man peering at him from atop a child's body.

"Don't know you," said James. "You fishing? That your boat?"

He saw the little man held a line that ran out into the river, and his curiosity quelled an initial touch of fear.

"Might say that, but it is not true," said the little man in clipped words.

James saw part of his face beneath a pointed cap, and it was chalky white. The line was being pulled, hand over hand, until a green jug was lifted, dripping water. It was carefully uncorked, and the stranger sipped.

James watched, then said, "I'm out of brew. Share?" He pointed to the jug.

"You might not want this," said the little man with a sad smile and a tone of caution. "Why do you drink?"

A deep laugh welled up in James. "To get away. To forget. To be free . . ." His voice trailed off when the stranger chuckled.

"I can't say about free, but this does get you away."

"What is it? Strong?"

"Yes. My people called it green port. I call it green death."

James reached out, but as the man released his cool treasure he shook his head and said to James, "Caution, lad."

"Packs a wallop, does it?" asked James.

"More than that, I would say. It goes up for some, and down for all. Truly has a downside."

To James his tone ran like a sad melody, but he was already drinking deeply. It burned going down, and then left a sweet aftertaste. He drank again.

"Easy, lad. You are not used to drinking green death. You won't even remember drinking it."

He ignored the warning of the little man who quietly observed him drinking. For some minutes James sought to drink it dry, hoping the pale stranger would not demand its return.

Then for some moments James felt nauseous. He could no longer see the little man. The tree outlines behind him began to circle, and waves of dizziness swept over him. A growing paralysis engulfed his senses.

The circling trees merged with foggy darkness like sentries swallowed by night.

CHAPTER TWO

Tote that barge! Lift that bale!
Get a little drunk, and you
land in jail.

-Oscar Hammerstein

James couldn't remember when he first realized that he was adrift on the river as he struggled with dreams. At first, he was only half-conscious and felt strangely reluctant to awake to an unknown day. A dreary, oppressive mist hung in the air. The lazy rocking of the boat was soothing, and it lulled him.

For a long time he heard no sound except a buzzing in his ears, which kept him from falling asleep again. He thought he saw shrouded outlines of trees, limbs moving eerily in dripping fog, and nameless fear began to nag his consciousness. He knew he was in a boat, and he suspected it was drifting.

Again he closed his eyes and tried to lull the fear with dozing, but it refused to release him. Something was oddly uncomfortable. At times his body felt very large, then very small. Although his senses begged for sleep, at last he knew he had to move and look.

James saw he was adrift in the middle of the river. The valley seemed vaguely familiar, yet he could discern no precise landmarks. He felt anxious about being late for work, and then remembered it was the weekend. Relief was short-lived. He recalled the stupid fight with Bethany that preceded his binge. He groaned.

His head hurt, his eyes felt dry, and his growling stomach felt like a rotted log soaked in salt. He was very thirsty. James dreaded facing a Saturday hangover destined to carry itself over into a bleak Sunday.

Through narrowed eyelids he watched a hostile, red sun which barely burned through the morning's shroud of fog and haze. He rose to one knee, groaning again. James stared into the mist and it dawned on him what felt so odd about the place: there was neither sight nor sound of anything living, not even birds.

There should be farms along here, he thought in mild alarm. There, that's farmland—isn't it?

James lay back in the boat, and tried to think clearly. Instead, with little effort he saw the bar, the rows of bottles, laughing faces, even Hefty setting him up with another beer and brandy. He gagged. The last blurry image was of throwing his empty beer pitcher—stolen from Hefty's bar—into the river's blackness.

What happened then? How far have I drifted? Bethany is going to be madder than hell!

James shuddered at the thought of fighting both her and a vile hangover. It had happened before. It had also led to moving out of his parents' house.

Time slipped away almost unnoticed as James struggled with the task of trying to paddle without oars. Gradually he worked his way out of the powerful main current into quieter water that felt unexpectedly warm. Moving slowly toward the closest shore, he was surprised to find that what he thought to be farmland was not farmland at all.

Sparse, dismal forest came into view, and it populated a swampy wilderness rather than the orderly cropland and pasture James knew surrounded Riverton. The air hung like a stifling tropical presence.

Something's very wrong, he thought, as he fought against panic.

The shore appeared too soft to support his weight. In places it oozed like dark pie filling, and all he could see was more swamp for at least fifty yards. Then the fog swallowed the pitiful trees which clung precariously to soggy half-land.

I've gone way too far downstream! Damn it! Got to try the other shore.

He started to paddle with his hands again, heading back into the river's current. James realized this would carry him even farther from his Riverton home. How far behind him that was, he wished he knew. When at length he found quiet water on the other side of the river, his hands dug into weeds and a green slimy material in the warm, soupy water. He gagged.

James took several quick breaths and drifted to a stop. He held his face in shaking hands as he tried to think straight and to make sense of what had happened to him.

Why in hell couldn't the boat have been tied or beached right? I could've sunk in this damned tub and drowned. Although its green paint needed touching up, James was satisfied the vessel was dry and shipshape.

When he looked to shore again, the outline of a large tree beckoned so he renewed his struggle despite the weeds. From under a sweaty brow James looked again at a seven-foot branch growing out from the base of the tree. If he could reach that he could pull himself onto dry land. Even though he knew it would place him on the wrong side of the river from town, he yearned for solid footing.

The large lower branch began to look more like enormous vines, intertwined, with the nearest one spreading out over a mossy bank. It seemed to move, and James felt more uneasy. He wondered if it was strong enough to pull on. Then, when the boat grudgingly got within a dozen feet he saw the vines moving towards him.

Snakes! Two snakes! Oh, God, there's more snakes than that!

For a terrifying moment only his pulse escaped paralysis. Oblivious to a sore shin and bruised knees, he pivoted in panic, digging into slimy water, paddling with his eyes closed. An agonizing minute passed before James dared glance back to see them writhing—ugly, sleek, and vigorously come to life. Others appeared, slithering over one another, spilling from the bank into the tepid water.

Damn!

He clawed for the current, refusing to look back again, paddling, paddling, and silently cursing his bad luck. Feverish imagination helped his arms and hands propel the rowboat.

He finally dared turn his head, and the fog had closed in again, concealing whatever danger—real or imagined—threatened him. Farther ahead, left and right, he searched for something safe and solid. Nothing looked good.

Staying with the current, he thanked fortune he'd not abandoned the boat and tried swimming as he'd had an impulse to do earlier. The mere thought of drowning in slimy, snake-infested water was almost more than he could bear.

Out of the corner of his eye, James saw a thick river root moving behind him. Or is it? He was unsure of his own judgment. Its outline suggested a huge, floating root, and then he visualized the earlier mass of snakes. It was as if they had somehow combined to pursue him.

Or is this in my mind? Am I going crazy? Can anything be that size, look like that, and actually swim in the river?

He shuddered involuntarily as images of an immense river serpent with glittering yellow eyes and darting tongue became too vivid.

He didn't dare look back. Uncanny currents or not, they carried him away from fear's mindless panic. Distance was all he craved. His legs stopped hurting and his arms were no longer tired. He stopped thinking about his stomach and head. He dug deeply into the warm water, pulling the boat faster and farther. He neglected the shores and did not yearn for land. James wished only to escape the nameless dread behind him, lurking in the fog.

To that end he applied all his will and strength. The old boat moved faster than he'd thought possible, and that was all he cared about.

From the sun's position, James calculated he'd paddled and drifted into afternoon. Only then did he permit himself to doze. He was determined to find hospitable ground before making another landing attempt, but now he was in no hurry.

· · ·

The boat drifted with the current. Only James's thirst kept him from sleep as an eerie sun grew hotter. It was shrouded by mist. He dozed fitfully as unpleasant dreams flitted through his mind. The morning fog clung tenaciously while the afternoon sun tried to devour what remained.

In the midst of a half-dream of snakes sliding through birthday cake, a violent impact jolted him awake. Almost immediately he found himself in the river trying to swim, struggling to regain the surface light.

A wave broke over his head as he surfaced. Spluttering and choking on water, he kicked hard, and blindly reached for what he thought was his rowboat. Instead, he struck a wooden object riding high in the river, but he was unable to grasp anything to hold him up. Sinking just below the surface, he banged his head and swallowed more of the river.

"Man overboard!"

Reaching once more for the light above, James heard that loud, gruff voice and thought it absurd. They must mean me!

There were other voices, male and female, muffled in the background. James choked again on brackish water, then found himself sinking deeper. He lost his sense of direction. More fearful now, he kicked harder, rediscovered the river's surface, and weakly began treading water with his eyes half closed.

How hard would it be just to let go and drown? he wondered.

He choked again, still dazed, and reached out for anything. Then a raucous, unreal voice reached his ears. "Oh, oh! Oh, oh!"

It seemed to be coming from a large, black bird perched on a man's shoulder. A crow! James saw the man's arm reach out to him, while the crow flapped its wings. Then others pulled them both back and upwards.

"That's it. Yank him up on deck. Give him some room to breathe. Rusty, grab a hold of that rowboat. Turf. Give him a hand there. We got us another passenger by the looks of it. Hey, this guy don't look so good. Here, give me a hand!"

James found himself facedown on a well-scrubbed deck that reminded him of his parents' kitchen floor. He groaned, coughed, and tried to focus on the noisy fellow that barked out orders. Turning his head to the side, James could see what appeared to be two cabins on a large, plain-looking barge. The man giving orders wore a captain's hat, and of all things, a cocky black crow of surprising size sat on his shoulder. James felt too weak to look any further.

"Don't worry, young fellow. I'm Captain Oxford. Reckon we saved your life, though I guess we knocked you into the drink to start with. Blasted fog. Hate the stuff myself."

He laughed a long, peculiar high-pitched laugh that made James relax, despite his misery, and force a smile.

"Hey, that's it! You're gonna be fine as a feather. Sylvia, bring me some of my brandy from below. It's in my cabin, under the nightstand."

"I know where you keep it, Captain," said a stern, elderly woman, "and I'm not about to fetch the filthy stuff,"

"All right. All right. I keep forgetting. Evelyn, you go." A middle-aged woman with tired blue eyes nodded curtly and left the deck, then disappeared down steps into the forward cabin.

"Blast them," said the captain under his breath.

By now James had glimpsed at least a half-dozen people gathered around, staring, and he felt fenced in. The mere suggestion of brandy caused him to gag, and that moved people back more quickly than the captain's orders.

"All right!" Captain Oxford sounded like a man used to giving orders. "All right. Back off, and get back to what you were doing. This guy's gonna be okay. He just needs a little rest. Ah, here's Evelyn. Plus some brandy, okay?"

Oxford's laugh came spilling with the alcohol. James wrenched away, gasped, and struggled for precious breath. He got to his knees, but lowered his head towards the worn deck.

"No brandy. Just let me . . . let me get my breath."

For a full minute he worked on just that, then added, "Thanks, thanks to all of you for pulling me out." His voice sounded weak to himself. "Think I was about done for."

Oxford laughed. "Forget it, at least for now. I deliver passengers for cash, but I'm not about to collect from you." He and a strong, deeply tanned man in overalls lifted James onto a cot near the railing. Soon James felt cool water on his forehead.

A young woman with intense, dark eyes was applying a cloth to his face. It felt so good that James managed a genuine smile of appreciation. She didn't say a word, but their eyes met and held. Her eyes were very expressive, reminding him of a doe, or some such forest creature. He thought it odd she didn't smile in return, or speak, but her gentle touch and haunting eyes made a deep impression on him.

• • •

James heard the distant sound of voices buzzing like gnats as he struggled to get up. He realized he must have passed out. With an effort, he forced his eyes to open.

"Lay back and rest, young man. You have a touch of river fever I expect. You're safe here."

This time it definitely was the voice of the older woman, her hair in a gray bun, maybe in her seventies. He recognized her as the one who had refused the captain's request to get his brandy. James wondered about the young woman with the unusual eyes he'd seen earlier, and whether she'd been for real.

He tried to speak but couldn't. Then he heard the faint strain of music from a single instrument, most likely a violin. It sounded so melodious he was content to keep his eyes closed and simply listen. It seemed to be coming from directly above him, and that puzzled him.

"That's it, you lie back and rest. Can you hear Elf's music?" The older woman fairly radiated care and attentiveness, and spoke in a singsong voice. "From your face I expect you can. That's from up on deck. He usually plays at sunset, and if you listen real close you can hear Rachel dancing, too. Oh, my name is Sylvia. Evelyn and I are taking turns keeping you company till you can come up on deck. Anyway, it's nicer down here. This is the captain's quarters, and he likes the best for himself."

She paused for a minute, as if letting her disapproval of the captain register with James.

"Maybe I'm talking too much," she added in a more pleasant, grandmotherly voice. Then she was quiet, perhaps listening to the music and dancing feet James strained to hear more clearly.

One moment he was listening for footsteps, while the violin music gradually filled his consciousness, and the next he was drifting away, feeling the rhythm of the unseen river. He conjured up an image of the young, dark-haired woman dancing. He knew it was just his imagination, yet he kept that mental picture as long as possible. It made him feel better, and helped him forget how thirsty he was, and how completely lost he might be.

. . .

James woke up in darkness to the sound of a man snoring. There was a dim light in the room which permitted him to look around. He felt better. Soon it was growing lighter, and there was a quick, sharp rapping at the door.

"Time for breakfast. Rise and shine."

It sounded like Sylvia's voice. James saw Captain Oxford roll out of bed, pulling on shirt and pants. He stared at James, who sat on the edge of a cot, and laughed.

"All right, fella. You look almost ready to meet the world. If you forgot, I'm Captain Oxford, boss of this here barge. Never did get your name."

"James. You pulled me out of the river?"

"Right as rain. Yesterday afternoon. C'mon now. Wash up over here and we'll get us some chow. Looks like you could use a little grub."

. . .

Soon they made their way down a cramped hallway below deck, and turned into the barge's small dining area. Everything seemed worn, but well made and spotless: furniture, walls, steps and floors, with shades of brown and green the predominant colors.

People were sitting and standing around the room. In the center of the room there was a long table set for eleven. Food was being brought in by a tall man with a dark beard, and the young woman James had seen the day before. James felt somewhat ill at ease because of his own disheveled appearance.

While he happily confirmed the young woman's beauty, James became aware of the others staring at him. It bothered him less when the young woman glanced his way and shyly smiled.

"Everybody pull up a chair. C'mon, quit gawking. This here young fellow is James. He's joined our crew so to speak, at least till he gets his sea legs back. Right?"

"I don't know, Captain. I'm grateful for what you people have done, but I've got to get back upriver as soon as I can. I've got to get back to Riverton."

"Sure you do," Oxford laughed. "But for now we can all get down to eating. Rachel, start the flapjacks right here. And bring this lad a big orange juice. He still looks a mite peaked to me."

Her name was Rachel, and she was in her late teens, he thought.

"You would be too, if you swallowed that filthy river water," said Sylvia.

"Reverend, I suppose you got to say grace again?" Oxford spoke in a weary tone to the bespectacled, dark-bearded man, who seated himself last at the table's end opposite the captain.

The tall man nodded curtly, and prayed:

"We thank thee God for these thy gifts of food and fellowship; Be in our midst to bless and strengthen us with thy spirit. Amen."

James noticed that only the two older women and a young, red-headed boy with freckles added amen. Like himself, the other adult men and Rachel kept their eyes open and heads unbowed.

"Before we get busy filling our faces, let me give out some more names here. James, the gal is my daughter, Rachel. This here's her first long trip with me on the barge. She don't talk. Hasn't since she was ten, and that's seven years ago. Don't ask me why, because nobody rightly knows. The preacher is Reverend Dennis. Real educated, but not always smart, if you guess what I mean." Oxford grinned.

"Next to him, with the hat, is Turf. We ain't cowboys, Turf. Take off the hat. He's a farmer. Looks like one too, don't he?"

An embarrassed Turf, who was stocky and looked as strong as a bull, wagged his head after removing a worn straw hat.

"And next to him, the sly-looking thin guy, that's the shop-keeper, Rusty."

The farmer's weather-beaten face remained unexpressive, but Turf did nod toward James. His age was hard to figure, but James thought maybe fifties or early sixties. Next to him the younger Rusty grinned and reached out to shake hands with James, saying, "How do you do, James. Pleased to meet you."

James also nodded, guessing Rusty to be forty or thereabout. He seemed almost as out of place on a river barge as farmer Turf did.

"And," Oxford continued with diminishing interest, "guess you already met Sylvia and Evelyn. Evelyn's the one with tired blue eyes, but they're nice and so's her smile when she does, which isn't often. She cooks."

Oxford drew a deeper breath. "They been taking turns watching you since we carried you down to my quarters. And the boy, he's ten—real live wire, by gosh. Jesse is our orphan brat."

The youngster giggled, grinning over the table at James. "He's full of pep, as if a blind man couldn't see that." He laughed his peculiar laugh, but when no one joined in he frowned. James guessed the captain probably wasn't the most popular person on the barge.

"Get me the syrup, Rachel," Oxford said, "before these things turn cold."

James spoke to their silence. "I'm glad to meet you, all of you. Say, I'd like to ask who played the violin I heard last night. That was—," he stopped, and the intake of his breath was audible.

Another boy, no, a short man entered the room and quickly sat next to Jesse. His skin was borderline translucent, a milky color. Observing his colorless hair and pale blue irises, with center splashes of pink, James concluded the man was an albino.

"This here's Elf," said Oxford with a laugh. "Least that's what we call him. He looks a tad weird, I know, but you get used to the albo thing soon enough. He don't talk much more than Rachel." He laughed again, more forced this time. "But he sure can play the fiddle. That's who you heard. He's a traveler and that's how he pays his way. Now let's stop this here yakking and get on with the eating."

No one else spoke and James tried not to stare at Elf. Although he felt uneasy, the food smelled good and the orange juice tasted like nectar.

Oxford, short and overweight, came across as part buffoon, blunt to the point of being rude, yet also at times an amiable guy.

His clean barge was nevertheless shabby and worn by time above and below deck. James wondered aloud as to its size.

Dripping syrup on his faded shirt, Oxford replied, "About twenty-five by fifty-five feet. Nothing fancy, but a great-running barge ever since my dad left her to me. Left me some land down-river and this here spunky tub of trouble. Sleeps ten to fifteen people, depending. Sometimes more, sometimes less. I like less, but you got to make a living, right? Dad named her *Midnight*, and I call her the same. Never did tell me why."

James wondered where they were headed, and who was running the barge while they were eating. He thought the others unusually quiet. Only Sylvia and Evelyn whispered a few snatches of conversation. Everyone was eating except Rachel, who continued to mutely serve. She was tall, slender, and moved, he thought, with a dancer's grace. He found it difficult to believe she couldn't speak.

Oxford anticipated his next question. "The Port of Jossandra is my next main stop. In fact, the end of this here run. Sometimes I make brief stops, like for food and stuff, or if someone's got the price. But I don't stop long unless the price is real good. Know what I mean? Rough country. Rough waters."

"I've never heard of the Port of Jossandra," said James. "I'm from Riverton myself."

"Never heard of it," said Oxford, perhaps mocking James. "And it don't surprise me none about you not knowing the river." He frowned and gave James a cool stare, as if questions were a needless bother.

"Who's running the ship right now?" asked James.

Downing some black coffee, Oxford leaned back and managed a weak grin. "To answer that, we ain't moving. Blackie's on lookout though. My bird's the best damn sentry of the whole bunch of these landlubbers."

James studied Oxford as the feisty captain fumbled with a spot of syrup on his shirt, sighed, and tried to rub the stickiness off with his thumb. For some reason he found himself feeling sorry for the guy. That passed in a hurry as he also sensed how stubborn the skipper might prove to be.

"Did you see old Blackie before you passed out, James? Great bird. Super. Best crewman I ever had. Knows some words, too, as much as he needs. Some could take a lesson." He looked at the women, then Reverend Dennis. "There's too much talk nowadays. That's what I don't like."

James thought of at least ten more questions, but held his tongue, while Captain Oxford and Reverend Dennis engaged in a staring match. Elf was playing a game of elbows and knees with little Jesse. For the moment James was relieved to see that Elf acted as normal as anyone at the table.

But someone or something's crazy here, he nevertheless was thinking. I hope to heck it's not me!

CHAPTER THREE

The great dragon that lieth in the midst
of his rivers . . . hath said, My river is mine own,
and I have made it for myself.

-Ezekiel 29:3

James had hoped that when he got topside after breakfast everything would make more sense. That was not the case. Nor was he feeling much better. The breakfast had looked and tasted okay, and he supposed it was, but his stomach was not. The pancakes seemed to hurt. The only thing he could tolerate was orange juice, and he figured he must have drunk half a gallon.

The next shock was the river itself. It had never looked so alien or imposing, and yet he grudgingly admitted to himself there was an air of excitement, too. Now it widened to more than a quarter mile, and as the barge steamed downriver it was getting still wider.

It doesn't look like our river. This thing's got a wild look and feel. The excitement led him to acknowledge an aberration of reality without being able to explain it. He was unable, at this point, to either accept or dismiss what he perceived to be reality as he had known it in Riverton. James felt he had to get off the barge—soon.

If the landscape was alien, the barge itself was homey, maybe because it was worn and comfortable. The deck chairs, captain's wheel, and wheelhouse, everything, looked secondhand, even though clean and well kept. The forward cabin was boxlike, situated to the right of the wheel. A miniature crow's nest next to the wheel provided Blackie's lookout post. The aft cabin was dark brown, worn but solid wood, and rose some eight feet above the deck floor. Most of the barge's open space was centered between the cabins, and that is where the passengers usually gathered.

The engine, if there was one, ran so quietly James couldn't hear it. He decided it must be forward, below deck, opposite the galley. James paced, trying to decide his next move, when at midmorning Blackie pierced the calm.

"Oh oh! Oh oh!" The bird ruffled and pranced.

Oxford responded quickly, finding a six-foot black snake on board near the wheel. A few minutes later Elf whistled and pointed out another one he'd spotted on the rear cabin's roof.

"These ain't poisonous, James," said Oxford. "No sweat. Just a damned nuisance. Happens sometimes when I tie up at river's edge. That's why I like to keep *Midnight* at mid-river. There are no unscheduled stops. Least not till we hit desert country."

This time his usually ingratiating laugh irritated James. His stomach was still unsettled, he felt weak in the knees, and he couldn't understand the reference to desert. Oxford also kept brushing off his questions.

"Hey, kid! Be careful there!"

Jesse had a seven-footer by the back of its neck, and his other hand had hold of the snake's tail. "One, two, three!" the ten-year-old chanted, then sent the wriggling creature sailing overboard.

"Want me to start up my tractor and crush a few of those bastards?" said Turf with a gleam of undisguised malice in his eyes.

"Nah, there's just a few more," said Oxford. "The kid's got the right idea. Chuck them overboard. No need to worry as long as we don't run into Gargol."

"What's Gargol?" asked James, feeling an odd shiver.

"Well," said Oxford, "it's too big to call just a snake, but it's sure snake-looking."

Delirium images from the day before flashed within James's thought. Can Oxford be talking about what I thought I saw?

"I never seen the whole thing myself," Oxford continued, "but part of it swept under my legs one night when I was resting my feet on deck watch. And another full moon night it took a half-grown cow clean off my deck. It was right over there where we got Turf's tractor tied down. Happened quick. Let me tell you, watch your step strolling the deck at night on this river."

"Listen," said James, "I've seen some crazy stuff, and I don't want to see any more. I'm not interested in sailing on a floating zoo. I want off this crate."

The reference to *Midnight* as a crate turned Oxford's demeanor icy in an instant.

"Don't go getting your dander up, fella. And don't forget maybe this crate saved your life. It goes by the name of *Midnight*."

"All right," said James. "But I'm fed up with these snakes and this other weird crap."

"Settle down. We most likely passed the worst snake country, especially where old Gargol's concerned. And these black bull-snakes ain't gonna hurt nobody. Hell, even Jesse the kid catches them like you seen."

He stabbed a stubby forefinger at James. "You better rest up some more before you think of jumping off my ship, mister. Matter of fact, you don't look so good right now. Maybe Sylvia's right. From your white face I'd say river fever, too. Ever had it before?"

"Never even heard of it," said James. But he noticed the dizziness again, and it began getting darker although his eyes were wide open. His head hurt. It was as if Oxford's suggestion of the malady had triggered an attack. Rooted to the spot, James felt himself powerless to resist the soft-swaying motion of the barge.

"Hey, Dennis. Turf. You guys help James here! This guy's conking out on me again. Damn! I hate picking up non-paying strays."

James barely heard Oxford spluttering, but felt strong hands lifting under his arms as his knees gave way. That was Turf's gruff voice saying, "Easy now," in his ear. Rev. Dennis had his legs. He was surprised how easily they carried him below deck.

"You want him in the men's bunkroom, or in your quarters again?"

"Ah, hell, there's more room for him in with me. Unless he starts throwing up. I won't have that kind of stink in my cabin. Okay. Put him in the same place, at least for now."

James wanted to stand up and assert himself. He'd seen his rowboat swinging at the railing like a promised lifeboat. He wanted to take off and be on his own again. Now he sensed there was nothing to do but wait until he felt stronger. An irrational thought came to him as he settled against the pillow.

I wonder if they put something in my food?

• • •

Sylvia was reading in a chair near Oxford's bed when James awoke. His eyes scanned the small gray room. Despite the dim light he could make out a watercolor of a schooner sailing over ocean swells, which hung alongside Oxford's bed. Other than a dresser, desk, and two lamps, and an old gun on the wall, a traditional ship in a bottle was the room's only other decoration.

Sylvia looked up and smiled. Her cranky look melted away in grandmotherly concern. "Well, well, James. I hope you're feeling stronger. You sleep sounder than my dear departed husband." She stopped smiling and changed the subject. "Would you like me to fetch you some broth? The others are finishing an early supper now."

"That's very kind of you, Mrs.—"

"Just call me Sylvia. Everyone does."

"I wouldn't mind some water. Maybe I could just—" He struggled to get up.

"You lie back there. I'll get it, and a little soup. Evelyn made it special. It's good for river fever."

James felt too weak to refuse, so he merely nodded. As soon as she'd gone he gathered his strength and propped himself up. Gingerly he swung his feet over the side of the bed, pushing a sweat-dampened sheet aside. He was dressed in nothing but shorts.

Looking around the dingy room depressed him. It had looked better when he was feeling okay. He didn't see his other clothes. He walked unsteadily to a porthole and looked out at a calm river. He was feeling some better, he thought. Weak, but the natural light of day somehow cheered him.

Sylvia returned with a glass of water in one hand and a steaming bowl of soup in the other. Seeing him out of bed, she hesitated, then pulled out the captain's card table from behind the headboard. She pulled out a chair and gave brisk orders.

"Sit down and eat some of this. Evelyn does most of our cooking, and her feelings get hurt easily. Come. Sit down."

She smoothed her gray hair and ran thin, capable fingers along her sleeves. "Don't worry about parading in your underclothes. I raised three sons of my own while teaching school."

"Where are my clothes?"

"Rachel's washing them. No, she already washed them. They're drying on the deck. Just a minute. Let's try this." Sylvia pulled on a short rope dangling above the captain's bed, and within minutes Rachel appeared. Color came to her cheeks when she smiled at James.

He felt ridiculous eating soup clad only in underwear.

"Check his clothes, child, and see if they're dry yet."

James was surprised to find Rachel taller than he'd remembered. He was a shade over six feet himself, and she was only several inches shorter. She appeared quite shy and he thought that added to her attractiveness. She hesitated for some moments, as if awaiting further orders, then gracefully turned and left.

Sylvia easily caught the gleam of appreciation in his eyes. "Yes, she's a lovely child. The captain has her working too hard, if you ask me. Washing, helping Evelyn with the cooking, and watching Jesse, it's small wonder Rachel seldom smiles."

"Why do you think she doesn't speak?"

"I don't exactly know. She's evidently been that way since her mama died from some kind of river accident. It seems relatives did most of raising her until now. This happens to be the first long trip Rachel's made on *Midnight* since way back then, and it's a mistake, if you ask me. Of course no one else agrees with me."

James nodded, more puzzled than before. "What about that . . . that little—"

"Elf? That albo Elf? That's what we all call him. He doesn't seem to mind. Somewhat sad. Turf says he's an outcast of some kind. His father used to be the leader of a clan that made their home in the forest. With that large head and those strange eyes, well, Evelyn and I were afraid of him at first. But he's quiet and really gentle as a kitten. Seems to be an unhappy wanderer. He's an amazing primitive musician. If you come out on deck before dark, you'll hear him play for Rachel. I think he loves her in his own way. The kid, Jesse, likes him better than anyone, except perhaps Rachel herself. But if you ask me," she said, "that child should not be gallivanting on the river with the likes of Oxford. Or Elf, for that matter."

"How do you mean?"

"Well, for one thing, he and Rachel ought to be in school. Rev. Dennis felt very sorry for him, being an orphan and all. He tried to help him with some problems, but Jesse doesn't much want anyone's help. He and Rachel work too hard for youngsters. Jesse will scrub down the whole deck, and help in the galley, asking for chores. He even cooks and can sew clothes. It's not natural. It's just my opinion, but he should be on land and going to school—and Rachel, too."

"Maybe it's from being on his own, but Jesse sounds okay to me, just pretty independent for a kid. Ah . . . Rachel, you've brought my clothes. Thanks a lot."

James touched her hand and smiled. "I hear you dance. Will you be dancing tonight?"

She nodded a shy affirmative. Sylvia said with a frown, "I don't see why she has to dance every night the weather is right. In my day a girl didn't show herself so much, but I suspect she's Oxford's pride, and he'd be the one for cheap entertainment."

Sylvia handed over the clothes Rachel had set on the foot of the guest cot. "You get dressed, James. Ring the bell if you need anything. We'll be on deck to watch the sunset. Hurry along now."

James nodded, handing Sylvia the empty bowl as she left the room. "Tell Evelyn I like her soup. It's the first food that's felt like staying down. I'll be up in ten to fifteen minutes."

He gulped down the rest of the water as Sylvia and Rachel departed. After they'd gone he searched the room for anything unusual, any clue to where Captain Oxford had been, or where they were going. He spied a small piece of paper with scribbles on it, near Oxford's dresser, evidently dropped on the floor. There was a crude sketch of what could pass for a meandering river, and at one bend there was an X labeled Cool Water, and later XX marking Port of Jossandra. Farther down from that was a childish skull and crossbones with the words Great Falls.

James was unable to make much sense of the scrap of paper, but he stuffed it into his front pocket. He'd heard Oxford mention the Port of Jossandra, yet the name remained otherwise unfamiliar. The same was true for Great Falls, as well as for Cool Water. He lay down on his cot, propping the pillow behind his head.

He wondered what Bethany was thinking had happened to him. *I'll bet she thinks I drowned, or ran off.* He sighed. "Maybe it's just as well."

· · ·

When James finally came up on deck he felt a surge of unanticipated excitement. For the first time he fully sensed the sheer adventure of this unique, new existence—himself a stranger among other strangers, traveling to an unknown destination. He was caught up in an extraordinary set of bizarre circumstances.

James gravitated to a natural gathering spot between the two cabins where the others had assembled. They knew Rachel would soon be dancing to Elf's violin. The hardwood deck was polished spotless, and *Midnight* seemed less scruffy to James, and actually solid and seaworthy. He was allowed to recline in the captain's special hammock, because the captain himself had insisted. Everyone was waiting for Rachel.

Oxford said he was not surprised that his daughter had naturally taken to the art his wife had once practiced. It was an emotional outlet, and from his very practical standpoint, Rachel kept the passengers entertained. James sensed the captain's pride, a desire for all to see and approve Rachel's ability.

Rev. Dennis and Sylvia sat on folding chairs against the starboard railing next to James, and Evelyn stood farther away, fidgeting near the door of the forward cabin. Oxford sat on the port-side deck, passing a jug with Turf and Rusty.

The three men seemed to be making private jokes. Oxford's long, high-pitched, forced laugh triggered Rusty's mid-range cackles, and Turf contributed bass chuckles. Blackie was perched near the men on the railing and was parading up and down while they were laughing. He offered a croaking "Hi!" from time to time, his black coat reflecting fading sunlight.

"Blackie's education seems as limited as the captain's," James said to Rev. Dennis. The waiting was making him irritable, and the men's drinking and laughing didn't help his disposition.

When the barge swung briefly northward around a bend, James mused to himself. It doesn't really matter where we are. I can always follow the river back from where we came from. He knew they had to land eventually, although James had a definite feeling the Port of Jossandra was yet far downriver.

James continued to be astounded by the passing terrain. Swampy wilderness had given way to desert, and the heat was growing more oppressive. Only a cool river breeze at sunset kept it from being truly uncomfortable for most of the passengers. James liked one aspect of the heat, and that was it seemed to begin drying him out.

"Where is Rachel?" he asked Sylvia when Elf began playing a soft melody from his perch atop the forward cabin's roof. The tune was so subdued it was all but carried away by the breezes.

Sylvia shrugged, but Evelyn approached them and said, "She's getting dressed. Sometimes she doesn't come up until almost dark. Rachel has her moods. She has to have a feeling for the music first. Same as her ma, Oxie says."

Evelyn continued, "I think it's shameful though that he has her flaunting her looks, and before strangers, too. Oxie even put up those special deck lights for her night dancing." James thought Evelyn was as straitlaced as Sylvia, and that she herself tended towards moodiness.

"Sunday night Rachel doesn't have to dance," Rev. Dennis said in a resonant voice. "Captain Oxford assured me that was optional for her. It's curious though, that's the night she usually dances best. Wouldn't you agree, Sylvia?"

"You might be right."

Dennis said, "I don't suppose Oxford notices though, because he treats all nights pretty much the same. I'll tell you what, James, I wish I'd had those two in my old congregation. We'd have filled the pews then. Listen to that music. People love to be entertained. My sermons put most of them to sleep in weather this warm."

"I can believe that," said James.

Rev. Dennis laughed, taking no visible offense, and James liked that about him. Just then Rusty sauntered over like a fox bringing stolen grapes, carrying instead the communal jug of wine.

"Anyone over here want a swig? James? Evelyn, you take a drop now and then."

Evelyn wrinkled her nose in disgust, turning her head away, and Sylvia looked like he was an idiot.

"Just being polite," said the wiry man, patting his slight pot-belly. James studied the nearly middle-aged man who strutted like a rooster, and guessed he was already feeling the wine's effect. Rusty stood about five feet, eight inches, maybe less, and James decided he didn't hold his wine very well.

It's funny how you can tell, James thought. They seem to get silly or angry and this guy could go either way.

• • •

Finally Rachel emerged through the cabin doorway onto the barge's deck. She took James's breath away and he was glad not to be drinking with the others. Somehow that seemed inappropriate.

Everyone stopped talking as the violinist acknowledged Rachel's presence by switching from strains of melancholy to a faster tempo. James felt transfixed as she began a series of pirouettes. Blackie flapped his wings, then froze at the railing behind Oxford like an attentive statuette.

Spinning faster now, Rachel's eyes closed as if to absorb a magical mood. She seemed to be performing for the group of four, and the three men gradually moved around to get a better view. Only Jesse the kid was absent.

Rachel wore a pale yellow peasant blouse that was gently scooped at the neck and shoulders. The skirt was quite long, nearly to her ankles, and the hemline was lightly weighted so that the shimmering green swirled rhythmically in response to her graceful movements. Even to James's inexperienced eye, she was a natural-born dancer. If she lacked anything in polish, it was made up for by magnetic exuberance. He could not tell if she followed the music or it followed her, for they were a perfect match.

After five or six or seven minutes James expected the high-spirited dancing to subside. Instead, it grew in intensity. The men started rhythmic clapping, but that did not last, for clearly the music's pace tired them, and they had seen at other times how long Rachel's dances could continue.

Suddenly Rachel leaped up a ladder to where Elf stood playing his precious violin atop the forward cabin's roof, joining him in silhouette against a fiery sunset. James glanced to see the captain put aside his jug, and heard him gruffly caution, "Careful, girl!"

The dance gave way to the dancer's abandon, and she became exhilaratingly free in movements. Rachel whirled around Elf with no apparent concern for the edge of the cabin's roof, yet somehow her flying feet stayed just far enough away from the edge. Her waist-length, dark hair was flying, shining auburn in the last sunlight.

The music itself was unbelievable, even fantastic. James was amazed the passengers had spoken mainly of Rachel's dancing rather than giving the unusual violinist priority in their comments. Clearly Elf was a superb musician who inspired dancer and listener alike.

Rachel's rare ability was in giving dynamic expression, image, and fine movement to those haunting tunes. They sounded slightly familiar, yet James came to realize he'd never actually heard them played before. It was as if they should be popular folk music, but were dramatically new and original.

At last, Rachel held to one place and circled ever faster. Around and around she spun, skirt and hair straight out, yellow panties flashing over curved buttocks. Her head arched slightly back, large eyes gleaming as if she were entranced. Rachel's lips parted as she gasped. Then she dropped in a spent heap of green and gold. Instantly the music stopped.

Elf gallantly abandoned his violin to help Rachel to her now unsteady feet. But her eyes were normal again: shy, dark, and luminous. She fastened them on James, basking in his obvious admiration and approval. Then, to an unspecified cue, Rachel and Elf bowed deeply in unison.

"Never better! Never better!" Captain Oxford boomed out, breaking the spell, grinning from larboard to starboard.

There was a sudden commotion behind the captain even as he issued his praise, and everyone on deck heard Turf's muffled roar, followed by Rusty's high-pitched scream.

"It's that damned Gargol! Serpent! Giant river serpent! Off the port bow!"

CHAPTER FOUR

But never met this fellow
Attended or alone,
Without a tighter breathing
And zero at the bone.

-Emily Dickinson

The beast loomed out of eerie shadows as startled passengers, frozen by fear, tried to grasp what was happening. It was Captain Oxford's bellow that finally set all of them into action, although it seemed to James that none of them had a clear plan.

"That don't look like no Gargol to me!" yelled Oxford for all to hear. "That looks more like Gargol's daddy!"

Oxford sprang to the foredeck wheel, trying to maneuver away from the approaching reptile. With Blackie screaming caws of encouragement overhead, *Midnight* headed into a U-shaped bend that pointed south.

James loathed the foul-smelling creature as soon as it appeared. Doubts about this being reality as he had formerly known it disappeared. So be it, he thought as he ran to get a better view. There was still enough light to see not only the beast's darting head, but also to sense that the black river concealed a powerful body. It continued to move menacingly closer to the barge.

"Faster!" screamed Evelyn to Captain Oxford. "Make it go faster!"

James kept scanning from the boat to the beast and back again, hoping the distance would stop narrowing. He saw its sinewy neck more clearly now—at one moment taut, the next flexing. It reminded him of a large elephant's trunk with an attached head. The head itself looked to James like a cross between an enormous python, and of all things, a giraffe.

"You women, get below deck! Find the kid!" shouted Oxford, who clung white-knuckled to the wheel. "Rachel, you two get down from that roof!"

Rusty stumbled to the deck, got up and raced after the two older women, and breathlessly returned with the captain's old shotgun. James remembered having seen it on the wall and had thought of getting it himself. Instead, James had abandoned the hammock and climbed after Rev. Dennis atop the front cabin's roof to get an even better view. They stood next to Rachel and Elf, urging the captain to go faster.

A clap of thunder sounded the beginning of a rare desert rain. Rachel was still breathing heavily from her dance, and in the excitement of confronting the monster, James suddenly felt protective.

Now he tried to think what he might do to challenge the beast, but James remained rooted to the spot with the rest of the passengers, waiting to see if *Midnight* would gain full power in the main current and outrun the giant serpent.

They all heard a hissing sound, as if cool water were hitting a huge, hot frying pan. All of them strained to see more clearly when the rainfall increased. The greenish-black darting head came closer.

Oxford screamed again, "That gun is empty, you damned fool!"

Rusty looked sheepish, and James suddenly scrambled down the roof ladder to search for a weapon. He was the closest to the creature as it glided within fifteen feet of the barge's port railing. At that distance, downwind, it reeked. Its sinuous neck grew more taut; its rounded serpent's head rose higher, now looking blue-black to James in *Midnight's* lantern light. Double rows of jagged, yellow teeth became visible.

James's legs felt weak, but he aspired to be a defender of Rachel and the others. He spied long cane poles in a pile of fishing equipment, grabbed one, and ran to Turf's tractor, hoping his legs wouldn't give out. After yanking off a protective canvas that covered the red tractor, he climbed into the seat of the sturdy machine and began to joust at the monster's head.

Turf was the next to grasp the idea, grabbing another long fishing pole, and Rusty did the same after he'd dropped Oxford's useless gun. While they jabbed and rammed at the elusive head coming alongside the barge, it lunged to bite off the end of each pole.

"Come on!" yelled Rev. Dennis. "Let's give them some help!"

He scrambled down the cabin ladder with Elf and Rachel right behind him, and soon six of them were madly poking and jousting at that purplish head with its hateful, glowering eyes.

Oxford stayed at the wheel, bellowing orders that went largely unheeded in the heat of battle and falling rain, as were Blackie's raucous caws from the crow's nest. James glanced from the tractor and saw Rachel lunging with a pole, her wet hair looking black and wild.

The hideous beast lunged at James on the tractor seat, missing only by inches. By then Oxford had *Midnight* near full steam, and the creature eased back alongside midship where the others kept thrashing away with their cane poles. James was surprised by the athletic prowess of Rev. Dennis, who despite rain-splashed glasses scored repeatedly about the reptile's head as it went by.

Once the foul beast was being left behind, a cheer went up, including one from Sylvia and Evelyn, who watched and cheered from the cabin doorway with Jesse safely behind them. Blackie flew from stem to stern, cabin to cabin, issuing defiant caws. Finally he settled down on the tractor's wheel, where James had slumped back in the seat to wearily bask in victory over the river serpent.

· · ·

The encounter left everyone exhausted or drained, and soon, not knowing what else to do, they made their way to the cabins, patting Oxford on his back and shoulders as he remained at the wheel. All of the men, including Jesse, stayed in the forward cabin, while the women returned aft to the smaller quarters.

With James feeling stronger, he was advised to move from Oxford's room into the men's quarters, adjacent to the galley area. Oxford himself did the advising, and James's receptiveness to the idea made the transition easy. His was the bottom bunk of one of three bunk beds in use, which it turned out he shared with Elf, who had the berth above him.

Rev. Dennis lay quietly except for reaching up now and then to tickle the feet little Jesse hung down from above him. Rusty and Turf shared the remaining bunk unit, with Rusty above and Turf in the bed below.

"Why did you get on the tractor, James? I still don't understand that," said Rusty, who remained excited even after a couple glasses of wine.

"My legs were none too steady after the fever stuff," said James. "So I thought I'd sit and joust at the serpent from Turf's tractor—not stand."

"I'm glad that river scum didn't drag *Big Red* overboard. Me and that tractor got some plowing to do yet, downriver wherever the good Lord says. Like I was telling the Reverend here, me and that machine's been through good times and bad. We stick together. When we get through these blasted swamps and deserts, why we're going to work new fields. Yes sir, that's it. New fields or bust, and I'm not waiting much longer."

It was a long speech for Turf. Evidently the river serpent scare had affected him, too, as he worked to empty the wine jug before thinking of sleep.

Rusty said, "I still don't get it, but those cane poles sure did the trick, didn't they, Reverend? Hey, James, that was quick thinking. Here, have a slug of wine before me and Turf kill it."

This time James tried it, taking a long, sweet swallow that turned bitter on the way down. It burned his stomach, and immediately he regretted it. He noticed Rev. Dennis remained quiet, and wondered why he didn't join in talking and drinking with them. When Rusty passed the jug to Dennis, he merely handed it over to Turf, who took a long pull and rolled over into his bottom bunk with a loud sigh. Rusty had poured his into a glass and continued to sip.

Suddenly feeling dead tired, James rolled back his own sheet. "Where's the captain?" he asked.

"Still at the wheel with Blackie," said Rev. Dennis. "I'll go up and spell him in a little while, but he doesn't want anyone but himself at the helm right now. He'll keep *Midnight* in the main current until dawn. Then we'll see where we've gotten to. This is wild, desolate country that we're going through."

"How'd you happen to come on this trip?" James asked.

"My congregation thought I needed a rest," he said with a smile that revealed even teeth. "They were right, but I don't think we anticipated all this. Still, once we reach the Port of Jossandra I intend to research Jossandra's writings and the archives there. It might be exactly what I'm after. They do healing work. Almost everyone on board is going there to solve one problem or another."

"Who is Jossandra?"

"She was a Christian prophetess. I was having trouble with my eyes, and I came across something of hers that helped me. Want to hear it?"

"I suppose," said James.

Rusty groaned from his bunk. "Don't let him get started. He'll never stop."

Reverend Dennis grinned at James, and undaunted he began, "Jossandra said to her people: 'You don't understand the nature of sight. People see what they believe. Sight is really understanding given by divine intelligence.'"

"So maybe we see monsters because we believe in them?" said Rusty with a cackle.

"I never thought of it just like that, Rusty. You might have something there," said Rev. Dennis.

"It's sort of interesting," said James, feeling glum, as he wanted to steer conversation back to questions about river travel. He also sensed Rev. Dennis had a philosophical bent that might prove unbearable, given time.

"How about you men? Why do you travel with Captain Oxford?"

"What, this trip?" asked Rusty. "It's none of your business, but my store was going busted. I had three stores at one time. Also promised my wife before she died that I'd look into this Jossandra thing, although I myself don't put much stock in it. And Turf here—Turf, you gone to sleep? Like you heard, he's looking for a new spread. Doubt if he'll last until the Port of Jossandra. He wants to get back to farming real bad, the sooner the better. Like yesterday."

"And the women?"

"Boy!" said Rusty. "You sure ask a lot of questions, James, about other people's business. Hope you don't keep prying like the Reverend here. No offense, Dennis. Let me see. Sylvia taught school, I guess, and her husband died. They turned her out to pasture as Turf might say."

"But she's only—"

"She's well into her seventies," said Rusty. "I know, she looks younger. She must have really been something in her day. A certain class about her. I think she wants to find the right place to finally retire." He drained his wine glass. "And Evelyn—they say she's dying of something or other, right Dennis? But she looks okay to me. If she didn't get so damn bitchy sometimes she might make some guy a nice, ah, friend. Guess she wants to get to the Port even more than Sylvia."

Dennis added in somber tones, "Oxford said she was dying, according to the doctors, and Sylvia says so, too. It doesn't show in her behavior, at least not that I've noticed. My guess is medical people gave up on her and she's looking for a special cure. It's said they discovered a way to heal hopeless cases at the Port of Jossandra."

Jesse and Elf remained quiet in their bunk beds. Then Jesse piped up. "Evelyn heard Jossandra had revelations about healing, Reverend Dennis," his voice came down in a boyish soprano. "She told me our problems would be solved once we got to the Port. I really hope to have a home again, like with family."

Finally the talk subsided, and the jug was empty. All that remained from the happenings at dusk were fading recollections and a rare desert rainfall that pattered atop the cabin's roof.

Before going to sleep, James thought of the joy he'd felt at being alive when he'd been instrumental in protecting Rachel and the others. Then he realized he'd nearly forgotten about his girlfriend Bethany, the love of his life. Guilt surged up. He wondered if the jolts of wine were part of that feeling.

But the old thoughts and feelings were driven back as his mind invited a new image: violinist Elf and youthful Rachel atop the cabin roof, etched against the setting sun's crimson sky.

· · ·

Just before dawn James heard Elf rustling covers in the bunk above him. His large head peered over the edge. Seeing James awake, he quietly spoke his first words on *Midnight* to him.

"It's a fell rain, mark my words. It should not last so long, nor trumpet that way in desert lands." As if to punctuate his words, another clap of thunder rumbled overhead. Despite its volume, the others remained sleeping, although Rusty groaned and rolled over when the barge lurched more than usual.

James said, "Maybe we've passed the desert area by now. There can't be that much of it because I never heard of one in these parts—wherever we are."

Elf gave a muttered laugh. "It's still desert all right, Jamie." James had never let anyone but Bethany call him by that name, yet from Elf it sounded natural rather than overly familiar. He let it pass as Elf continued. "There's not a good stand of forest within a hundred miles by the way that I feel. Make that fifty. My bones sense when a good one's at hand. But let's slip up on deck and see for ourselves. It must be close to dawn."

James enjoyed the lilt of Elf's speech, and he readily agreed. He'd slept in his clothes, and Elf was clad in green tights and T-shirt over which he'd thrown on a thin, blue jacket. They quietly made their way into the hallway. While passing the narrow galley-way, they were shocked to see a rotund stranger helping himself to coffee and pastry.

The stranger scowled at being spotted, but kept on eating. Elf looked back at James and they both shrugged. They whispered together for twenty seconds or so and decided to continue up the steps, which they did without speaking to the stranger.

Topside a fierce wind blew, thunder cracked, and streaks of lightning lit up the barge. Oxford was frantically working to tie a rope to a large palm tree that was nearly bent double in the gale. By the looks of it, he was having a terrible time.

"Let's see if we can give him a hand!" James yelled above the howling wind.

They were in a small cove in almost barren terrain, and it offered *Midnight* some protection. When the lightning flashed, James could make out five palm trees of varying size along the shoreline. Oxford had attached ropes to two of them, but was struggling with the third.

James and Elf leaped to shore and pulled on the rope to give Oxford sufficient slack to finish tying his knots. While they held and pulled, James noticed that the rainfall had ceased. If that was odd, the area's desolation was shocking. As far as they could see by lightning flashes, sand dunes and a vast wasteland stretched away from the river. The rolling water hues were ghastly shades of green.

James shuddered. It's like Elf said, he thought. It's a strange kind of storm. And where the hell has Oxie landed us? A quick survey told him it would be impossible to strike out on foot in such terrain.

Within fifteen minutes *Midnight* was secured, and Oxford's long laugh of relief was swallowed up in the howl of desert wind. He grinned and wiped his brow, pointing to the main cabin and yelling hoarsely, "Let's get our tails below deck, lads, and let this bastard blow over!"

Going down the cabin steps towards the dining area, James remembered the man he and Elf had seen eating by himself. Oxie was on a collision course with the stranger if the fat man remained where he had been. They turned the corner and James saw Oxford tense, stopping with a surprised whistle. Elf grinned at James.

"Hey now, what's this? Who the devil are you?" asked Oxford, and the stranger took his cue from Elf and merely grinned, popping half a doughnut into his large mouth.

He leaned back in the chair with relaxed ease and placed chubby hands on his stomach. "Name's Snyder, Captain," he said. "I thought you saw me come on board when you were hitching to those trees. I've had a speck of trouble myself. That hot, bitching wind is friend to no man. I'm a river traveler like yourself. I buy and sell."

"Ah, a merchant like our man Rusty. But I sure didn't see you topside," said Oxford, stabbing a forefinger at the composed stranger. "And you've no right stepping in here bold as buttons and snitching my best rolls. Hey now! Hold off on them chocolate ones. Evelyn made those special for me!" Oxford looked and sounded more hurt than angry.

"There's no need to get upset. Any port in a storm, it's said. And wouldn't I do the same for you? River hospitality. Of course I would, Captain. You can rest easy on that."

"What exactly is your business?" asked James.

"Yeah," said Oxford.

"Whatever opportunity comes along." He smiled inoffensively. "Mainly policies made to order. Life policies for people like yourselves who travel in dangerous lands and times."

"Well and good, I suppose," said Oxford, drawing himself up to full height. "Just how do you explain being in the middle of nowhere?"

"Same as yourselves. Oh, to be certain my craft was smaller and sleeker. But it was taking on water during the night. I had to scuttle it and take my losses. Your barge sure looked like an adequate temporary, ah . . . substitute, so to speak."

"I know, I know," said Captain Oxford. "Any port in a storm."

"Exactly. I have seen better ships," said Snyder. "But who knows, I might even make you a handsome offer on your barge, if it meets my needs. You never know."

CHAPTER FIVE

'Tis the wink of an eye; 'tis the draught of a breath,
From the blossom of health to the paleness of death,
From the gilded saloon to the bier and the shroud;
Oh! why should the spirit of mortals be proud?

-William Knox

About midmorning the wind quieted, the storm retreated, and all the passengers except Snyder met on deck. Sheet lightning flickered in the distance, and an odd darkness continued over land and river.

"Dark as dusk," said Captain Oxford. "I'm open to some notions on this fellow we got sleeping in my cabin." At once James wondered if they'd had such a meeting after pulling him from the river the day he'd almost drowned.

"Well, he's a big one. It's too bad we're not a whaling ship," said Rusty. "He's dark as a gypsy and twice as sly from what I see. But a good salesman, no doubt about that. Sold me a policy when I'd hardly got done eating breakfast. Said my credit's good. Sharp. He's also in the market for buying a boat, Oxie."

"He's too big for our regular bunks, Captain," said Turf. A grin spread across his weathered face when the ladies tittered. "And as far as Rusty's credit, maybe this guy isn't so smart as we think. That goes double if he's got a notion to buy *Midnight*. He doesn't strike me as a sailing man, or anybody used to working with his hands. Now what about his sleeping in our bunks?" Turf grinned again.

"Maybe we could ask him to sleep on your tractor," said James. As quickly as he deadpanned the suggestion, Turf lost his smile.

"Hey now, look at this," said Rusty. "We're already listing to that side. See what you think, Oxie."

"Nah. That's the way I got her tied up. Let's stop running at the mouth. I'm serious." Then he lowered his voice. "I can't keep taking on every stray that comes along. No offense, James, my boy. Maybe we ought to hear from the ladies. Sylvia, what's your opinion?"

"I haven't seen enough of the man. Obviously he's stranded out here. I think he's something of a con man. My, did you ever see such a sky?"

Then Evelyn spoke. "It's our duty to do all we can for the man, Captain Oxford." She had a face that was rescued from plainness by a warm, loving smile. Her slightly curly hair couldn't seem to decide if it wanted to be light brown or dark blonde. "After all," she said, "the Lord says it in his book, right Reverend Dennis?"

"Why, that's right, of course Evelyn. Captain, have you asked the man about his destination?"

At that moment Snyder himself appeared in the front cabin doorway. His clothes looked rumpled, but he was smiling. He seemed almost cherubic to James, having a round face yet handsome features. For all his size, the ladies probably did not find him unattractive or without charm.

"Don't let me interrupt here, folks. Go on about your business. I left a few things on shore when the storm drove me to your good captain's vessel." For a man who looked like he weighed over three hundred pounds, Snyder nimbly navigated a side plank from the barge to shore.

"Don't you 'good captain' me," said Oxford, while they watched Snyder lift a box and backpack from behind the largest palm tree.

From the box he took two ornate bottles of whiskey, lifting them up for the captain and all to see. "These are for you, sir, tokens of my appreciation. Hope I didn't put too big a dent in your pastry supply."

Oxford beamed. "Not at all, not at all, Mr. Snyder. We was just saying how nice it was to make new friends, right, Rusty?" Then he burst into an old tavern ditty:

"Rye whiskey, rye whiskey, rye whiskey I cry.

If I don't get rye whiskey, I surely will die."

That was followed by an excellent rendition of the peculiar, long laugh that was Oxford's trademark.

Blackie flew to his shoulder and screeched, "Hi! Hi!" When Oxford kept right on laughing, Blackie offered a noisy encore.

Snyder lit up a cigar and grinned. "Listen folks, since I may have to journey with you for a few days, let me mention my life policies. Fine for your protection, and my friend Rusty here can verify, for any who care to ask, just how small an initial payment we're talking about. I'd also like to enter negotiations with your good Captain Oxford to purchase his fine barge."

Snyder smiled and Oxford frowned. "Don't let me trouble you anymore right now," he continued. "But realistically we can't forget about doing good business, not even in times as difficult as these. And a tip to those of you who think about their loved ones from time to time in this perilous world—plan ahead. After all, none of us live forever, right, Captain?"

Oxford nodded while sniffing the contents of one of the gift bottles, appearing to ignore the comment about buying *Midnight*. Sylvia had placed a sympathetic arm around Evelyn, who was dabbing at a brief flow of tears evidently caused by Snyder's mention of loved ones and not living forever. Then a clatter of footsteps brought Jesse from behind the women's cabin, alerting everyone that something unusual had happened.

"Captain, I saw that monster coming into the cove! He's not more than fifty yards astern!" Jesse used the nautical term he'd picked up from Oxie. "We've got to get out of here!" he yelled. The stark fear on his open face prepared everyone for the worst.

Oxford shouted, "Rusty! Turf! Make ready to ship out! Elf, you get back there. I'm with you. C'mon, tell me what your eyes see. Look sharp now! I don't see nothing!"

Again he ordered the women and Jesse the kid below deck. Rachel disobeyed, staying close to James, and Oxford was too preoccupied to notice. And Jesse nevertheless stayed topside, following Elf and anxiously pointed to where he'd spotted the monster.

The water broke twenty yards back, just as the barge edged away from the shore. James and the others argued over what they'd glimpsed. Elf alone was dead certain.

"It's Gargol! That foul beast will come up under you, Captain, or board you! Speed!"

· · ·

Oxford had raced back to the wheel, spelling Rev. Dennis, who'd filled in during the hectic moments of getting *Midnight* underway. With agonizing slowness the barge lumbered into deeper water like an old cow moving to familiar pasture. James held his breath and wondered if they might not be better off to leap for shore and abandon the barge. In split moments that choice was gone. He gripped Rachel's hand. She squeezed his hand in return, smiling, and that was but one more oddity to add to his collection.

James had difficulty forgetting something Snyder had said about loved ones, and in the midst of turmoil a vivid picture of Bethany gazing on their familiar river, near their apartment building, choked him. He thought of the thwarted birthday picnic.

Then water burst across the rear deck with such force that James and Rachel were knocked from their feet and sent sprawling onto the deck. As the creature's dark head slipped across the railing, jaws gaping, Elf sprang forward with the rear cabin's fire ax and sliced a notch into the monster's scaly neck. The beast thrashed through the rear railing as if it were made of toothpicks, at first ignoring the wound. From the force of Elf's blow, James expected to see blood gush from its dull-green hide. Instead, it reared upwards, oozing a slimy, colorless fluid.

Rachel looked stunned and little Jesse began to scream as loud as he could. James scrambled to his feet to help Elf and slipped again, falling heavily on the deck as the beast grazed him. The immense serpent drew back, forked tongue slithering in and out, its yellowish eyes gleaming hatred during its retreat.

It submerged except for its repulsive head, soaking Elf's inflicted wound in river water, and then at fifteen yards began again to advance on *Midnight*. At ten yards a sharp explosion, much louder than a gun, rocked the barge.

James backed away from the railing debris, turned and grasped Rachel and Jesse by their wrists, then looked up at the rear cabin roof. Snyder was outlined against the sky, clutching another stick of dynamite in one hand, a bright-tipped cigar clenched between his teeth.

Another toss and there was another explosion near the beast as it sought refuge in a strategic dive. Snyder hurled a third stick, but this time it failed to explode.

The barge was now reaching swift current, and as the passengers issued a collective sigh of relief, there was a mighty lurch that sent them reeling—and that was the end of it. Everyone waited, anticipating another blow to the barge, but none came.

Oxie waved exultantly to the others from the wheelhouse, while Blackie cawed, and *Midnight* once again found safe waters. The passengers sent up rounds of cheers. They cheered Elf's courage, then Snyder, then James, then Oxie, and finally everyone. All of them had survived together. Only Elf remained unsmiling, seemingly pained or paralyzed by the terrifying nearness of the foul beast.

James wondered if the last violent thud had come from a delayed explosion, or from the angered creature, although he freely joined in the celebration. Oxie called for whiskey and wine, and at last Elf managed a modest smile. Soon everyone but Jesse and Sylvia were imbibing, even though it was still morning.

It had been another frightening encounter, and more than one openly wondered if Gargol had drowned. None were very optimistic about that, but they did have cause to celebrate, and celebrate they did.

• • •

Afternoon wore on as *Midnight* steamed by riverbanks that began to show occasional trees, but it became apparent some problem resulted from their encounter with the beast. Water had begun to seep into the women's cabin, and Elf was ailing.

Bilge pumps took care of most of the excess water, but Evelyn and Rev. Dennis were quite concerned about Elf. He unhappily announced he would not be able to play the violin at sunset because of soreness in his bow arm.

"I don't see why he ain't coming up," said Oxford to Rev. Dennis. "Evelyn here says he hasn't got but a touch of fever and that his arm aches a little. Hell, I work every day with hurts worse than that."

"It's more than meets the eye," answered Rev. Dennis. "For one thing, there's the belief in what he calls a fell beast that troubles his mind. He holds the creature foul to the extent of imagining it to have certain evil powers. Our doctors might call it nonsense, but Elf is badly touched by fear."

"He's greatly afraid of evil spells and such things," said Evelyn. "He mumbles about getting off the barge. He says *Midnight* has tempted fate too often, or something to that effect. And he called the attacks omens of dire things to follow. It may be the fever's touched him, like Reverend Dennis says, in his mind. Believe me though," she said ringing her hands, "he's got me plenty worried."

Oxford grimaced. "I've got to keep this crate moving and take care of a leaky keel, and now play nursemaid to Elf, who might be crazy. Listen you two," Oxford pointed to Rev. Dennis and Evelyn, "it's your job along with Sylvia. All right, all three of you, keep the little guy off my back. Evelyn, you fix his favorite grub, whatever he wants. But don't let him come whining around me with no jinx talk. I got no time for that."

They nodded, and Sylvia said, "We'll take care of things, Captain. You just keep the barge moving away from that critter, and keep the water out of our cabins."

At that moment they heard an ominous scraping along *Midnight*'s underbelly. They all recognized the sound of stones and small rocks grinding against the keel.

"Damn all your blasted talking. See what you gone and made me do. Where was the buoy? Oh, crap!" He struggled with the wheel, which spun away. Then Oxford ran to starboard and portside.

"Dead Man's shoal! That storm must have took out the buoy. Hey, Rusty. You guys help me check this out. We've got to get—"

A yanking force stopped Oxford short when *Midnight* swung sideways in the current. The passengers milled around on deck between the cabins. Evelyn cried out, and so did Blackie, whenever the barge lurched and scraped unnaturally. Snyder looked to James like he was contemplating jumping ship. Jesse looked scared, and Turf feared the worst for his tractor. Only Elf remained below deck.

"Don't say your thanks too quick," said Oxford. "We ain't off the sandbar yet. That's just stones and such on the shoal—or else we might be sinking right now."

"Good heavens," said Evelyn, "doesn't this ship have any good luck?"

James stared at her and said, "Didn't you hear the captain say it could be worse? We're alive, aren't we, lady? It still beats swimming in this river."

Evelyn looked flustered, and said, "I'm beginning to think—"

But then Rachel came waving her arms, bolting from the rear cabin doorway. She could only make moaning noises, and James saw her stark fear.

"Sylvia. James. You go with her and see what's scaring her," said Oxie. "Calm her down. Hurry up! See what's wrong and come back and let me know, pronto. I got to stay and somehow work this old tub free."

• • •

While the men worked topside to free the beleaguered barge, Sylvia, James, and Rachel surveyed the damage in the women's cabin. Furniture, clothing, and cushions were afloat in two feet of water. It was Sylvia's turn to scream, while James just stared and patted Rachel's shoulder.

Sylvia was distraught. "Oh, my books! My papers! James, you get the captain down here. We've got to stop this or everything will be ruined, if it isn't already."

Sylvia waded into the mess, shaking her gray hair, while Rachel joined her, looking to salvage what they could. James turned and raced back up the steps to find Oxford at the wheelhouse.

"Captain! You'd better take a minute and look below deck. We might be sinking!"

Oxford seemed to barely hear him. Wrestling with the wheel, *Midnight* lurched one way and then the other.

"We're getting it! We're getting there. Turf! Drive your tractor to the stern. Go on! Snyder, you get back there, too. The current's making its grab, but we need rear ballast. Move it! I think we got us a chance!"

James held his tongue, trying to get a better perspective on what was happening. He saw their need to pull free from the treacherous shoal, but wondered if *Midnight* might not immediately sink. Oxford seemed to read his thoughts.

"Don't let a little seepage worry you, James. Bound to happen on a keel scrape like this one. Don't fret, my boy. Old *Midnight's* come through worse than this, right Blackie?"

Midnight's mascot had stopped screeching and now squawked a sporadic "Bye-bye!" That didn't make James feel any better, and he wondered if Oxford really knew how fast the water was coming in below deck. He decided not to risk making a further fool of himself, however, and kept quiet for the moment.

James watched with fascination as Oxford instructed Turf on precisely where to position his tractor. The weight shifted once more, and the river's current caught *Midnight* with greater impact.

More scraping sounds brought another grimace to Oxford's face. That was transformed into a broad smile when the barge began to swing free. Rusty and Turf sent up cheers, and little Jesse joined in. Snyder looked as if he was amused by some private joke. Perhaps, James thought, it's because his own great weight was put to good use.

Elf wandered up on deck looking dazed, and Evelyn took it upon herself to guide the diminutive fellow back to his bunk, gently scolding him as they went. From the opposite cabin, Sylvia emerged with an armful of soggy books and papers, as well as soaked clothing.

"We're darned near up to our waist in water down there," she snapped at Oxford.

"Well, why didn't you say so, James? You don't want the womenfolk drowning, now do you?"

"Less mouths to feed," said James, pretending indifference.

"Hey, Rusty, Turf, you guys get that tractor lashed down again and get below working them bilge pumps. The women will be sleeping with the men tonight if you don't get a move on." The two men grinned at Oxie's attempt to embarrass Sylvia, but quickly finished securing *Big Red.*

Oxford battled with the current for a while longer before he got *Midnight* properly headed downriver again, and then he yelled at James. "Here you go. Hold her to center current. I got to get below and see what me and the boys can do to get things squared away. You got to start earning your keep anyway, like all my working passengers." Oxford then gave James the wheel, adding a shrill laugh while he patted James on the back, and left him to face the river on his own.

· · ·

There was an hour or so left before darkness fell, and James knew the barge was making good time. He had assumed there would be smooth sailing for Oxford to trust him with the wheel, and so it proved to be. He laughed to himself, feeling exhilarated despite being worried that *Midnight* might not stay afloat.

It's quite an adventure, anyway you look at it, he mused to himself. He had to face the fact he felt more alive and happier than he had been in Riverton before this journey began. James wished his factory boss, Ollie, could see him at that moment. Or Bethany, when we battled the river beast. Wouldn't she be knocked out?

Then he noticed more trees ahead on the left bank and dimly perceived a small mound of land with more tree clumps.

Oxford returned with grease on his clothes. "Good job, lad. At least you haven't run us onto any more shallows. With a month's training I could make you into a pretty good river pilot."

James was about to ask how much the job paid when he noticed the humorous twinkle in Oxie's eyes. Still, Rachel and the others had gathered to watch another sunset, and James was pleased they'd all seen him take a turn at the wheel.

"Is that civilized land coming up on the left?" asked James. "That's not the Port of Jossandra, is it?"

"Portside, off the larboard bow," said Oxford with a snort. "Nope. It's more like the Port of Oxford. Some of the land my daddy left me, and fact is, most river pilots call my place Cool Water. I don't charge anyone though—just a place in the middle of nowhere to take on fresh water. We'll put in for repairs and see what me and Turf can do about them danged keel leaks. Maybe we can patch them proper. Like most good farmers, Turf's got repair skills. We got a fair cove to work in up there, if no Gargol catches up to *Midnight* again."

"That devil sure wouldn't come this far after us," said James.

"I don't rightly think so, lad. But let me tell you this ain't no ordinary trip. I can't remember when we had so much stuff going screwy in a long time."

He lifted his captain's hat, scratched his thinning hair, and took the wheel from James without another word. They both welcomed silence as a setting sun painted the western sky red and pink across a desert landscape.

James surveyed the passengers and the peaceful scene. As the barge had drifted farther downriver, he realized his thoughts of a return to Riverton had also drifted. He felt mesmerized, as if floating within a waking dream. For the time being, he merely concentrated on the prospect of arriving at a desert oasis that promised fresh water, and an opportunity to get solid land underfoot again. But somewhere in the back of his mind, curiosity was growing about a place all of the passengers referred to as the Port of Jossandra.

CHAPTER SIX

The nights are cool, and I'm a fool,
Each star's a pool of water, cool water.

- Bob Nolan

The sun had already set and a full moon was rising over the desert when Captain Oxford and *Midnight*'s passengers finished cleaning up. The clothes and bedding salvaged from the women's cabin had been hung out to dry. The morning sun would be required to finish that task.

"It really looks to me like the women will have to sleep in the men's quarters tonight," said Oxford. His voice was firm, and his studied nonchalance told James the captain expected resistance to that idea. He didn't have to wait long.

"Now see here, Captain," said Sylvia. "I'm not bunking double with the likes of these men. I draw the line. If my man were still alive he'd box your ears for even suggesting such a thing. And since he's not here, I've a mind to—"

"Hold your horses, Sylvia. There's no need to get yourself all riled up over nothing. Can't you wait till I've had my say? Geez! The men will sleep on deck, right here, or ashore if they like the ground better. We're going to have to place double watches tonight anyway. Meanwhile, you gals will have to make yourselves as comfortable as you can in new quarters. Just for now."

"It's going to take a heap of work," said Evelyn. "How long has it been since you men properly cleaned in there?"

"Just a doggone minute," said Rusty, irritation animating his wiry frame. "We aren't a pack of animals, you know. See how you women go getting worked up over nothing? Didn't the captain just say we'd be up here, without beds, on hard wood and ground? I'd think you'd be grateful to have dry mattresses, if for nothing else."

"He's right," said Sylvia. "Captain, my apologies. You could learn to communicate more precisely though."

Oxford grinned. "All right, the gals can start fixing up the dry cabin's bunks. And us men have to set at least three watches tonight. Make that three watches of two men each. One guy will take the point, right over there, to keep an eye on the river. The other will stay right here on the larboard bow, by Turf's tractor, to watch for land trouble."

"Like what?" asked James.

"Prowling animals, people, whatever," said Oxford.

"And at the point?" asked James. "What are we watching for—Gargol?"

"Maybe," the captain answered in a weary voice. "Whatever might come along to disturb my sleep. That's what I'm going to try and get right now. Rusty, you and Turf take the first watch. Me and Snyder will take second. James and the Reverend can take the dark to dawn lookout. Anymore fool questions? Good. Let's get on with it."

· · ·

The first watch seemed to go smoothly enough, but it was nearly midnight before the women finally settled down in their temporary quarters. Elf was the only male to remain below deck, and he slept fitfully in the captain's quarters. Oxford remained on deck with his men, falling asleep almost as soon as he curled up with a large blanket in his hammock along the railing closest to land. Rusty had taken the point watch, and Turf kept lookout from his tractor seat.

Although the waves lapped a lulling rhythm against *Midnight*, James found it difficult to sleep. At first he had a strong impulse to explore the oasis by moonlight, but eventually his tension eased and he also slept. Restlessness and dreams kept him tossing and turning. He'd wake up with a start, and then gradually drift back into dreaming about Bethany, and Riverton, and his factory job.

• • •

Below deck, all was quiet except for an occasional moan coming from the captain's cabin. Rachel took turns with Sylvia and Evelyn, cooling Elf's brow or giving him something soothing to drink. At best he merely dozed, and at worst he wrestled with a terrible delirium. The fever had not broken.

During the middle of the night, Rachel tiptoed to the captain's quarters and peered in at the figures beside the dim table lamp. Sylvia was soaking a fresh cloth, and Elf twisted slowly about, his eyes closed.

"Come here, child," said Sylvia to Rachel, who still stood in the darkened hallway. "What are you doing up this time of night? His groaning woke you?"

Rachel nodded a silent, sleepy yes.

"Button up your nightshirt, dear. I think he's quieting down, although his face is still too warm."

Rachel stayed near the edge of the bed, while Sylvia felt his forehead again. They sat in silence a long while before Sylvia spoke again.

"I can't keep my eyes open any longer, child. Would you like to sit with him awhile?"

Rachel shrugged, then nodded yes.

"Good girl. Don't stay too long though. Keep his brow cool, and if he turns for the worse, or if his fever breaks, come tap me on the shoulder. I just have to get a few winks of sleep before dawn."

Sylvia sat Rachel down in the chair, offered a motherly hug that Rachel brushed aside, and left the room half-asleep on her feet. Rachel wished that for just a few moments Elf would awaken and speak to her. What was he thinking?

• • •

Images of near-forgotten homeland, forest creatures, and woodland maidens moved through Elf's feverish dreams. He could not find his way, and he felt threatened by unknown beasts that loomed from dark shadows.

Elf's pale, milky skin reflected lamplight, and it seemed strange that his skin should sweat so profusely. He thrashed about for several minutes, then calmed as he felt the damp cloth. He heard Rachel dip it again before she bathed his entire face. He even imagined her trying to hum to him with a voice that could not or would not speak. As his hand came up to hold her slim wrist, he gave no thought to her being afraid.

Elf saw his woodland nymph through a yellowish haze, and he imagined green garlands in her tousled chestnut hair. In her arms she cradled stalks of flowers and fresh fruit. He tried to grasp her soft arms, but he was not strong enough to keep her. He clutched again for his elf lass. The damp sheets fell away and Rachel gasped. He saw her rise and turn in awkward surprise. He viewed her as a woman for the very first time. He hoped she saw him as a man, and not just a strange companion who made splendid music and spun delightful moods.

His right hand clutched her nightshirt as she spun away with a dancer's move. The buttons tore off, bouncing on the hard floor. He glimpsed the roundness of her breasts as she spun away from him. With her back to him, Rachel yanked free, fleeing the silent room without her nightshirt.

As Rachel fled in panic, Elf fell back into his tortured sleeping dreams. Never did the beasts of night overcome him, but neither did he find his forest home. And the lovely woodland nymph vanished into mist, gone for good.

. . .

As the time approached for the second watch, Oxford stirred and felt Rachel nudging him. There were few clouds. The night air was warm and dry. "I know girl, no need to wake the whole barge. It's my watch, and I know it. I got a clock in my head. Why are you running around in that half-open robe? Get below and go to sleep before you catch a night chill."

Rachel noiselessly disappeared down into the cabin. Captain Oxford managed to awaken a reluctant Snyder, and James continued to doze, knowing his watch would come soon enough.

Oxford said, "Hey, Snyder. C'mon, roll it out. Rusty and Turf here need to get a mite of shut-eye, too. You want the point, or to park yourself over by the tractor?"

"I'll take the point, Oxford. You just show me where to stand and what to watch for."

Oxford grumbled, but led the large man ashore. They walked some fifty yards from the barge to a point of land at the north end of the natural inlet.

"This here's the place. You can see where Rusty pushed down the grass walking here.

There's plenty of moon tonight, too, so if you see anything that spells trouble, hightail it back to the barge. Can you whistle?"

"Yes." Snyder put chubby fingers to his mouth and was about to demonstrate.

"No need for that," said Oxford, clenching his teeth. "If you can do it loud enough, send one of them out. One loud whistle, got it? Otherwise come running—or both."

"Sounds all right. How long do I watch?"

"I'll send James or the Reverend out a few hours before sunup. Keep a special eye out for that bastard Gargol trying to come sneaking up. I'd hate like the devil for it to get onto the deck with everybody half asleep."

"No need to worry, Captain. First of all, I think my explosives already did the trick. Second, I don't think it goes feeding at night. And third, I've still got more of these." He reached under his shirt, sucked in his belly, and showed several sticks of explosives.

Oxford gave a low whistle of his own. "Say, how much of that stuff have you got, anyway? I'd be willing to make a deal for some of that."

"We'll talk deals sometime soon," said Snyder. "I hate to waste explosives on that reptile, but you saw what I can do with these. So don't worry, I have access to more."

"That a fact? And why wouldn't you really want to go and blast Gargol with them? I mean, if you got plenty like you say."

"Let's say I have a certain admiration for the way that beast patrols its domain. It's the largest living thing in a wild river. It's got to be doing something right, and who knows, maybe it keeps riffraff down to a minimum."

"That thing is rotten to the core of its damned belly," said Oxford. "I could tell you a story that'd raise the short hairs on your neck." He stared at Snyder, trying to make a decision.

"Be my guest," said Snyder. "I've heard some tall tales from river people like yourself. Some of them are quite amusing."

Oxford bristled. "All right. Listen, this ain't no tall tale like you said. This here's something I seen with my own eyes ten years back under a full moon just like that one." Oxford stabbed his finger skyward, lowered his voice, and began his story in earnest.

"Me and the woman was doing some night fishing when Rachel was still a little girl. Right off *Midnight* there. A couple hours after dark Rachel went down to nap in the forward cabin, and me and the missus kept fishing. I guess maybe I dozed off, too, after a long, hard day. Anyway, I woke to this here horrible hissing and sucking sound with my wife thrashing something awful." His voice broke.

Oxford's gaze wandered across the river. He was breathing faster. Snyder stood silently, looking mildly incredulous, as if this could still be just another tall river tale.

"Listen to me, Snyder, and then try to tell me this here beast don't feed at night or is fit to live. It had my woman stuck in its head, a head like a huge watermelon. Had her by the top, and it must have stretched its mouth wider than you can believe, like a snake with a chicken. You ever seen that?"

"Affirmative."

"Well," he shuddered, seeing it all over again in his mind's eye. "It was like that thing with a chicken. Her head and shoulders were gone by the time I started beating on that slimy bastard from hell." He sobbed. "And when I could see it was no use, Rachel—" His voice broke again. "Rachel came walking up on the deck just like she done tonight when I was fixing to come out here." He wiped his eyes.

"Come on, man," said Snyder. "Get control of yourself. There's no monster here now. Rachel's safe. I saw you send her below deck just before you got me up."

"Yeah, yeah. Okay. So Rachel comes up and sees her ma being sucked down. Listen to me, you cold fish!" He grabbed Snyder by the arm. "When the thing backed off the railing, only her legs was left sticking out. One of her shoes fell off. She never said a word, never even screamed that I heard."

"It was merciful," said Snyder. "Fast kills are best. She probably never knew what hit her, Captain." He put a huge arm around Oxford and gave him a pat.

"And my beautiful daughter, Rachel, even better-looking than her ma, never spoke a word since. I don't really know if she remembers what happened. She might."

"Captain, I take it back. If I ever see that beast again, or any like it, it will be my pleasure to kill it with these." He brandished a deadly stick of explosive.

With shoulders sloping forward and his head bowed, Captain Oxford turned and walked alone back to the moored *Midnight*.

• • •

Just before the third watch, James felt as if he himself was being observed. He turned toward the railing, and while only half-awake he saw a head against the sky. He bolted into a sitting position from his covers on the deck.

It was Rachel, beautiful in the moonlight. She was standing there in her robe, barefoot. There was a glass in her hand, and her thick hair moved slightly in the night's desert breeze. James sensed her vulnerability and was drawn to her. He would have given a great deal to hear her speak just one sentence from those tempting lips.

"Can't sleep?" he whispered, rising to her side.

She didn't move away from him, but her eyes remained wary. Impulsively, James leaned forward and kissed her on the forehead. When she closed her eyes and didn't move, he kissed the fullness of her mouth and lingered for a moment. When her lips parted he was surprised by the smell of wine.

"Rachel? Try to sleep, but not with wine. It's . . . it's almost daylight."

He wished he knew what she was thinking. He felt protective. Her youthful face was flawless under the moon, he thought, but her expression remained placid, and therefore more mysterious than ever.

James suddenly remembered Oxie was on watch, and so he scanned the quiet deck. With a feeling of relief, he saw the captain dozing on Turf's tractor, evidently having fallen asleep while on second watch. James grinned and pointed at her dad. Rachel nodded with a slight smile.

"I've got to wake him, Rachel. I think it's my turn to stand third watch. You better get back to your bunk before he wakes up and finds you wandering the deck."

Once more she stood expressionless, inscrutable, and James wished again for some way to communicate more deeply, to discover what she thought and felt. He sensed she was troubled, and that intrigued him. Without knowing why, he wanted to help her, but he wondered if he was really being honest about that.

James guided her to the cabin doorway. He entertained a notion of pulling her to him and kissing her again, but resisted the impulse. Maybe some night when there's more time, he thought, or when it feels exactly right.

For fleeting seconds he remembered when he had first kissed Bethany, and the intoxicating reaction. He patted Rachel on the cheek and smiled his goodnight, wishing he could take time to toast her youthful beauty with his own glass of wine. She must have sensed his indecision. She breathed an almost imperceptible sigh before she wordlessly turned and descended the cabin steps.

Again his thoughts returned to his own summer of youthful passion with his girlfriend in Riverton. It had been great, yet there were also signs of trouble. There was always Bethany, but also too much drinking on his part. Rachel reminded him of how very much he missed angelic Bethany.

CHAPTER SEVEN

Money can't buy back your youth when you're old,
Or a friend when you're lonely, or a love that's grown cold.

- Red Hayes

"I wasn't sleeping," said Oxford.

"No," said Rev. Dennis. "You were just painting the tractor with your nose." He laughed at Oxie's feigned indignation, and together they decided nothing much was happening anyway. It was still dark.

"It looks like James is already up, Captain. It's time one of us got out to relieve Snyder and start the third river watch," said Rev. Dennis, "Hey, I can see Snyder from here. Isn't that the glow from his cigar?"

"Yeah. Are you going out there, or James? Don't matter. That's between you two," said the captain, just as James joined them. Within minutes Captain Oxford wrapped himself up in a blanket, secure in his hammock, and was ready to sleep.

Rev. Dennis spoke quietly to James, "Whatever's your preference, I really don't care either way."

"In that case," said James, "I'll stay here by the tractor and take the land watch. You can head out and send Snyder in from his river watch."

Rev. Dennis turned and slowly walked along the inlet's grassy edge, gingerly avoiding things he could not clearly see in the predawn darkness.

• • •

"Time to get some shut-eye, as the captain says," Dennis said as he approached the bulky watchman.

"I'm not sleepy anymore, but thank you Dennis for coming out," said Snyder. "I am getting hungry," he said, puffing on his cigar. "It gets boring as hell out here."

"It's rather hard to predict if hell is boring, isn't it," said Rev. Dennis.

"Negative. I've been everywhere, seen almost everything, and talked to about every type in the world. You know what the upshot is, Dennis? The bottom line? Boring. That's spelled b-o-r-i-n-g, with a capital B."

"Would you say that about our encounter with Gargol yesterday? It seems to me there's more excitement on *Midnight* every day than most people would want."

"You're talking about average people, Dennis, if you don't mind my saying so. Now I've been around the world more than once, traveling, selling, wining and dining. You name it, I've done it. A run-in with some poor river beast once in a blue moon is my idea of dull." He stopped and chuckled. "Unless, of course, you're in the process of being killed or eaten, or shall we say swallowed alive."

He paused for effect. "But people interest me from time to time. Yourself, Dennis, for instance."

Rev. Dennis detected a glint of mischief in Snyder's eyes, and said, "I'm afraid you're putting me on."

"No way," said Snyder. He pulled deeply on his cigar butt, then threw it into the river as he rose to leave. "For one thing, you've got a nice speaking voice. Men and women go for that, especially if you're selling something. Know what I mean?"

"No."

Snyder was undaunted. "Say you spend most of your working time trying to sell people on heaven or church or whatever is the latest religious vogue. That's wasted talent. You could work for a man like myself. That's big time. You'd travel, see the great world, and have an opportunity to grow. I'd set you up. Then someday if you got tired of all the money and women and adventure, well, you could always give up the good life and go back to preaching."

"I'm not in the active ministry right now. I am traveling. This is what I desire for the time being." He spoke with quiet conviction.

"Maybe so. But what about money? Income? Don't forget what I said. And you may not be preaching to these peons right now, but you still think preaching. I can tell by the way you act. And you can't see clearly enough through those thick glasses of yours to realize a new experience, of a different kind, is exactly what you need. I see it as clearly as I see your black beard. I could teach you how to make what you're good at pay off. Handsomely. Think about it, Dennis. Handsomely. Don't decide anything on the spur of this moment. Snap decisions are for fools like Oxford."

Rev. Dennis cleared his throat to speak as he watched Snyder take several steps towards the barge, then stop, evidently being pulled away by the thought of breakfast.

"Don't get me wrong, Snyder. I appreciate your interest in my career. But you and I actually appear to be going in different directions. I'm rather surprised, you being a man of the world, that you can't see something so simple. Peace of mind, for instance, interests me far more than fighting boredom or getting rich."

"Maybe they're all the same thing." Snyder spat in the river. "Dennis, you're a sad case. I hate to say it, but you're more naive than I first calculated. You're an amateur, so far from being professional it isn't funny."

"Maybe you're right, but I'm my own man, and I don't owe anyone," said Dennis.

"Maybe you're right," said Snyder. "And maybe you're afraid to try a novel approach." He left quickly without turning to look back at a puzzled Rev. Dennis.

Dennis did more thinking. He wondered why Snyder said some of the things he had. The man was pleasant one moment, and arrogant, or surly, the next. What bothered him most, however, were his own thoughts.

He knew Snyder most likely was a rascal, but he wondered if he had conned himself about this pilgrimage to the Port of

Jossandra. A latent fear arose that perhaps he'd studied religion so long that he'd lost track of where he was really headed. Finally, Rev. Dennis concluded he was still on the right path, but that he simply didn't know yet precisely where that path would take him. That's natural enough, isn't it? he wondered.

• • •

A tomato-red sun spilled over the eastern horizon as dawn was breaking on the third watch. With its appearance Rev. Dennis felt more alert. He had felt weary and afraid of dozing off since the night river tended to lull a man. Sunrise was a welcome sight.

When he heard water breaking halfway across the river in the strong current, Dennis expected to see a fish had jumped, or birds feeding. Instead, he was greeted with the unmistakable head and neck of the dreaded beast, Gargol. It was submerging and rising again in repeated movements with the current, like a dark, bloated swan. It's got to be following us!

Every muscle seemed to go rigid in Dennis's body. His throat went dry. He couldn't move or speak. It was the greatest fear he'd experienced since childhood, and never had he felt so alone.

What if it comes for me, or towards *Midnight?*

After a full minute seemed to take an hour to pass, Dennis knelt down to peer from behind a clump of bushes. He looked away from the reptile, and glanced in the direction of the moored barge. To his disbelief he saw a lithe woman poised at the railing. She dove perfectly, barely making a splash.

Rachel! Can't she see the beast? She must see! My God, she's swimming towards Gargol!

Moments later, Dennis saw James leaping from the barge and running along the bank, frantically waving to Rachel, but not yelling.

He sees the monster, too, I think they both see it!

Dennis's own reaction was inaction. His body felt frozen as he watched first the beast, then Rachel who swam towards it, and finally James who sprinted along the bank.

As James got closer to Dennis he tore his shirt off and began to fumble with his shoes. Dennis guessed that James hoped to cut Rachel off by swimming across the mouth of the inlet, from the point. Still, Dennis felt unsure of what to do. He felt like a rooted spectator.

Then Dennis observed that the serpent swam on a fixed line, now drawing even with the moored *Midnight*, but still far out in the river. It's not coming our way! It's not coming our way!

"James," he called in a harsh whisper. "Don't alarm the beast! It may swim past us!"

James appeared not to hear the preacher's plea. His eyes were fixed on Rachel as she swam, and he neither looked nor listened to Dennis. He ran closer to him, and when the bespectacled minister blocked the path, James sent him sprawling.

Dennis saw James hurl himself from the grassy bank, diving into the water where river met inlet. With powerful strokes, the young man quickly reduced the intercept point between himself and Rachel. She appeared oblivious to everything except an irrational compulsion to reach the creature.

Dennis could only watch and pray. Disaster was inevitable if the two swimmers alerted the beast, but only then, since the giant serpent apparently had seen or heard nothing to divert it from its downriver course. Finally, Dennis removed his sandals and waded chest deep into the warm water.

Dennis caught his breath as James accosted Rachel and began to struggle with her. From the beginning, he now realized, she had no chance of reaching the powerful beast on her own. It would have had to turn toward her and the barge.

Thank God it did not! he thought.

Rachel pulled James under, and for frightening seconds both swimmers disappeared.

Gargol continued past them, downriver and out of sight. Dennis then began to swim to the aid of the struggling couple. They came up choking, gasping for breath, and then James forced his forearm around Rachel's neck. She went limp as James struck out for shore. Dennis joined them and added his help to James to get her out of the water, up the slippery bank, onto the grass where they placed her inert body facedown.

Someone had sounded a general alarm aboard *Midnight*, and both men heard a whistle. Looking up, they saw Oxie, Evelyn, and Rusty running pell-mell in their direction.

• • •

Rachel moved to her elbows, coughing and breathing raggedly. James managed a weak smile to Oxie. "I owed you one," said James. "I don't know where she got this crazy idea, but she's going to be all right. Aren't you?"

Rachel, unsmiling, weakly nodded agreement. Oxford stared at his bedraggled daughter with what looked to James like both concern and unasked questions.

"You men did a good job," he said. "James, we're more than even." The two men shook hands, "I seen her swimming from my porthole," he said. "It's my fault, but I can't be both her daddy and mama every minute. Tell them what happened, Evelyn." Oxford sank down beside Rachel, trying to untangle her soaked hair.

"A tragedy," said Evelyn, her voice choking. "Sylvia found Elf gone this morning. Just plain went missing. We were looking everywhere below deck. He was so weak last night, and now he's gone. Rachel sort of . . . went crazy. I thought she was going to search topside and then I guess this happened."

Rachel rolled over on her back, taking great gulps of morning air while tears trickled down her cheeks. Evelyn tried to wipe her face, but she rolled over again on her stomach, burying her face in the wild grass. Everyone else looked at one another without speaking, sinking into sympathy. Her slender body shook, and there was little they could do to console her.

Finally, Oxford said, "Her ma was lost to the river, you know. Maybe she thinks the river got Elf, too." His voice trailed off.

"There, there," said Evelyn, softly rubbing Rachel's back.

"C'mon you guys," said Oxford. "Let's go see what's become of Elf. There's got to be some clues or something. Evelyn, you tend to my girl. She'll cry herself out by and by. She always does."

The men found no trace of Elf on the barge. At length they transferred their search to the riverbank, while Sylvia and little Jesse continued to comb the barge, searching for any clue that might help solve the mystery. The only evidence of Elf's existence was his ornate violin, which rested precisely where his body had last been seen. According to Sylvia, Rachel must have been the last person to see him. For the most part, Rachel lay motionless and sullen in the captain's hammock on deck.

"What's wrong with her, Sylvia," asked Jesse. "Why can't she come and help us look for Elf? We looked in every closet, every nook, and I even looked in the engine room."

"Never you mind, young man. Rachel nearly drowned this morning. She'll be herself before too long." The older woman combed Rachel's hair, which despite its thickness and length had nearly dried in the brisk desert breeze.

Meanwhile, the men gathered at the ramp, trying to decide what to do next. "If he's got himself drowned," said a sweating Captain Oxford, "then he's done it without leaving a trace. Jesse, you people found anything yet?"

"Nope. But Evelyn is still looking for him or for clues. Can we start searching back there?" The red-haired boy eagerly pointed to the oasis palm trees farthest away.

"I think we'd better go over the entire oasis very thoroughly," said Rev. Dennis. "Maybe we'll find something beyond the trees."

"Not too likely," said Oxford. "It's grassy around the spring and pond, then comes the palms and more grass. Out there," he pointed with a sweeping gesture, "tracks cover over real fast. It's sand and not much more. Besides, Elf don't barely leave no track to begin with, is my guess."

"We could divide up the oasis into sections," said James.

"Yeah, yeah," said Oxford. "Okay, spread out. James, you and Rusty take the left. Reverend and Snyder the right. Turf and me got the middle."

"I could use some sleep," said Snyder.

"What about me?" said Jesse.

"You kind of take all over the place, young fella. Just don't wander out into the desert. Fill in between us. And let out a yell if you see anything important."

The men and boy spread out as ordered, moving slowly across the sloping oasis. Its physical configuration reminded James of a horseshoe since the trees formed an open ring around the water with both ends touching the riverbank. The land sloped upwards away from the river. Everything was grassy within the rings of trees, but James was surprised to see such little variety of vegetation.

Beyond the ring of trees there were sparse patches of grass, which varied in size, and did not venture much into the desert. Beyond that was mostly rolling, shifting sand, scrub brush, and bleakness. Soon, from the outer perimeter, the ten-year-old squealed.

"Over here! I got something!"

"What you got, kid?" asked Oxford, arriving first on the scene.

"Tracks!" said Jesse in an excited voice. "Think they might be his? Elf's?"

Oxford knelt down to examine them. One by one the men gathered around the site of possible discovery.

"Maybe, maybe not," said Oxford. He scratched his head. "But I doubt it. Why would he go straight out into the desert?"

"Looks like they could be rabbit tracks to me," said Turf. "Or a polecat or fox. Can't tell much the way the ridges fill in with sand. See that? The wind could have these completely covered in an hour, or even less."

"Shouldn't someone go out into the desert?" asked Dennis. "I mean follow these out in that direction, just in case. If Elf was feverish like the ladies say, he could have been disoriented, wandered out there, and fallen. He could even be behind some of that brush, or behind a sand mound."

"He's right," said James.

"He's partly right," said Snyder. "Look at the size of that wasteland. You could search for a year and lose yourself in the process."

"I kind of agree more with Snyder on this one," said Oxford. "I'd hate to leave my fiddle player behind though, and have Rachel pining for him. Tell you what. While the rest of us fill up *Midnight*'s water barrels and make ready to ship out, you two, Dennis and James, might have yourselves a look-see."

"How long do we have?" asked James.

"Couple hours. Aw heck, make it by noon. Keep these trees in sight at all times, Reverend, or you'll end up going to your own funeral. I mean it." Oxford tried to joke, but his laugh was absent.

. . .

After filling their canteens, James and Dennis headed out in the direction of the unidentified tracks. The others began the arduous task of filling large wooden water casks and rolling the barrels one by one onto the moored barge. While they worked, gloom settled over the passengers, and more than one prayed the magical violin and its player had not been silenced forever.

"I've heard it said that when an elf dies they sometimes go poof and merely disappear," said Evelyn while coming up on deck with Rachel.

"For heavens'sake, Evelyn, not in front of the girl," said Sylvia with a disapproving frown. Rachel looked pale and sad. Sure enough, the tears began trickling again.

"I don't mean Elf actually died, child, or that Elf is even an elf," said Evelyn. "It's just so strange we can't find him. There's nothing except that gorgeous violin you dance to. If there were a body, or if we found him sick or hurt, we could at least tend to him."

"You're going from bad to worse," said Sylvia. "Can't you see Rachel's sorrow? Maybe the men will turn something up in the desert search. The Reverend and James are still out there looking, honey." She hugged Rachel about her shoulders when the troubled young woman rose. "Why don't you go below and get some decent sleep? I know for a fact you scarcely slept at all last night. So many times a good sleep makes all the difference in the world."

Suddenly, Rachel bolted. She broke away from the women, ran down the gangplank past where the men were filling barrels at the spring, and headed for the farthest trees that encircled the oasis.

"Stop her!" Oxford scrambled after Rachel. "Don't let her get out in the desert!" screamed the captain, puffing after her but losing ground.

After ten minutes of hectic running and dodging by Rachel, the men were able to corner her. She ran like a wild gazelle, but they kept cutting her off and circling around until Snyder came up behind her, pinning her flailing arms.

Snyder carried her like a sack of wheat over his broad shoulder, back to *Midnight* and down into the cabin where her bed had been the night before. Captain Oxford strapped Rachel down with a white sheet around her slender waist.

Finally, she closed her eyes and lay still. Sylvia, after being persuaded by Oxford, agreed that the cabin door should be secured from the outside until after their departure from Cool Water.

"We'll be underway at lunch, I mean, after lunch," said a shaken Captain Oxford. "Unless James and Dennis come up with something in the desert. I told Elf when he came aboard I'd deliver him to the Port of Jossandra, or else to a first-class forest. You hear me, Rachel? If I can do it, I will. No one wants to go off and leave your friend if he's still alive."

Rachel did not move. She merely opened her large, brown eyes and stared blankly at the cabin ceiling.

CHAPTER EIGHT

For the Lord sees not as man sees:
man looks on the outward appearance,
but the Lord looks on the heart.

-1 Samuel 16:7

"Maybe we shouldn't go any farther," said James. "You look tired."

"I guess I am at that," said Rev. Dennis. They trudged together through the desert sand, trying to decipher the tracks they followed from the oasis called Cool Water. "My thoughts start to wander. I think about some things Snyder said to me last night and I wonder who's the one who is really lost." They stopped and looked back at the semicircle of palm trees that were barely visible. "For one thing, I'm not used to standing night watches."

"I know exactly what you mean," said James. "In fact, I may have nodded off during my watch. That bothers me. You know, that's most likely when Elf slipped overboard or came out here."

"You blame yourself?" said Dennis.

"Not really," said James. "And no one's accused me either, although Oxford hinted. But maybe if I'd been wide awake—"

"Forget it," said Dennis, who stopped to wipe his glasses. "If he came this far, and intuition tells me he did, then Elf was purposely avoiding detection. He would have sneaked around you one way or another."

"I suppose," said James. He studied the terrain, waiting for Dennis who finished cleaning his glasses. "Hey, Dennis, let's make for that small tree down the incline there. It looks like a bit of shade. We could rest a few minutes and decide what to do. This trail is going nowhere."

"That'll take us out of sight of Cool Water. Don't forget what Oxford said," warned Rev. Dennis.

"Ah, c'mon. We can easily follow our own tracks back. We've got less than an hour left. Let's hurry." James sensed the risk, yet felt if should be taken. "No more tracks to follow," he said to Dennis over his shoulder. "But this is the way he'd have to come, if we were on the right tracks to start with."

As they half-slid down the sandy incline, James mentally wrestled with his own doubts. If I saw green or a town out there somewhere, I'd keep on going alone by myself. The land feels so good for a change, even desert, he thought.

"James, look at this!" Dennis held up a small blue jacket, its thin material nearly buried under the fine sand.

"That's his!"

James knelt, fingered the cloth, then looked away. "Down to that tree," he said. "He'd head there for sure. Dennis, we're going to find Elf!" Like a kid on a scavenger hunt he felt excitement building.

"We've already found him," said Dennis. "Look closely at that tree." James followed the suggestion, and grinned at his companion.

• • •

Captain Oxford and Turf were filling the last barrel with the fresh water that gurgled from under a massive boulder into a small pond.

"Listen, Captain," said Turf, "this might be the end of the line for me. You told me once you'd like to find someone to work your dad's land now that he's gone."

"I thought you was keeping kind of quiet, even for you. Hell, Turf, you can do better than this water hole in the middle of nowhere. Sure, I'd love to have a hard worker like you go fifty-fifty with me, fix it up and all. But what about the valley where the Port of Jossandra waits for you and Big Red? That's great farmland. Or even hang on another fifty, maybe seventy-five miles. As soon as we spot some decent acres . . . ," Oxford's voice trailed off.

"Nope. I decided. You said before I could if I wanted. Me and that tractor have had it with river travel, Oxie. Listen, that Gargol clinched it. That damned thing is waiting for us downriver somewhere as sure as that Great Falls you told me about. I'm not getting any younger, and I don't want any more of that beast or risk sinking Big Red in the river. Let me go."

"Now, Turf, you know we still got this here understanding," said Oxford, lowering his voice. "You produce on my land, like it was your own land, see—and I get the produce you promised at cost, on my trips. Plus half of any cash we get on what I sell for you. So I'd rather find some good land instead of this little patch of oasis for you. We both want what's best for you."

"Hell yourself, Captain. It's always easy to talk tomorrow to me. But look here, today, at this supply of pure water." He let it trickle over his gnarled fingers while Oxford capped the last barrel.

"So?"

"It's gold. All this here countryside needs is to get it. It'll be more than a bit of hard work, you bet, but I'll make stuff grow good with this water source. You'll see. I got plenty of seed: corn, potatoes, lettuce, squash, melons, you name it!"

"Yeah, yeah. Well, I got to think on it some. The other passengers might not like it either."

"They won't care. And so what if they do? Just tell them my tractor is tilting the barge, or something. Anything. You've told a lie or two on this trip already, I reckon. I never did think the Port of Jossandra could be as great or fantastic as you said. Plus, Oxie, always remember you get my produce at cost, or sometimes free. I just crave some land that's not already taken, and a chance to work it. Maybe next trip you can bring me a cow or two, and maybe some chickens."

"And maybe some pigs?" Oxford began the long, forced laugh that had been absent awhile. Turf joined in.

"Shut up now. Here comes Snyder and Rusty," said Oxford. "No need getting them riled up or asking questions."

While Turf maintained a triumphant silence, all four men helped to roll and carry the final barrel back to *Midnight*. It was hot, sweaty work.

"We about ready to ship out?" asked Snyder, who appeared very impatient.

"Right after lunch," said the captain, puffing. "You wouldn't want to miss fish again, would you? Fish and them thin-fried taters." His laugh bounced off every palm tree that encircled the pond. Blackie joined in with raucous cawing.

The trees stood like guards, bristling outward against the harsh wilderness. Blackie swooped to the top of one tree, with a "Hi there!" Out of that bleak desert two figures were approaching.

James and Rev. Dennis weren't far off, and the absence of Elf was conspicuous. It appeared they had failed in their search-and-rescue mission.

· · ·

Elf was sipping fresh water from a small stone jar he carried. He looked very small. His pursuers circled around the isolated palm tree he leaned against, confronting him in dramatic fashion. As his pale eyebrows arched, his face showed only the faintest hint of surprise.

"Never thought to be seeing the likes of you two again," said Elf. "At least not before the misty beyond."

"Why did you do it?" asked James. "Is this your Elf idea of grown-up hide-and-seek?" Irritation tinged his question.

"We're happy to find you alive, Elf," said Rev. Dennis. "You've given everyone a scare. That's not like you, and I for one had almost given you up for dead."

"More's the pity. Sorry for the grief I caused on *Midnight*, gentlemen. I've been knowing in my heart for many miles this river trip is wrong for the likes of me. It's not what I was promised for playing the fiddle by your Captain—namely, escape from my own misery. And mostly it's not what was promised by me to myself."

"Why run off like that though?" asked James.

"When that terrible fever broke at dawn, I felt done in by dreams gone sour. Homeland and beasts and lasses—my head was all in a jumble. Then I struck clear thinking on Cool Water and this wild-free land."

He looked far off and added, "My new home is here, came the sweet thought. I can make myself a home right here."

"In the middle of a desert, with no trees to speak of?" asked Rev. Dennis.

"In your way of speaking, I guess that is true," said Elf. "But my people have passed away, and I am tired and worn from wandering in waking dreams. *Midnight* is taking me far away from what my needs are, farther and farther every time the sun sets. My music is getting low in spirit. And then into my life comes this fell beast with violent ways that are alien to my true nature. Such things from the darkness of the river must be avoided or destroyed."

"Maybe I'm stupid, but I still don't get it," said James, finding a place in the small area of shade. "Why run off into the desert? Why leave your violin behind? Did you want us all to think you'd drowned?"

"Perhaps. It was in part a decoy, for my getting clear. I knew Oxie would never agree with my thinking. As for my violin, it is for Rachel, or whoever comes along one day to play tunes for her. Enough of why. My plan was to hide here in the waste, coming back to Cool Water after the ship leaves."

"But how would you survive? What would you do for food and shelter?" asked Rev. Dennis.

Elf chuckled. "It's true I love the forests, and that's what I'd do with all my time. See these packets? I have seed from twelve different kinds of trees. My favorites. I will be planting them along the river and such. Then when they are thriving with good water, a new forest gradually begins. So it will take years, but I have nowhere left to go that I can see."

They all sat silently, and Elf continued, "And I love fishing for my meals, especially at dawn and dusk. Grapes and olives would come along, too. See how clear a real dream can be? It would be a finer life by far than forever serving on a ship, riding her to drowning or darkness in the end. Gargol was the omen to open my blind eyes. Then the fever brought everything to a boil, as they say. I am only sorry for loving . . . leaving, I mean, the lass." Again, he looked far away and into nowhere.

"Maybe you do make some sense," said James. "You won't come back to *Midnight* with us then?"

"Never. I am as set as I can be," said Elf.

"You sound like a man who knows his own mind," said Rev. Dennis. He removed his glasses and wiped the sweat smears away.

"Not really, my friends," said Elf. The small man smiled. "It is what life designs for me. I was created to live and dwell free, and to play my songs to the wild. Since I cannot find a suitable forest, it seems I was meant to grow one or to die in my efforts. But you can do me one small favor."

"If we can," said Rev. Dennis.

"Tell Rachel how sorry I am and that I love her with a brotherly affection. Don't you see? She stole my heart the very day I first spied her dancing to a wind-song near the captain's ship. I am perhaps a fool to be leaving my violin, but it is hers to have."

Elf paused in silence for half a minute. "I do know how simple of me this must sound. There are no words to say." He turned his face away from them.

"I understand," said Rev. Dennis. "Leave it to me. The lass, as you call her, will calm down with the passing of time."

"She is upset? Oh, what a fool I am. I should have spoken to her, yet I could not. Break free, said my inner voice. A clean break. Run for your free life. And that is what I have gone and done."

"You may have been right," said James. "I've had my own thoughts about leaving the barge. But I couldn't make a home out here like you might be able to. I almost envy you. Good luck."

"Envy no man anything, Jamie. Your time will come when life has it prepared for you." He gave a smile, knowing what he alone knew.

• • •

After shaking hands with Elf, James and Rev. Dennis turned and walked away, and within a few minutes Elf was left alone with his dream. From the top of the desert rise the two searchers hesitated, and then waved a final farewell to Elf.

"It's just crazy enough an idea to work, you know, Dennis. I can't help but envy his freedom, though I suppose the odds are against him."

"If God is with him, that's all he needs. He spoke of his inner voice. So is it God's design for him, or human will? That's the question. But I keep thinking there's more debate or advice or warning to give him," said Rev. Dennis. "I agree with you in part though, James. In some ways I think he could do better than we might expect. At least he has a clear idea of what he wants."

"That's what bothers me most," said James. "I'm having some trouble ever seeing a forest here. Aren't you? But who knows."

The two companions then walked on in silence. Both were solidly convinced that Elf was wedded to a great experiment, for better or for worse.

. . .

As they approached the dot of oasis, James and Rev. Dennis concluded a short, earnest discussion.

"Then the best thing all around might be to keep Elf's escape secret?" said James.

"I tend to think that's best, although I won't directly lie about it," said Rev. Dennis. "Once we're well downriver and the circumstances appear right, then it's a different story. What bothers me most is Rachel's sadness. One of us ought to tell her the truth as soon as possible."

"I've got a feeling Oxford won't like losing his fiddle player," said James. "He might even blame Elf for Rachel's near drowning, but you know what isn't right? The violin. Elf will need it in the days—"

"What's this?" James interrupted himself, startled by what he saw. He couldn't have been more surprised if the barge were gone.

There was Turf ashore with his tractor, Big Red. Oxford and Rusty had already pulled back the makeshift gangplank, and they appeared to be making ready to get underway. It looked to James as if Turf was also going to be left behind. James saw him hastily inventory his plowshares, a planter, sacks of seed, lumber, and other supplies.

James and Dennis began to run, and James gave a quiet reminder to his companion. "Say nothing specific about Elf if we can help it. If it comes to lying, I'll do the talking. Elf's got to stay free."

"Agreed," said Rev. Dennis. "But what's this? It looks like Elf might have some company when he stays behind. Maybe there's been a change of plans for Turf."

"Hello, boys! Any luck?" asked Captain Oxford from *Midnight*'s deck. "I thought not. He's drowned himself in water or sand, and it's sad and all but I guess it don't matter much which. Good news here though. Turf's found his little farm without going all the way to the Port of Jossandra. That's right." His laugh was more artificial than usual.

James and Dennis stared briefly at one another, thinking along similar lines: a two-man settlement!

"We're sailing in five minutes. If you fellas want some fish, there's plenty of Evelyn's leftovers in the galley. Snyder ain't eating as many as he used to. Say, did you find anything at all?"

"Yes and no," answered James. "It's so damned big out there an elephant could be swallowed up. I'm afraid we've returned empty-handed. If he's still alive, at least he'll have plenty of fresh water. Now, what exactly do you mean about Turf finding a farm? This sure as heck isn't any farm."

James saw at once he'd struck Oxie's funny bone, or maybe it was the way James said it, because the captain laughed so hard tears actually came to his eyes.

After a bit, Oxford held his aching sides and gasped, "Nah, that's just what I tried to tell old Turf. But he's gonna prove us all wrong and turn it into a farm. If anybody can do it, it's him. Right, Turf?" Oxford wiped his eyes as Turf approached *Midnight*'s railing. The sturdy farmer clapped James and Dennis on their backs as they prepared to board.

"Yep, go ahead and laugh if you want. All I can say, Captain, is you kept your word and found me new fields to plow. I'd like to see you get going before you change your mind."

"You heard him, men. All aboard!" said Captain Oxford.

James and Dennis had grown more uneasy, but said nothing and did nothing except exchange hurried glances.

I sure hope Cool Water's big enough for the two of them, thought James.

Captain Oxford, assisted by Rusty, heaved the last restraining line on board, and still neither of the newly returned searchers spoke of Elf.

"Shouldn't there be more time to think this out?" said James. "I mean, Turf's tractor has come in handy before."

"We'll just have to get along without him and his tractor. On my future trips it'll mean more to us, Turf being right here on shore. I'll get more supplies, like fresh produce—cheap."

James saw it was no use stalling without spilling Elf's secret, and he didn't want to risk that. Then he suddenly turned and ran below deck, coming back up in seconds with Elf's violin.

"What the heck are you doing with that?" yelled Oxford. James grinned a silent message to Dennis before he answered the captain.

"If Elf should ever turn up around here, he'll need it more than us," James yelled back as he leaped ashore. He ran along the bank while the barge was moving away, and he stopped beside Turf with a broad grin.

"What the devil are you doing giving me that blasted fiddle?" said Turf. "I accept your best wishes and all, but I don't play the thing. I've got a tin ear. You better get your butt back on that barge, James. No offense you understand. You're going to have to swim for it."

James thoughts raced as he tried to find some diplomatic way of breaking the Elf news to Turf. He saw *Midnight* easing away from the bank, so for certain his time was short.

"Turf, listen. We found Elf's jacket out there, the blue one. Remember? Yeah, that's a fact. So I can't say I'm positive, but, well, just don't be too surprised if he turns up after we've gone downriver."

Turf's mouth dropped open.

"So if he turns up, you guys make the best of it, hear? And he'll need this, believe me, he will." James patted the ornate violin. He left it in front of Turf, turned and sprinted away without waiting for any comment.

Turf bent down, rose up again and stood alone, holding the newly acquired instrument in clumsy fashion.

James raced along the grassy bank, then dove into the inlet's water before *Midnight* had gotten up much steam. Captain Oxford was stomping around the deck, waiting to pull his passenger on board again. He and Rev. Dennis finally grabbed the young man's arms and yanked him onto the deck.

"That was a fool thing to do," said Oxford, not realizing what James had really accomplished.

"Just giving Turf a quick lesson on how to play the fiddle," said James. "It's going to be a long haul for the farmer if he doesn't learn to appreciate good music."

Rev. Dennis stood at the stern railing, shaking his head. Captain Oxford wrapped up the last mooring lines. *Midnight* swung out into the river proper.

The rest of the passengers, except for Rachel, stood on deck waving their goodbyes to the solitary figure of Turf. He stood on his tractor seat, waving the violin which caught and reflected the rays of the desert sun.

James had not sorted out all of his thoughts, but he was pleased to know the violin was where it belonged.

CHAPTER NINE

Swiftly, swiftly flew the ship,
Yet she sail'd softly too:
Sweetly, sweetly blew the breeze—
On me alone it blew.

-S. T. Coleridge

Tension, based on envy, settled in among the remaining passengers like a stowaway while they watched mile after mile of sparse desert roll by. Seeing Turf with a tangible version of his heart's desire made them think in terms of their own goals, and how long it was taking to attain them. Never mind the fact that Turf settled for less than what he'd set out to gain, or that Elf had failed altogether. All that was overlooked.

Evelyn finally began to vent her frustration on Captain Oxford. "I don't see why Turf should have been given special treatment. What did he do for you to end up with that entire oasis? Captain, do you hear me? I'm tired of seeing others get ahead, while I keep on cooking and waiting and cooking and waiting. Why don't I ever get anything?" She complained for everyone to hear.

"And I'm tired of having people sniping at me while I knock myself out doing my job, mile after mile, taking all the risks with my ship *Midnight*. You're getting closer to the Port of Jossandra all the time, ain't you? And that's where everybody wanted to go in the first place, right?"

He was quiet for a minute.

"And nobody told you it was easy or cheap, which is why you agreed to work along the way," said Captain Oxford. "All of you had agreements with me, just like Turf did. So why don't you dry up and let me keep this ship in fast current?"

"That's easy enough for you to say," said Rusty. "Evelyn has a point. And now I'm expected to do a lot of Turf's chores, too. It sure seems like he got special favors, and we could have looked harder or longer for Elf. That entire layover was—"

"Hold your horses," said Oxford from the wheel.

"Maybe they both have a point," said Snyder. "If I ran this ship, you could expect equal treatment for all passengers. Why was it Turf got that land? Did you consult the others about that or his leaving *Midnight*?"

"Hear, hear!" said Rusty.

"Now just a doggone minute," said Oxford, redness creeping up his neck. "What right do you have to stick your nose in this, Snyder? When I rescue strays, it don't give them the right to argue with me." He stamped his foot for emphasis.

"As far as Turf," said Oxford, "he worked harder for me than anyone else on this ship. He's been here the longest, and we talked land deals before I took on anyone here. That was my business. I get some payments at the Port of Jossandra, too. That's my own business. Back to Turf. There's work he done I didn't want to worry you about."

"What a leader," said Snyder under his breath.

The others remained silent and attentive as the captain continued to explain.

"Old Turf solved a slew of problems sailing this barge, and he got his reward. First off, when he was working on this last keel leak, last night, Turf came up to me and volunteered metal from his machinery to seal off leaks coming in below deck."

"Is that really true?" asked Rusty.

"It's a dad-gummed fact. He gave up extra plowshares so the strong metal would support *Midnight*'s hull against river pressure and scrapes. That was his own property, and he did all the work himself, while others was sleeping or on watch."

"He must have done a fair job, too," said Sylvia to the others. "Rachel and I checked the rear cabin, and it appears we can move back in there. There's hardly a trickle of water seeping through either floor or wall."

"See!" said Oxford with a beaming smile. "And that's not all. If Turf gets that farm of his going proper, he says the passengers, you and me, would share his harvest. Cheap fresh veggies and fruits and grains and such. Plus he'll tend to the spring, not to mention putting it to work for once to make the whole oasis better. No siree, old Turf more than earned his way. I'm surprised you people didn't see that right off," said Oxford.

"You'll have to admit we weren't informed about everything," said Snyder. "You've got a high-handed way of running things, Captain, if you don't mind my saying so."

"I do mind," said Oxford. "Like I said, I think you forget you're a guest here, mister. I think I made it clear I'm not going to sell *Midnight*, and maybe that's why you join in these here complaints that got nothing to do with you. You'd be better off to mind your own business."

Oxford turned from Snyder to face the passengers. "Now I want to say something to all of you. I'm the one running this ship. We're due into the Port before too long if we can keep this here pace, and that's my job as I see it. Not to play nursemaid to every little doubt and problem you got. Now bug off and let me think about what I'm supposed to be doing next."

"He sounds right to me," said Rev. Dennis. "Let's help move the women's things back into their cabin. What we need is more positive action and less arguing."

"Reverend, that's the smartest thing I've heard you say yet," said Oxford. "Sometimes I think you've got the makings for running one of these here riverboats yourself. You took the words right out of my mouth."

That was Captain Oxford's ultimate compliment, and he punctuated it with a laugh that told everyone things were back to normal. They all settled down, pitching in to get the women's cabin on *Midnight* back in order.

• • •

The afternoon passed quickly, and the riverbank scenery remained monotonously the same, although a few gulls and a single, high-flying hawk were welcome visitors.

James looked for an opportunity to talk alone with Rachel about Elf. They still hadn't told her of their discovery, and that revelation remained uppermost in his thought. She looked so forlorn it made his own heart ache.

When she hears, I'll bet she smiles again, he thought. Then he remembered the music was gone, and James wondered if she'd ever dance again without those magical tunes.

At dusk, the passengers gathered from force of habit to watch another sunset. James noticed that Rachel failed to come up from the women's cabin. He approached Rev. Dennis, who stood astern in his favorite place watching *Midnight*'s wake break the river's peaceful flow.

"Have you spoken to Rachel about Elf?" said James.

Rev. Dennis looked up and said, "There hasn't been a good opportunity yet. Maybe one of us should go down now and talk to her."

"Now? If I had a chance during supper I would have. We've got to make her understand before she gets too . . . despondent."

"Don't be surprised if telling her doesn't make much difference," said Rev. Dennis. "Oh, she's bright enough, and I've no doubt she'll be relieved that Elf's alive. But she's still apt to mourn for him and his music. Rachel's moody to start with, and one way or another I'm afraid Elf's gone from her life."

"I don't know," said James, "but I'm going to try and cheer her up. I can't stand to see a woman mope and sulk like that. Sometimes Bethany does the same thing, and it drives me crazy."

"Bethany?"

"My girlfriend. We'd been together quite awhile before . . . before all this river stuff happened."

"You miss her a lot?"

"More than I can say," said James. "But sometimes out here Riverton and Bethany seem like another lifetime. I want to get back to that world and have another chance to patch things up. The sooner the better. Once we get to this port the captain's always talking about, I'll check the place out and see why everyone thinks it's so special. Then I'm out of there! I'll go by land or by river, whatever's the best and quickest way back. I'll have to get around the desert somehow. I'll figure all that out, check out this Jossandra place, and then decide how to get home."

"You may have problems there, at the Port of Jossandra," said Rev. Dennis. "From all I've heard it's a very isolated place. A lot of people stay there and never come back. Captain Oxford seems to be an exception. He's been there before, but doesn't actually go ashore, so he scarcely knows any details of what it's really like. He knows how to get there, but he never seems to talk about return trips."

"He has to get back upriver himself, doesn't he?" said James. "Remember what he said about seeing Turf on later trips? Back and forth. Back and forth. That's the picture I get. Man, you'd think he'd go nutty." James laughed. "Maybe he already has. In this world it's not that hard to go bonkers."

Rev. Dennis shrugged. "You've got a point. Say, Rachel just came up on deck. Don't turn. She'll think we're talking about her, and she probably feels bad about not dancing."

James said, "We could flip a coin to see which one of us has our little talk with her. I'm dying to tell her about Elf, if you want the truth."

"I've got an idea," said Rev. Dennis, glancing around the deck. "You stay here, away from the others. I'll see if I can steer her back this way. Or else everyone's going to hear the Elf news, and I think we agreed to wait longer on that?"

"Agreed. I'm game. It'll be my pleasure to try and make her smile again."

"I know exactly what you mean," said Rev. Dennis. "Hang on a minute. Here goes nothing. Whatever you do, don't get her overexcited. Gently. Break it to her gently."

"Right," said James.

Rev. Dennis moved forward amid the gradually descending darkness. The western sky still cast a sliver of pink and red-tinged brightness. Captain Oxford's wheel light was lit, but he hadn't yet signaled any intention of landing for the night. Evidently he wanted to make up for lost time.

• • •

Fifteen minutes of waiting seemed like a long time until James saw Rachel coming towards him along the railing. Then his chest felt lighter, and time was forgotten.

"Did Dennis tell you that we have news?" asked James when she was several feet away. He peered over her shoulder, half expecting Rev. Dennis to be following her. They were alone. Rachel nodded her head yes, shaking dark, lustrous hair in the light of a rising moon.

"Did he tell you we have news about Elf?" He heard her intake of breath, yet he detected no change in Rachel's expression. She moved a step closer. Again he searched her face for signs of hope or fear. She was simply alert, waiting.

"Rachel, listen carefully. When we went searching in the desert at Cool Water, Dennis and I found Elf's blue jacket." He was trying to build slowly, to give her time to prepare herself. "And then we kept following what we could of his tracks."

She came closer, reaching out, and James instinctively took her warm hands in his own. She trembled.

"We found him alive and well. He was drinking spring water he'd carried with him out into the desert. His fever seemed gone, and he was only waiting for the barge to leave."

Rachel slapped James across the face. He stepped back, stunned. She stepped forward and swung at him again. He caught her right arm at the wrist and held it firmly. Rachel uttered a small cry and instantly he released her.

"I don't understand. Rachel, Elf is alive. He said to tell you he was sorry, and that he loves you like a sister."

She had regained control of herself, and her dark eyes stared intently, apparently trying to determine whether James was telling the complete truth. Rachel motioned with her hands that he should continue talking. James breathed more easily when he saw she wasn't going to get hysterical.

"He wants to plant a forest, Rachel. Elf said he had to leave *Midnight* because it wasn't taking him where he wanted to go. He couldn't wait any longer to find a special forest, not another day. And . . . he said he wanted you to have his violin. But, of course

I took it back and left it with Turf, to hold for Elf. I hope you understand why."

Pulling away from James, Rachel's hands moved to her face. In a long minute she composed herself.

"There's not much more to tell. Dennis and I wanted to let you know right away, but we didn't want the others to know yet. It's really Elf's secret. He only wishes to be free. And I think he loves you very much."

Rachel stepped closer and grasped his hands, squeezing them. For the first time she managed a smile. It was fleeting, yet it showed James she understood. Her brown eyes were brimming.

With Rachel so close, an awkward feeling kept him from responding. He wanted to kiss her, to feel her lips again. He wanted to kiss her before she got away.

Rachel studied him, and James felt like she was reading his thoughts. Her smile faded, replaced by a hint of uncertainty. As she began to draw away, James reached out, took hold of her hand and drew her back. She froze like a young sparrow before a night cat. When he offered a gentle smile, however, she relaxed. "I'm sorry you don't have the violin to remember him by," he said. "Do you understand why I returned it to Elf?" She nodded as he hoped she would.

James kissed her cool cheek. Rachel's lips parted without hesitation, and she freely offered him a grateful kiss. She stepped back, gently pulling her hand from his. Rachel offered her most beautiful smile as she turned away. Even if she could have spoken, there was nothing more to say. He knew she was leaving before she left, and James realized he wouldn't stop her if he could. His heart was pounding like the first time he had kissed Bethany.

James was recovering his poise when Rev. Dennis stepped out of the shadows.

"I'm disappointed in you, James. It appears you took advantage of Rachel."

"Then you got the wrong picture," said James. "I don't know if you get your fun spying on people, but that was completely innocent. Rachel was just happy to hear Elf was alive and cared so much for her. You can make anything out of that you damned well please."

"There's no need to flare up, James. I think I understand."

"I don't think you do. Next time we have a message for Rachel, tell her yourself." At that moment he detested the mere presence of Rev. Dennis, yet something in the pastor's demeanor restrained his anger.

"Listen, Reverend Dennis, I suppose you might be partly right," said James. "I've got a rotten temper when I'm riled, and I'm tense and tired."

"Forget it, James. Why don't we join the others and have a nightcap. Oxford said to help ourselves to the wine. He'll be tying *Midnight* up soon for the night, once he finds a lighthouse that's supposed to be out there, somewhere on the right bank."

"That sounds good to me. Sounds like what I need to relax," said James.

CHAPTER TEN

Wine is a mocker, strong drink a brawler,
and whoever is led astray by it is not wise.

-Proverbs 20:1

James thought, maybe we're finally past the desert, as he stumbled over the top step onto the slick deck, immersed in a foggy night. He was also very much aware of his unsteadiness but knew he was quite capable of handling wine. And yet, with the memory of his last drunk at Riverton, James didn't want to overstep himself again.

"Captain, how goes the river? I brought you up a full flask of wine here. If you've got a notion, why not join our party?"

"Been doing some sipping of my own, James. Got me some of Snyder's leftover whiskey. You leave that here though. I'm running kind of low, and once we tie up for the night I'll have my wine nightcap. I hate to mix good whiskey and wine." He sipped from his own bottle. "But that don't stop me from doing it." He laughed.

"Dennis said something about a lighthouse. Is that what you're searching through the fog for?" James squinted into the blanket of foggy darkness and wondered how the captain could possibly know where they were.

"That's part right," said Oxford. "You see, it gets kind of tricky about here. It ain't never quite the same way two times by. We got no exact charts on these waters." He smiled mysteriously. "I can tell you we always hit bad water before the Port of Jossandra.

First we get a lighthouse warning on the right. Soon after that it's fast water and rocks to dodge. Usually in the morning I pull her across to the left, take a backwater route—and before you know it—poof! Clean and clear running the rest of the way into the Port. Yep, we're getting close."

"It sounds too darned vague to me, Oxie. Maybe I've had too much of this." James held up his bottle. He grinned. "I guess I'm not too much on river jargon either. I don't see why this isn't more exact—your course and all."

"James, this here's an art. River running the way I do it ain't no true science, so to speak, and it's never going to be. See that current? It don't come from nowhere and it's not sure where it's going. Or I'm not sure. She's only waiting to trick me if I make the wrong move. I do make a mistake now and then." He laughed. "And then we run into that lurking Gargol. It's always something."

James felt dizzy for a moment and sat down on a wooden bench about ten feet behind Oxford, who was intently peering into the fog. James breathed a heavy sigh.

"You all right, boy? How's the party going below deck?"

"Oh, not too bad," said James. "Sylvia got upset because Snyder offered Jesse some wine. The kid said it tasted funny and spit a mouthful on the galley floor."

"No kidding?" Oxford laughed.

"Then Sylvia took Jesse off to bed and she went herself. She's done for the night on half a glass. Rusty's trying to dance with Evelyn. Hard to say which is more excited. Evelyn's had too much to drink. She's let her hair down for the first time since I met her."

"How do you mean?"

"Well, her hair really is down, she's unbuttoned a few buttons, and her face is kind of flushed from dancing too fast."

"Yeah, she gets into it once in awhile. She's almost pretty if the light ain't too bright. And Rusty thinks Evelyn likes him," said Oxie, "so he pays attention to her, especially when he's drinking. Say, what a pair when they get wine-sipping. Always good for a laugh. You know what happens? Evelyn eggs him on, trying to look sexy. Then Rusty makes one too many passes or gets fresh. She gets mad, and then they fight."

"Yeah, I can see that coming," said James, taking another swallow. "And Dennis and Snyder are arguing about religion and money."

"That a fact?" Oxford laughed again, never taking his eyes off the river.

"It's getting all mixed up. They're both drinking too much for straight talk. Rachel was taking it all in for awhile. Now she's in a corner, reading. Poetry I think."

"That's Rachel. She must be getting into one of her moods. She ain't drinking too much, is she?" Oxie shot him a quick glance. "I hate to see her with the stuff at all, but I can't make a big deal out of it. Her ma drank too much. And if I start riding her about it sure as heck she'll drink all the more. Know what I mean?"

"She's only had a couple of glasses. I don't think she really likes it that much. She just wants to act cool or older. Know what I mean?" James mimicked Oxie, who didn't seem to notice.

"Good. Hey, before you go back to partying, James, could you bring me up some of that fresh baked bread Evelyn made? Maybe one of the end slices, with butter on it. I'm getting kind of hungry. And tell them who want to know, we'll most likely be docking for the night in an hour or so, maybe less. Ask Evelyn to save me a dance, too." His laughter rippled out across the dark water.

Oxford then found the bottom of his whiskey bottle, and he threw the empty out into the river. James heard the faint splash as he left, and an image flashed in his mind of that last night in Riverton when he'd thrown the empty beer pitcher as far as he could out into the river before passing out. Then he dimly remembered, for the first time, a fragment about drinking green death. For just a moment, a little man who looked like Elf in a foggy haze appeared briefly in his mind's eye. It was like a fleeting dream image, and just as quickly it was gone.

James shook the cobwebs of his tangled thought, then looked back at Oxie with mild disgust and wondered if the captain was fit for night river running. He swayed at the cabin doorway, then went down to search for the fresh bread requested by the captain.

• • •

Somewhat later James felt the room moving in circles and realized it was time to rest. Oxie had not yet appeared below deck. Rachel was curled up, sleeping on the floor. Rusty and Evelyn were making out in a dimly lit corner of the dining area, still nursing a bottle of red wine.

Midnight moved unsteadily to James's sense of things, and he was barely aware of Dennis and Snyder. They continued to drone on in a meaningless conversation at the other end of the long dining table. Normally James would have slept off the wine's effect, but the river's ceaseless motion made that difficult. He felt nauseated.

"James, you don't look so good around the gills," said Rev. Dennis.

"Better stick your head out the porthole," said Snyder. "Trouble with these youngsters is they don't know how to hold their drink. They don't pace themselves. Or would you care to debate that, too?" Snyder asked of Dennis.

Dennis looked weary and said, "I know I've had enough. Before I turn in I'm going topside to chat with Oxie. I'd better let him know Rachel didn't make it back to her cabin. That's it, James. Hold your head in the night air. That'll clear the fuzz," he said in a sympathetic tone.

At that moment the barge lurched erratically, and Snyder bumped into James, who was still leaning out of the porthole in the evening air. James pulled his head back into the room, swearing. "Watch where the hell you're walking, elephant! What the devil are trying to do?" James glared at Snyder, and felt the fury build from nowhere.

"And watch your tongue," said Snyder.

Without further warning, James put his shoulder down and charged into Snyder's bulky midsection. The two of them went down with a crash, breaking a chair in the process, while Dennis exited up the steps to advise Captain Oxford.

As Snyder slowly rose to his feet, James shoved him into the wall with an angry burst of energy. Rusty tried to stand between the two men, but was rudely shoved aside by Snyder as he squared off against James. Snyder picked up a piece of the broken chair and advanced on James just as Oxford came quickly down the steps.

"What in blazes are you bastards doing? Wrecking my ship? For two cents I'd—hey there! Snyder! You drop that piece of wood!"

"I'm going to teach this foul-tempered pup a lesson," said Snyder. His usual cool indifference appeared to have fled in the heat of revenge. "Nobody pushes me like that!"

"Now, now," said Oxford. "Just some drinking here that got a little out of hand.

Happens once in awhile, ya know. You sure ain't going to take on James and me and Rusty all at once, are you?"

Rusty looked bewildered, as if trying to guess whether the stocky captain was bluffing. James stood glaring, feeling flushed with anger, his body taut. Half a minute passed as the four men positioned themselves for a fight. Then Evelyn spoke up from the corner.

"You men stop this nonsense. You'll wake Rachel," she said in a reprimanding whisper. Rachel's skirt was riding up across her thighs, and Oxford snapped his next orders.

"Evelyn, you get Rachel on her feet and back to your cabin. We're either going to fight or discuss here and we don't know which. So stop your whining. C'mon now. You never should have let her sleep on the floor like that."

At Evelyn's urging, Rachel stirred, then sat up quickly and looked at the broken furniture. Evelyn pulled her from the room just as Snyder let fly with his stick of wood. James ducked, then picked up the missile after it bounced off the wall.

"All right! That does it! Now you got me mad!" screamed Captain Oxford. "Any more fighting here and you're off my ship! Either one of you. James, you get to my room! Snyder, you get to your bunk! I don't want to hear another damned drunk word from either of you! Now get out!"

For some reason, Oxford's potential instability worried James more than Snyder's physical threat.

"I'm sorry Oxie, but he—," began James.

"Oxford. Captain Oxford. Now get out!"

James grinned as he left the room, making a final defiant gesture to Snyder, who automatically moved forward. Oxford grabbed one of his massive arms, and Rusty struggled to hold the other arm.

"Let him go, Snyder," said Oxford. "The lad ain't used to drinking on a moving barge. Hell, he ain't done no real harm that I can see."

Snyder shook free, but with a baleful expression stood his ground. "Out of respect for you, Captain, I'm going to bed. You better keep that young pup out of my sight. I've broken men in half that were a head taller and weighed fifty pounds more than him."

"Yeah, yeah," said Oxford. "You just keep the lid on your own temper. I can't keep people apart on a ship this size. You get some sleep and cool off. We'll be docking near the lighthouse, and I got to get topside before Dennis runs us all on the rocks. You got it? I ain't got time to stand here and argue."

"Rusty, you get this mess cleaned up. If there's any more trouble, come up and get me, pronto. Snyder," he paused for emphasis. "You behave yourself!"

An eerie scraping sound punctuated his command, and Oxford scrambled back up to the deck without further comment.

• • •

Oxford, followed by James, came running to the sound of roaring water, as Blackie screeched "Oh-oh! Oh-oh!" from his perch atop the wheel-guard. The bird's excitement and the panic of Rev. Dennis might have proven amusing until he cried out, "Captain! I think there was a lighthouse back there! We went right by and I didn't know what to do!"

"Get hold of yourself! Where? What'd you see?"

"It was high on a great pile of rocks, off to the right, jutting out into the water. First there was nothing but fog, and then I saw the rocks and this shining light. I yelled but no one came. I wanted to get you, but I was afraid to leave the wheel."

A pale Captain Oxford held the wheel and demanded facts. "How far back? I mean how long. C'mon!"

The captain seemed rattled and that bothered James, who knew Oxie to usually be fairly cool under pressure.

"Not long. Gosh, I'm not exactly certain. It was there, over the cabin roof, and it stayed clear a few minutes before things fogged over again. I'm sorry, Captain, I didn't know—"

"Shut up! Get the others awake and on deck! Everybody! We're already sucked into whitewater and *Midnight* ain't responding to the wheel like she should. Hey! You hear me? Get all them people on deck! Pronto!" He wrestled with the wheel while the huge craft picked up speed.

Soon all the men gathered together near the impotent wheel. Evelyn ran to wake the women and Jesse. James noticed enormous shadows rising beyond the bank and saw the fog had started to thin out.

Oxford looked scared.

"Look here, you men. I ain't never run this here rough stuff but once, and that was by day and clean sober. Damn the luck! We missed our last chance at the backwater. Now we do it the hard way. This ain't going to be no picnic run. Everybody brace by the cabin there. Keep the women and Jesse close to the deck floor away from the rails."

He said something more James couldn't hear, then urgently continued, "Listen up! Don't let anyone bounce away when we hit something hard. Okay, you women there! All of you! I'm going to try and ride this one out in the dark. Fast water, you hear?"

A roaring noise like muted thunder began to drown out Oxford's harsh yelling to the huddled passengers.

There was a splintering sound as the barge squeezed by a rock island, then tore into open water. *Midnight* seesawed in the darkness while Oxford clung vainly to the nearly useless wheel, trying to stabilize his tormented ship. He flung his cap down and mopped a furrowed brow.

"Damn! I could sure use me some sipping whiskey." Rusty stepped forward and offered the captain some wine. Oxford swore into the wind, grabbed the container and threw it overboard.

"You damned fool! If you all hadn't been drinking and James hadn't got into that fight with Snyder—"

Then a horrendous grinding noise from the port side and keel tortured fearful imaginations. Sylvia grabbed Jesse, and Evelyn was bravely fighting tears. They started crawling for the cabin door.

"Don't anybody go back down! No one below deck!" Oxford screamed. "If she sinks you'll never get topside! James! Rusty! Get everybody to brace!"

The wheel spun crazily one way, then the other as James and the rest of the passengers looked on, hoping for the best.

"That's it," Oxford shouted. "Everybody brace themselves on the deck!"

They huddled close to the deck floor. Spraying water soaked everyone. A bit of moonlight had begun to filter through the darkness and disintegrating fog, and James saw the huge shadows were mountains, or else fog banks that looked like mountains.

"Oh for the quiet backwater," moaned the captain. "We're headed into Devil's Canyon. Ain't no way to treat a ship, not even a scruffy old barge."

He scrambled for one of the lifeboats, peeling back wet canvas. Oxford was knocked off his feet, but managed to crawl back to the main cluster of passengers.

"Now hear this, you landlubbers! I ain't going to say it twice. If *Midnight* starts to break up, it's into the smaller boats. You hear me? I'll man the regular one. James, you take a few in your rowboat. Just ride it out if it happens. It's all luck anyhow."

"You gals hold tight like you're doing. We'll all get in the lifeboats at my order. Not before! Snyder, you get back here!"

"Watch him!" yelled Rusty. "He's trying to get away with our lifeboat!"

"He can't lift either boat alone," said Oxford. "Calm down everybody! Here now, the water's getting some smoother. Let me see if I can beach her!"

He sprang to the wheel. Nearby Rev. Dennis prayed aloud for the benefit of those ready to trust a greater power in time of desperate need. He concluded his prayer with the expressed thought, "Thy will be done."

CHAPTER ELEVEN

Sweet are the uses of adversity,
Which, like the toad, ugly and venomous,
Wears yet a precious jewel in his head.

-William Shakespeare

The next ten minutes dragged on forever, as the battered *Midnight* rolled and pitched like a leaf in a windstorm. James tried to stay on his feet but couldn't. A violent shudder wrenched the barge from prow to stern. For one moment it hung across a line of submerged boulders, then teetered over and continued downriver, faster than before.

"Doesn't this thing ever get over with!" screamed Rusty to Oxford.

"We got us a fifty-fifty chance," Oxford shouted over the roar and spray. "What more do you want?" He was grinning, but James noticed he kept eyeing the two smaller boats.

With the fog now melting away, James caught glimpses in the moonlight of large trees along the shoreline. *Midnight* was speeding along about forty feet from the right-hand shore, and he could see walls of weathered rock behind the trees and more trees growing atop the cliffs. Farther back, gray shadows looked more and more like actual mountains.

Then the river suddenly divided, and *Midnight* was involuntarily drawn into the steeper canyon gorge. The barge steadied, then shot forward ever faster. One by one the passengers dared to stand, and they saw the captain brave a smile.

He's beginning to regain some wheel control, James thought.

"We may be through the worst!" Oxford yelled. "Don't get your hopes up yet! Maybe!"

"What about Great Falls?" yelled James. "Is that a danger?"

He recalled the ominous sketch he'd seen earlier in the captain's quarters and moved closer to the wheel. He attempted to read Oxford's expression as well as his words.

"Not yet, my boy." Oxford grinned. "If we get past Devil's Canyon, then we hit us some quiet water before the Port. If we can just clear this gorge without a breakup, then there's a nice valley. Real pretty with lakes and trees and such. Just hold your horses a mite longer, folks! We're getting there!"

James could feel the tension easing, lifting like the fog. Then came a totally unexpected thud against *Midnight*'s prow and underbelly. Everyone was thrown forward. Oxford slammed into the wheel casing and slumped unconscious to the soaked deck with a gash across his forehead.

James and Dennis grabbed for the wheel as soon as they could rise. Rusty dragged the captain towards the forward cabin. Rachel stayed amazingly calm. James saw her carefully lift her dad's head onto her lap, tear a white strip of cloth from her T-shirt, and quickly fashion a compress bandage with Evelyn's help. Bending over Oxford's inert form, Rachel began slowly rocking him back and forth. Sylvia also moved to assist her. No one else reported suffering anything worse than bumps and bruises.

"Check for water below!" hollered James to Rusty. "See if it's coming in either of the cabins. The captain said we've got to try and ride this out if we can."

James thought for certain the jarring collision had halted *Midnight*'s progress, but somehow it lumbered forward once again, moving like a wounded elephant in search of an ancient burial ground. Movement was life, however, and the barge surged again into the swift waters of that uncharted canyon.

Where are the backwaters Oxie talked about? James wondered to himself. He made it all sound orderly. Just hold the wheel and ride it out.

"Keep her steady," Dennis said to James, then yelled in his ear. "I hear Rusty calling from below deck. I'll check it out and get back as fast as I can."

Water's coming in, thought James. Never had he yearned for daylight as he did that terrible night.

• • •

Finally *Midnight* came to a scraping halt, resting precariously on rocks that held the craft not twenty-five feet from shore. She groaned as the force of water pressed against her walls.

"I can see the shore clearly," said Evelyn. "It's the closest we've been to land."

"We'd best stay with the ship," said James. "That's what the captain wanted. Here comes Dennis. How's it look below?"

"Not good. Water is seeping in again, this time into both cabins. But not as fast as before. Why aren't we moving?"

"We're hung up here, somewhere in the middle of this god-forsaken canyon," said Snyder. "James says we should stay put, and I disagree. I'm for getting people on shore. At least that's what I'm aiming to do. This scow isn't going to take much more pounding without coming apart at the seams. I'd think you could tell that yourself, James."

Snyder paused, and asked, "Dennis, don't you agree with me?" The big man appeared to have forgotten his recent quarrel with James, although, under the circumstances James barely noticed his adversary's tone.

Rev. Dennis spoke, breaking an indecisive silence. "I vote with James. Let's stick with *Midnight*. That's what Oxie would say." He paused. "Rusty's dragging up a mattress for the captain. I'm going to give him some help."

Dennis disappeared, then reappeared in seconds, accompanied by a dour Rusty. They placed the mattress next to the main, forward cabin and lay Oxford on it, trying to make him as comfortable as possible. Rachel hovered there, her dark eyes always fixed on her dad's face.

The passengers moved closer to the starboard railing, where they strained to get a better view through the darkness. "It does seem too treacherous to try for shore in the darkness," said Dennis. "And we've got to think of the captain. He's in no shape to be moved. All things considered, I think we should pray for direction."

"Save your preaching for someone who wants to hear it," said Snyder. "I'm taking the lifeboat, and anyone who likes their chances with me can come. But remember one thing. I give the orders. On that boat I will be in absolute command."

"A fat lot of good that does you if your boat capsizes in the dark," said James. "And I doubt you can get that thing down into the water without our help. Like the captain said, it's too heavy."

Snyder guffawed and threw up his chubby hands. "Have it your way. When you start sucking up river water, remember Snyder gave you an opportunity." He turned his back on the others and sauntered into the darkness astern.

"Going off to pout," said Rusty with a snicker.

"You don't suppose we ought to let Snyder take his chances alone, do you?" asked James with a wry grin.

Dennis laughed softly. "Not really. Not only would he probably tip it over in the dark, as you said, but we'd be out a lifeboat in case—"

A mighty splash from the back of the barge interrupted Rev. Dennis. They ran to the rear railing, which had previously been heavily damaged by Gargol.

Snyder's bulk was sprawled across the fishing boat James had once capsized himself. He was afloat, clenching a fist and waving it at them as his stolen craft hit swift-moving water. Within fifteen seconds he bobbed out of sight, gone in the darkness.

"How in hell did he—" began Rusty.

"Look at this," said James. He held up the sliced ropes which had bound the boat four feet above water. "He sure must have hit the water like a ton of bricks."

Blackie screeched from the railing, "Bye-bye! Bye-bye!"

"And good riddance," said James.

"Amen," said Rev. Dennis. "But I truly hope he hasn't committed suicide in the process."

• • •

Although everyone agreed *Midnight* might resume its helter-skelter course at any moment, for the time being it stayed wedged on the treacherous rocks. Oxford's state remained unchanged, but his ship's did not. There was now a definite list towards portside.

"I say it's from that fat Snyder jumping off the barge," said Rusty.

"Nonsense," said Rev. Dennis. "You saw the water in the cabins. It's like this, James. We've run onto rocks that are partly submerged and come out of the water over there. That's tilted *Midnight* away from shore, and the water seeping in adds to the tilt."

James nodded. "Any chance of . . . of tipping?"

"I really don't know. It's anybody's guess with the captain out of commission. Maybe we should try to get a line to shore," said Dennis. "You know, around some of the large trees or rocks. That way there'd be some insurance against being swept away, or worse yet, capsizing."

"Pretty risky before dawn, for one thing, and that's not exactly shallow water between ship and shore," said James.

"He's right," said Rusty. "I studied it a bit on my own. If you ask me, it might be suicide to try to get to land. It's a worse chance than Snyder took, and believe me he calculated the odds on both actions before he took off with the rowboat. On the shore side the water's pretty fast, it's still night like James said, and there's slippery, hidden rocks. Forget it, Reverend, unless you want to try and be a hero."

"I don't like sitting here, just waiting," said Dennis.

"Me either," said James. "When you've got trouble, what's worse than just standing around and waiting?"

"Drowning," said Rusty.

"Then your troubles are over," said James.

"How long would you guess until daybreak?" asked Dennis. The men were quiet for a moment, then James took a guess.

"Half an hour—an hour at most."

Rusty disagreed. "This night's taking a long time to get done, and it might be two or more hours till full dawn."

"I tend to agree with James," said Rev. Dennis. "We could wait—" He stopped when *Midnight* shifted its position. Evelyn uttered a small cry. Everyone froze until stability was restored.

"We could draw straws for one man wading or swimming with a rope to shore," suggested Rev. Dennis. Rusty appeared to be mulling over his personal odds, but James shook his head.

"Nope. We stick together until more light comes. See the way *Midnight* is tilting now? It's either going to—"

He didn't finish his thought before the barge shifted yet again. The forward portion slid off the rocks, and along the stern there was more scraping. Then *Midnight*'s list was slowly corrected as she slipped into the water like a long, dark otter, completely free.

"Yahoo!" yelled Rusty. "Here we go!"

"One more time!" said James. "Rusty, you keep an eye on the passengers and captain. Dennis and I'll do what we can with the wheel."

"Aye-aye!"

Midnight soon found its way into swift current, and for all its wounds proved seaworthy, at least for the time being. James and Dennis looked at one another, grinning. For better or worse, waiting was a thing of the past.

"Can you imagine," James called out over the noise, "if one of us had been trying to get to shore with a rope tied around him when she finally broke loose?"

"God is with us," said Rev. Dennis through the spray. "Don't put your trust in men or women or boats. Trust in God!"

Wrestling with the wheel, sweat and spray soaking his grimy shirt, James yelled to his comrade, "One thing Snyder was right about, you never stop preaching!"

Most of the passengers seemed to be getting used to the sound of their vessel striking rocks. As long as the rocks were not too large, they weren't afraid. There was newfound confidence in *Midnight*'s ultimate survival that lifted their spirits.

• • •

Faint light finally appeared above the canyon's steep walls and with it came the promise of dawn. Rachel, half-dozing, was more awake than asleep. She was cradling Oxford's head when he stirred.

The captain quietly moaned. "Was it you that hit me with a bottle?" He spoke from his daughter's lap, but he appeared to look at Evelyn. She sat next to Sylvia on a deck bench with Jesse.

"Was it you, Evelyn? I didn't mean nothing by whatever I done, you know that." He groaned. "My head feels as big and ugly as Gargol's."

"Hush your mouth, Captain," said Sylvia. "Don't mention that creature's name. And you're talking out of left field."

Rachel smiled, perking up from her semi-sleep, while Evelyn's laughter joined with Sylvia's. Jesse added his giggles. The shoreline passed by more slowly, and bluish-gray fog dispersed in the wake of the day's first light.

"You banged your head on the wheel when *Midnight* hit shoal rocks," said Evelyn. "Since it was your head that got hit, no real damage was done. Don't touch it, Oxie, it's healing. We're coming through this canyon, and it looks like we're almost out. What a lovely sunrise."

Oxford seemed quite concerned despite Evelyn's patient reassurances, and he tried to rise.

"Take it easy, Captain," said Rusty. "James and Dennis are working the wheel as well as I could myself."

"That ain't saying a whole lot," said Oxford, muttering mostly to himself. "How did we—"

He appeared to study the exotic landscape, trying to identify landmarks. "It's always different." He shook his head. "This time I'd say the mountains had grown up from hills, like they been eating too much fog and getting fat on it."

Rachel was happy, clapping her hands to hear her dad's voice, with its familiar air of complaint. The other women smiled, too. Rusty winked at Jesse the kid.

"Don't let that mean-looking bandage fool you, Jesse. The captain will be back at the wheel before noon, or I miss my guess." He also laughed, and for dour Rusty that was a special occasion.

"Lookee that orange ball of sun creeping around the peaks over there," said Oxford, still stretched out on his back, "If that ain't the prettiest sight."

"You can tell his head was rattled," said Sylvia. "Next thing you know he'll be reciting poetry."

"By gosh, I would too, if I knew any fit for mixed company. You know, it looks like them mountains are floating between blue-gray river and blue-gray sky. Ain't that something? And see how the gold mixes in with the orange and blue. It's plumb beautiful."

"Snap out of it, Oxie," said Rusty, who sounded worried again. "You got your hard head in a soft lap, and you've not had any breakfast. Plus you got knocked pretty hard in the noggin. Take some deep breaths and stop talking crazy." Rusty shook his head and looked to the women for agreement.

"I like him this way," said Sylvia. "He sounds more sensitive, and he can't run us onto anymore rocks if we keep him quiet and flat on his back."

That was enough to bring things back into immediate focus for Captain Oxford. He evidently began to dismiss poetic images of a mountain sunrise from his thoughts the way most people forget night dreams the moment they open their eyes from sleep.

CHAPTER TWELVE

And the Lord spoke to the fish,
and it vomited out Jonah upon
the dry land.

- Jonah 2:10

Captain Oxford stood on *Midnight's* deck, swaying in the morning breeze which was soft and cool. He touched the bandage on his head, then saluted James, who now had the wheel. Oxford smiled and nodded approval to see that his barge was being kept in the river channel's deep water.

He took several deep breaths, then James saw Oxie staring at Rachel's T-shirt, which she'd torn around the waist to make her dad's bandage. "You get below and find a good, clean shirt, young lady."

"He's really back to normal now," said Evelyn. "Giving orders as soon as he stands."

"It had to end sometime," said Sylvia, with a mock sigh. "Captain, as far as her going below deck for a clean shirt—your last order was that all of us should remain topside."

"That's right," said James.

"I just changed that order because we ain't sinking. All right? At least not that I can see. Rachel, stop gawking and go get yourself fixed up proper and decent. I ain't raised you to be no river rat."

He stalked away, checking the bilge pump hoses, before moving forward to the wheel that was still manned by James.

"I don't rightly know how you guys done it, but you got us through Devil's Canyon in a banged-up ship at night and with fog thick as soup," said the captain, voicing puzzled admiration. "You're either darned lucky or better at navigating than I thought."

"The man here says it was because God was with us," said James, with a good-natured wink at Rev. Dennis. "Maybe he's got something there?" Oxford scowled, perhaps not realizing James was making light of their ordeal.

"Give me the wheel, lad, I want to see right off how she handles. Look here. This here's the valley I was telling you about. This should be real pretty coming up on portside. Ain't got the mountains like back off starboard, but wait till you see them lakes. One after another if we're where I think we're at. And all kinds of trees and green grass everywhere. Sheep-grazing country."

Rusty and Jesse joined the men. "Don't pay him too much mind," Rusty said to the others. "The captain's been spouting some poetry this morning. Seems after that knock on his head he's gotten to talk a little weird."

Rusty ducked as Oxford threw his captain's hat at him, while Jesse ran to retrieve it for the skipper. James and Dennis laughed, feeling relief that the long, dangerous night had passed and harmony had somehow been restored.

Captain Oxford was back at *Midnight*'s helm. The morning sun was burning off remnant blue-gray shrouds of patchy fog, and their trusty ship was scarred but afloat on a peaceful river. Added to their pleasant surprise was the fresh, new landscape. Nothing remained of swampy wasteland or desert. As the captain had predicted to James, they were entering a green and pastoral country, and there was a lovely, clear lake already coming into view.

. . .

Watching the morning unfold to bright beauty, James nevertheless was feeling a growing sense of puzzlement. The problem once again was that everything seemed to float by like a dream. His expectation that each day might finally bring solutions, or find him headed in a homeward direction, had certainly failed. Try as he might to find answers or solutions, there were few that shed any light or changed his direction.

"What I don't understand, Captain," said James, while watching the scenic countryside pass by, "is why you seem so uncertain about exact locations or what to expect or how far it is to the Port of Jossandra. You don't even have a decent map from what I've seen."

"If I had one, and I'm not saying I don't, why should I be going over it with the passengers? It's like I said before, James, this here river ain't never run the same way. One day you got foggy blues, next day nice and like this morning, and the water runs the same way. It changes all the time. Now ain't this here a perfect looking day? It makes me glad to be alive."

Oxford took a deep breath, pointed out some river gulls, then several unique brown and white doves along the riverbank. "Ain't them pretty? I seen squirrels, rabbits, and coons this morning. And sheep grazing farther back by them lake meadows with the tall spruce. Didn't I tell you? We got to be getting close to the Port of Jossandra."

"But why don't you know exactly how close?"

"Because it ain't exactly set down. Can't you see how it is out here? You're getting to be almost as ornery as Snyder was, James. By the way, from what you said, we might be bumping into that river pirate again. He can't have got too far. That bum owes me one boat. But I guess it's really your boat." The familiar long laugh came forth.

"On the serious side, though, that guy tried over and over to get me to sell him *Midnight.* Can you believe that? I don't even think he had as much money as he offered, but you never know. I told him not for any price. He got madder than heck back at Cool Water when you and Dennis was out in the desert looking for Elf."

"You're getting off track again, Oxie," said James. "Tell me this. Why in all the years I lived in Riverton didn't we ever see or even hear of you and your barge?"

"What town you hail from?" asked Captain Oxford. He took his hand off the wheel to point out an agile doe that bounded away from the river's edge. Two speckled fawns looked up, and then continued drinking as *Midnight* passed within twenty yards.

"You know darned well it was just back where you picked me up. Riverton." James felt his exasperation grow bit by bit with the captain's obvious evasiveness.

"Ain't never heard of it. You sure they don't call it by something else? I know all my stops on this here river. Maybe your town just ain't one of them."

"Listen here, Oxie—"

"Captain Oxford."

"I'm telling you, Oxford—"

"Captain Oxford," said the captain without a trace of his usual good humor.

"All right. Captain Oxford. Let's say you don't stop there. But you can't go by some town and not have a name for it."

"The heck I can't. I do it all the time. I even make up my own names for places. If it has a bad smell, I might call it Stinktown. But I haven't done that lately. I don't pay no real attention to towns or anyplace unless I got business there. Some towns I avoid, like where I been locked up for being drunk. I try to mind my own business, and you'd be a sight better off doing the same."

Midnight moved smoothly downriver, with no one else on deck except Jesse. It was unusual for him, but he was jumping rope. Everyone else, except for Blackie, was catching up on sleep they'd missed during the harrowing ride through Devil's Canyon. James watched the boy playing and envied his apparent lack of concern as to what was going to happen next. Then he decided to give interrogation one more try.

"Captain Oxford."

"That's better, and if you smile like that, and no one's around, you can call me Oxie."

"Thanks. Do you remember any town near where you picked me up? You know, fished me out of the river in that fog."

"Nope. Nothing I can recall off the top of my head. Maybe there was, but I recollect you was out in the middle of nowhere."

"Okay. Forget about that. Do you know where we are now? I mean exactly where we are?"

"Yep. And nope. Now, don't go getting mad, James. I know we came down Devil's Canyon the hard way, and I know this valley is near as familiar as your face. We're coming into the Port of Jossandra. That's clear from all the signs."

"What signs?"

"Like I told you, lakes, trees, grass, sheep grazing, birds—everything. I ain't got every rock and blade memorized. But you can't miss the Port. So I sit tight, keep my mouth from flapping too much, and watch for the huge bay in the bend of this river."

"What's it look like?"

"Well, let's see. It's sort of like Cool Water back yonder, only lots bigger. Everything is greener, with more trees, flowers, and the great bay hooks up to a stream, and that stream comes out of a nice spring-fed lake. On that there lake is Abigail's house, at least one of her houses."

"Who is Abigail?"

"She runs the Port. I don't rightly take to her Christian do-gooder kind, but she's pretty as a picture. Beautiful blond curls down to here." Oxford tapped his shoulders.

"But can you actually say we're ten minutes from that bend, or the Port's ten miles from Devil's Canyon? You can't say that, can you?"

"That's right. I don't have to. When I see the place I know it. That's how I run my ship. We're getting close. I can almost taste the place. Ain't that good enough for you?"

James simply stared, opened his mouth to ask another question, then closed it and turned away from the captain. His head hurt and his eyes smarted.

I need some sleep, he thought. Oxie's running me in circles.

"Where you going, James? You'll miss our coming into the Port."

Oxford sent his laugh ringing after the retreating James, who was already descending the steps of *Midnight*'s main cabin. James was certain he'd felt more frustration in his life, but he couldn't remember when. For the moment sleep seemed to be the answer.

• • •

By midafternoon the revived passengers began assembling, one by one, on deck. The sky was a faultless azure, the temperature mild, the breeze moderate and refreshing.

Evelyn was truly her sober self again, still looking apprehensive as the valley's beauty continued to unfold. James thought it odd that she alone among the passengers didn't seem happy amidst the lush, pastoral scenery passing by them. Even Rachel finally appeared contented.

Sylvia was also evidently struck by Evelyn's inappropriate mood and said to her, "Look at that perfectly gorgeous woods. See the oak, pine, birch, and look at all the evergreens."

"But think of poor Elf," said Evelyn, almost brought to tears. "Here is his heart's desire, and now he's gone."

"Why, Evelyn, you hardly ever spoke to him when he was alive. I didn't know you cared the slightest about what he found or didn't find. For heavens' sake, can't you enjoy this instead of sniffling over what might have been?"

"I wish I could, but—"

"Just a minute, ladies," interrupted Rev. Dennis. "James and I can lift your spirits regarding the mystery of Elf. You want to tell them, James?"

"You go ahead," said James, gazing at the shore. "It's your turn to tell someone the good news."

"What's this?" Captain Oxford shot back over his shoulder. "You guys been keeping secrets?"

Dennis looked startled at the blunt question, as for some time they'd hoped to keep from being confronted by Oxford about Elf. At the moment, however, there remained little or no choice.

"He's alive," said Rev. Dennis. "We both saw him alive and in good shape."

"Who is that?" said Sylvia, sounding confused, or acting like she hadn't heard correctly. "You don't mean—"

"Yeah, c'mon," said Oxford. "You ain't saying Elf was alive back there at Cool Water, are you?"

"Yes," said Dennis in his resonant voice. "He couldn't stand the river and Gargol and all the rest. He's back there with Turf, ready to start planting trees."

"Thank heavens!" said Evelyn. "But that's all the worse. Look at all he missed by not waiting."

"I'll be darned," said Oxford. "I should have known something was funny when you two came out of that desert hike. James, you knew and didn't tell me? Who the devil can you trust around here?"

"Look at it this way," said James. "He got what he wanted—a chance to be free and start out on his own. Maybe that's what he was meant for. And darned if I don't think maybe the best thing for Turf was to have some company anyway."

"James is right," said Rev. Dennis. "Together they've got a better chance. One plants fields, one starts a forest. It was made to order," he said looking over his glasses, tugging at his dark beard. "At least that's what we're hoping for, although time alone will tell the outcome. God sees more than any of us, and—"

"Aw, shut up," said Oxford. "You don't know beans about farming and forests, so why don't you give your mouth a rest." He glared at Rev. Dennis, who wisely said no more. "And you, James. I'm real surprised by you."

"Captain, for heavens' sake," said Sylvia. "You'd think they were giving us tragic news. Elf is alive! I think that's the best news I've heard in weeks."

"Me too," said Evelyn, brightening. "Thank God someone we thought died now lives and breathes. You men did right." She looked at James and then Rev. Dennis, and offered an approving smile and hug to each of them.

Captain Oxford abruptly changed the subject. "Folks, look up yonder there. That's the Port bend! Dead ahead, everybody! Port ho!"

Seemingly endless minutes passed as *Midnight* rounded an enormous bend in the river lined with evergreens interspersed with delicate white birch trees. All passengers lined the deck railing, craning in hopeful, silent expectation.

"It's so pretty," said Jesse, clutching his jump rope. "Are we going to stop, Captain?" Everyone strained to see and hear.

"Hold your horses, young man. That's my job, but I can't go jabbering while I'm doing it. Stay with James there and just keep nice and quiet."

James was amazed at the size of the river's natural bay while they rounded its heavily forested shoreline. Evelyn may have been right, he thought to himself. What fantastic trees for Elf.

No one spoke as the barge veered left, following the wooded land. James had expected a town, or at least buildings, but everything seemed to be forested wilderness. Then he saw a large pier jutting out from an area with the tallest clump of pine trees. More trees bordered a fifteen-foot wide stream that entered the bay some distance to the left side of the pier.

Upstream James glimpsed a shimmering blue-green lake in the distance. He recalled Oxford's earlier description of it. Now the captain swung the barge past the stream and then the pier. It was quite clear *Midnight* was too large to enter the stream's mouth. James at once regretted that they couldn't steam straight up the stream to that jeweled body of water.

As Oxford slowly positioned the barge for docking, James saw the pier was indeed sizeable. He estimated it to be 150 feet long and perhaps 20 feet wide. Because it rose only several feet above the waterline and was an emerald green color, the passengers hadn't seen it until *Midnight* was almost ready to dock.

James's gaze wandered inland to a wide path framed by pine trees. He was startled to see two statues seated on either side of a large, flowered trellis. They appeared to be carved from stone, and were positioned facing one another on marble benches.

The green and white trellis was thickly covered with twisting vines and bright blue flowers. James guessed them to be an exquisite variety of morning glory. The statues were of handsome women in simple, flowing gowns. One had light skin and one was dark, one was blond and the other had black hair.

Beyond them the tree path was bowered by great trees rising from behind the pine trees—it was lush and boldly straight, evidently leading back to the placid lake. While *Midnight* was being secured, and the weary but hopeful passengers disembarked, James was utterly shocked to see those classically sculpted statues rise to meet them.

CHAPTER THIRTEEN

The two women rose together as if guided by a single, silent command. Both of them smiled and waved greetings to the passengers of *Midnight*. All of them disembarked, and they moved slowly, almost reverently, like strangers entering a realm of dreamlike beauty. Oxford remained a lone sentry on *Midnight's* deck, unsmiling, with hands on his hips, a dispassionate observer.

The blond woman, shorter and more voluptuous than her slender companion, wore a dark blue, almost black gown. The woman with black hair wore a pure white gown. The scoop-necked dresses draped their bodies like smooth satin. James guessed he'd mistaken them for statues because of their even features and flawless complexions, together with the fact that not the slightest breeze was blowing on shore to move their gowns or flowing hair.

"Welcome to the Port of Jossandra," said the slender woman in white. "My name is Feruka, and this is my sister, Jana. We are here to serve you." Her voice was as clear as the small pool of crystal water that bubbled nearby.

Faint color rose to Jana's fair cheeks as she smiled, adding her own welcome. "We are pleased to receive you as our special guests. Abigail is waiting at the lake, and we will take you to her."

"It's just simply gorgeous here," said Evelyn. Sylvia murmured her agreement.

James found himself staring at the women's configuration of face, hair, and build. Suddenly it was his turn to sense his face grow warmer. He realized he'd been gawking, as Oxie would say, like ten-year-old Jesse. Turning momentarily to the moored barge, he was baffled to see Captain Oxford silently waiting, holding back.

"Why isn't the captain coming?" asked Rev. Dennis in a whisper.

Feruka overheard the question and smiled. "Your captain does not like to leave his ship. He prefers the river to Angel's Lake."

"Is that the lake I saw through the trees?" said Jesse. "I can't wait to get there."

"Yes it is," said Feruka. "If you would like to see it better, and more birds and flowers, follow us."

The two hosts turned gracefully in unison and walked into the lush woods. Everyone but Oxford followed, although James and Rusty waved, gesturing to coax him into joining them.

"Let him remain behind if he insists," said Rev. Dennis. "He probably wants to guard *Midnight*. "I'll bet he fears Gargol is still following the barge, and he thinks Snyder may attempt to steal more than he already has. Anyway, he's got Blackie for company." The men laughed, following their group through the trellis, and into the cool, green woods that bordered the lake.

Towering pines, giant elms, and mighty oaks of many seasons guarded the path, forming a natural bower overhead. Even so, bright sunshine filtered through, and flowers of pink, white, purple, gold, red, and blue grew in scattered profusion along either side of the pathway.

Sylvia, Evelyn, and Jesse were oohing and aahing as they walked behind their gracious guides through the thick forest. The men and Rachel followed close at hand, and they were also impressed.

"I've never seen such perfect roses," said Rev. Dennis, adjusting his glasses. "Look at that deep red. Pink and white ones over there, too. And peonies in full bloom. Look!"

"There are so darned many kinds and colors," said James. "Just take a deep breath of that perfume."

The pathway narrowed and continued to rise slightly as they walked near to the stream. Then they reached a natural crest about a half mile from the river. There was a narrow meadow with sheep grazing, golden dandelions, and scattered royal blue wildflowers. And a hundred yards away, the peaceful lake sparkled before them in radiant sunlight.

To the left of the meadow were berry patches, and to the right, growing along the base of rugged, light purple bluffs, were a variety of fruit trees.

Jesse broke from the spellbound group, heading as fast as he could run for a wide, sandy beach. The sheep paused from contented grazing to watch the youngster with mild curiosity.

The spring-fed lake was set like a jewel in a three-sided frame of quartzite—its hills and bluffs rose hundreds of feet skyward, sometimes as sheer cliffs. Pine, birch, and oak trees grew among shrubs and bushes scattered along the rocky, rough-hewn slopes. Angel's Lake appeared to James to be a half mile across and several miles long with clear water.

The group of passengers followed silently behind Feruka and Jana, finally drawing abreast of the pleasant waters. Far down a twisting path through rocks and boulders on the lake's right border, James saw a small group of people gathered. One person appeared to be addressing the others.

"There is Abigail," pointed Jana. "She is instructing the children. We have a path among the boulders. Everyone please follow closely." Jana smiled and said, "Later on you may check the flowers, berries, and trees more carefully."

"I'll go get the boy," said Feruka, pointing to Jesse on the beach, wading in shallow water. "We will catch up with you on the Rocky-Dell path."

Adjacent to the sandy north beach of Angel's Lake another earthen path began, which wound through tumbled boulders along the western bluffs. Interspersing the giant stones were patches of lawn, flowers, and fruit trees. The adult procession followed Jana in single file—the last two were Rachel and James.

"You go ahead with the others," said James. "I'll wait here for a few minutes until Jesse can catch up. Feruka's bringing him now."

Finally alone, James paused on a large rock which was partially covered by soft, green moss. From there he had an unimpeded view of the sweeping beach. Feruka was walking knee-deep in the clear water, laughing at Jesse's banter. He held her hand and chattered as they walked in the shallow water. Suddenly James felt a pang.

It's like when I was a kid at my grandparents' cottage, he thought—I was just like Jesse!

Memories jarred him like an earth tremor, and the visions were haunting. For some minutes James really felt he was watching himself as a boy, and his eyes grew moist.

It quickly passed. As if coming out of a trance, he was awakened by shouts from Jesse. "James, the water's so clear!" His freckled face was beaming.

"You should see all the minnows and other fish," said Jesse. His jeans were rolled above the knees, but soaked anyway. "There must be a million minnows swimming in the shallows. They nipped on my toes," he said with unbridled amazement.

Feruka grinned at James and said, "He can return to swim and play later, or else swim at the south shore where we are going. We had best hurry after Jana and the others." James saw she studied him. "Are you all right, brother James?"

"Yeah, I'm okay. But a minute ago I'd swear I was dreaming while awake." He wiped his eyes. "How is it you know my name?"

"Abigail told us about you and the others," Feruka said with her eyes averted. She spoke in shy fashion, yet James was very impressed by her voice, smooth brown skin, and general beauty.

"If we hurry along all of you can listen to what Abigail has to say. That is what she desires and we had best adhere to those wishes. Come, Jesse. Perhaps I can take you for a swim after supper."

"Can we come back to this beach in the morning?" asked Jesse with a wistful smile.

"Yes." Feruka laughed. "You can swim and boat and play all day tomorrow, maybe until you're as brown as me."

Jesse clapped his hands, laughing with Feruka. As James followed them along the winding path, he thought again of his own childhood. He missed his family and Bethany so much at that moment his sight was blurred, and it was difficult to see the trail. What he wished for just then was to be alone, among the rocks with his memories.

It's darned silly, he thought to himself. I'd almost forgotten them, too. I've got to get home!

In his agitated heart he longed to recapture a precious glimpse of his mom and dad and brother. And Bethany. Soon, however, the ache was lessening amid the breathtaking wonder surrounding him. Yet how he wished they all could be with him at that moment, on that special day. He glanced skyward. Even at the highest point of those rocky bluffs he saw green trees growing against the sky.

• • •

Two dozen children, ranging in age from three-year-old toddlers to teens, dressed in swimsuits, noisily filed past the approaching group led by Jana, which now included James and Jesse. James heard the happy chattering of the new children, and that brought a broad smile to his face, as well as to the faces of all the *Midnight* passengers.

"What did you learn today, Loreen?" he heard Jana asking a pretty preteen girl.

"More about diving and swimming underwater. We've been diving from the rocks and holding our breath underwater." Loreen giggled and ran after the other children.

While James stopped and stepped aside to let her pass, he got his first clear sight of the woman who had been teaching the children. She was sitting under a large willow tree that grew within twenty feet of Angel's Lake. She slipped a pale blue tunic over the top of her white, two-piece swimsuit. As she rose to meet the passengers, she waved a greeting.

"Welcome, all of you, to our valley and the Port of Jossandra. I am Abigail, handmaiden of Jossandra."

When Abigail smiled and spoke to them, there was such radiant warmth it felt as if her message was meant for him alone. At least that's what James experienced, and then he sensed the rest of the passengers did as well. The intensity of her look was captivating. Her unique eyes, as blue as bright summer sky, reflected an unmistakable depth of caring. She seemed to see through James while radiating affection, and still there was a definite regalness in her bearing. Blond shoulder-length curls framed intelligent eyes and classical features. Her lightly tanned face bore no makeup, but this seemed only to enhance her compelling eyes.

"Where is Captain Oxford?" asked Abigail.

"Once again he chose not to come," said Feruka.

"Did you try to coax him?" said Abigail with a gentle smile.

"It does no good," said Jana. "He left no doubt his barge is where he preferred to be, but we have brought all the rest of *Midnight's* remaining passengers."

"I don't see Elf," said Abigail. "I didn't expect Turf to make it this far, but we do have a fine section of forest amidst the bluffs that Elf would love."

James turned his rapt attention away from her and exchanged a glance with Rev. Dennis. James felt her knowledge of the passengers uncanny, to say the least. In a word, he was dumbfounded.

Rev. Dennis spoke, "We are pleased to meet your sisters, and yourself, Abigail. We have waited long and journeyed far for this day. Elf left our company many miles back, at a place belonging to Captain Oxford called Cool Water. He plans to start a forest there, working alongside Turf, who says he'll start a farm there, too."

The strong voice of Rev. Dennis carried out across the water, and James thought Abigail seemed pleased with his answer. He was grateful that Dennis had dispensed in simple fashion with what might have proven to be a complicated story.

"May I invite all of you to follow this path with me," said Abigail, pointing to the long trail which continued on around the lake's west side, to the south shore. "We will have refreshments for all of you at our south shore chateau. For resting tonight, we have many cottages scattered in the bluffs and forests, or the mansion itself. Most guests prefer the mansion at first, before exploring, but I'm certain we have the right place for everyone."

"What about the captain?" asked Rusty, nervously clearing his throat. "Shouldn't we be going back to the barge tonight? That's where all our clothes and things are."

"It's your choice later," she said. "But first you should dine and sample our hospitality. As Reverend Dennis stated, it has been a long journey for each one of you. You can sample our food and see something of our lake home. I will send Feruka or Jana to invite the captain once more, too. I'm certain he would really like to join you. Perhaps it's his sense of duty, or some fear, that prevents him from joining us at the mansion."

"He probably thinks the ship should be guarded."

"I know, James."

When she spoke his name, he had a strange feeling that this striking woman already knew him well. There was a sense of unspoken kinship, although why such a thing should be eluded him. Even if Abigail was somewhat baffling on first meeting, she provided a comfortable puzzle which James felt sure time would ultimately solve.

"Feruka, Jana. One of you please return to invite the captain again, and one of you come with me. Everyone, single file," said Abigail.

They followed her lead through a marvelous section of white birch, silver-leaved poplar, and pine trees. The cool air was filled with a pine-scented aroma that made hiking an effortless pleasure, even for Sylvia. James was concerned the distance in warm weather might prove too much for her, but such was not the case.

Sylvia whispered to Evelyn as they hiked, "That woman is an old-fashioned beauty, like the women of my day. You know, I hate to say this, but she reminds me of myself in courting days."

Evelyn bubbled amiable laughter that she couldn't contain. "Oh Sylvia, you silly thing. You've been out in the bright sunlight too long."

After Jana left them for the barge, the group passed a number of rustic cottages nestled among the rocks and trees. Several were situated along the water's edge. Soon they found themselves at the southern shore of Angel's Lake. A single, great building dominated the central beach, and consisted of three levels spread along more than one hundred feet of shoreline. Part of it reminded James of a country palace with elegant turrets and spires, yet it had too much rustic charm to be considered a castle. The lower level blended with the beach, constructed over the water.

They went directly up winding steps from the beach level to the elevated main floor. Its central feature was similar to an immense ballroom at the front, with dining tables and huge glass windows that overlooked the lake.

The uppermost floor was not unlike an old-time hotel, with long narrow hallways leading to spacious bedrooms. After Abigail and Feruka had conducted their guests on a brief tour, the group descended steps once more to assemble at the central dining area.

The hungry guests washed up and were seated at a long, heavy oak table where they could look out across the splendid lake at sunset. Everyone was unusually quiet. Large green salads, with choices of several types of dressing, and baskets of fresh-baked rolls, were already set on the table.

James spoke first concerning Oxford's absence, saying, "Rachel wants Oxie to share everything with the rest of us."

"I agree," said Sylvia.

"No doubt about it. Maybe one of us should check on him after dinner," said Rev. Dennis.

"Jana will certainly see to his welfare," said Feruka. "When she returns, with or without Captain Oxford, your question will be quickly answered."

Abigail and Feruka seated themselves opposite the seven, who faced Angel's Lake. From left to right, facing the water, sat James, Sylvia, Jesse, Rev. Dennis, Evelyn, Rachel, and finally Rusty.

Men and women then began bringing in fresh-cut sweet corn, tomatoes, cucumbers, and potatoes prepared several different ways. There was a rice dish with savory herbs and seasonings, as well as cheese and an assortment of nuts. Fruit was in great abundance, especially berries—strawberries, raspberries, blueberries, and blackberries with cream and sugar if anyone chose. There were pitchers of cold milk, lemonade, and spring water to quench everyone's thirst.

"The captain's really missing a fantastic meal," said Rusty from his end of the table. "Say, are those people in small boats out there fishing, or what?" He pointed to three rowboats that appeared anchored about two hundred feet offshore.

Feruka laughed. "They're feeding the fish, and some of them are swimming, too. See."

They looked carefully. James saw that men and women were indeed diving from the boats and swimming around them.

Later in the meal, Abigail clapped her hands twice, and within moments an elderly man with white hair brought in cream puffs topped with melted caramel. Those were a great hit with Jesse the kid.

Evelyn critically sampled one, and said, "Rachel would love to share these with the captain. He has quite a sweet tooth, too, you know." There was unanimous agreement that the meal far surpassed everyday fare on the barge, and surprisingly, Evelyn's compliments led the way.

"I certainly would like the recipe for this rice dish," she said to Abigail. "And I've never tasted fruits and vegetables any fresher than these. Your chef has my admiration, and your gardener must be superb."

Abigail smiled graciously. James thought it somewhat odd that she herself was not eating, but merely sipped a clear liquid which he assumed was water.

"We all take turns with both the gardening and cooking," said Abigail. "Our function is to enjoy life and to serve river travelers like yourselves. When we please you and meet your needs, then we are pleased and satisfied ourselves."

"Well," said Rev. Dennis, pushing back an empty plate, speaking for all of them, "you've certainly pleased your guests tonight."

CHAPTER FOURTEEN

Even the darkness is not dark to thee,
the night is bright as the day; for darkness is
as light with thee.

-Psalm 139:12

A light summer breeze carried the sounds of crickets and frogs through the huge, open windows to where the guests sat sipping beverages, chatting quietly among themselves.

They had finished eating. The last remnants of sunset lit the twilight sky with fiery fingers, and pink reflections shimmered on the darkening water.

"Feruka will show you to your rooms, whenever you are ready," said Abigail, rising from her chair. "There is a separate room prepared for each of you. Tomorrow you may select your own cottages if you prefer. The captain usually stays three days, so you will have ample time to enjoy our lake and our hospitality. Some of you may choose to stay longer, and that can certainly be arranged."

Rev. Dennis rose and said, "I'm afraid we've grown weary from all our travel. If I may speak for the others, I for one would like to stay up and chat longer, but my eyelids are getting heavier by the minute."

"What he means," said Rusty, "is that we're all tired."

The women laughed and began to clear the table.

"Leave those," said Abigail to Sylvia and Evelyn. "Please follow Feruka to your rooms, and you will be able to get all the rest you need. James, would you please remain here for a few minutes?" Her blue eyes were riveted on him. "Good. May you all sleep soundly. If you have any needs during the night, ring the bell in your rooms. Pleasant dreams."

James watched them follow Feruka up the enormous winding staircase, as she led them to their third-level bedrooms. He remained seated and wondered why Abigail wanted him to stay.

Something tells me, he thought, that this has to do with Captain Oxford. I wonder if Abigail thinks I could help persuade him to come ashore and join the rest of us here at the south shore mansion?

• • •

Rachel felt uneasy. Her foremost concern was that Oxie join the group. But there was something else that bothered her. It was evening, her dad was alone on the river, and Jana might prove a temptation when she tried to coax him ashore. Oxie was like that.

It's dumb, Rachel thought, but I have to be sure what happens on *Midnight* is okay. Ma's not here to watch after him, so now it's my job.

It took Rachel one hour to return to the barge. She caught her breath when she saw Jana pacing the deck, looking out across the quiet bay, and then enter the forward cabin and disappear. Rachel waited impatiently for several minutes. Unable to bear waiting any longer, she made her way to the pier and cautiously stepped onto the deserted deck.

Rachel circled the rear cabin, and her heart skipped a beat when she saw the missing boat of James moored behind the barge. It was empty. Removing her sandals, Rachel tiptoed across the deck to the forward cabin. Taking great care not to make any noise, she moved carefully onto the steps. From the cramped hallway, Rachel was finally able to make out Oxie's voice.

"I ain't going on shore tonight, and that's that. I already told you that twice, and here you come waltzing below deck again!" His voice came from the galley, and he sounded very irritated.

Jana's soft voice, by contrast, was patient and understanding. "I'm certain everyone would like to have you join your passengers, Captain Oxford. If you'd give us the pleasure of—"

"Ain't you got ears under that blond hair? I got to finish this lousy supper, and then get back topside on lookout, where we already been through this twice. Someone's got to protect my ship, and the best one to do that is me. But you're welcome to sit here and chat a spell if you change the subject. Matter of fact, I could use some company. Blackie don't talk much."

"Abigail instructed me to try and bring you back. If you still refuse to join us at the south shore, my effort here is done. I can't force you."

"You're darned right."

Rachel was trying to decide what to do next when she heard creaking on the steps behind her. A strong hand cupped her open mouth and she was hoisted off her feet, up onto the deck, then carried over to the rear cabin. As they were going down the cabin's steps she heard the familiar voice of Snyder issue a stern warning.

"Stop struggling, Rachel, or you'll regret it. Behave yourself, and I'll treat you like a lady." His voice had a smug tone, and Rachel kicked him hard in the shin.

"Damn you. I can see you're as stubborn as your old man. You're going to need restraints again, bitch. So be it."

Without another word he proceeded to tie Rachel to the bed, running a sheet around her waist as had been done before at Cool Water. This time he was not as gentle, however, and he also tightly bound her wrists and ankles.

"This is nothing personal. Oxford's got something I want, and he refuses my fair offers. You're in my way at the wrong time. I'm not about to be left high and dry. Whatever it takes. If somebody gets hurt, that's tough."

Within minutes Snyder finished tying his silent captive, and he left her alone without saying anything more. Rachel struggled against the restraints until she realized they were only getting tighter.

Someone will come, she thought.

. . .

A sleek boat, its white sail bluish under the starlit sky, moved slowly across the darkened water of Angel's Lake. James sat in the center of the boat, with Feruka behind him in the bow. Abigail, who faced him, operated the tiller.

James studied her exquisite features. "Why did you pick me to go with you?" he asked.

Abigail's smile was enigmatic, but her words were frank. "Why not? I doubt that Rachel and Jana are in serious trouble, but we saw her running from the mansion, and your help may be required. Actually, our first choice was Reverend Dennis, but as you heard, he was sleepy." She laughed. An aura of inscrutability about her continued to puzzle James.

"I'm tired myself, but not sleepy." James smiled in return. "Now I think this night air perks me up. That, or the fact I have such lovely companions tonight." Abigail did not respond to his compliment.

"Seriously," he said after a pause, "I'm glad you asked me to go along. I've been concerned about Rachel ever since I—well, ever since I met her. She's like a child sometimes."

"Yes, I agree," said Abigail.

They rode for a time in moonlight and silence. James found himself wondering more about Abigail than Rachel. She was unlike anyone he'd ever known before—serene, but not haughty.

He thought Abigail was also analyzing him, and he wondered if she could read his thoughts. Without knowing why, she made him feel as if she could read thoughts that even he had hidden from himself.

"Why do you look so worried, James? Is it because you're so far from home and with strangers?"

"Maybe." He looked at the cliffs which encircled most of the lake like enormous shadows. "Just nerves, I guess, and the fact I no longer seem to have control of things. Oxford runs his barge, *Midnight,* and you seem to run things here at Angel's Lake. I got caught up in Oxford's world by accident, and every mile since then I got more tangled up in it until it was too late to get back to Riverton, where I belong."

126

"Your decisions are your own, are they not?"

"Yeah, but—"

"What?" She looked mildly amused, although it was difficult to gauge her exact expression in the moonlight.

"I seem to have lost direction, or else I've gone too far in the wrong direction. This lake and all looks like a really cool place, but what the heck, there's no way I can stay here very long."

"Why not?"

"Because I know I can't. In some ways I'd sure like to, but right now I just can't. I've got to keep moving. After I turn my direction around, I guess, or get my thinking straight. It's like I haven't been able to do that for so long, and even though I've got to change I keep putting it off. Like now, we'll find Rachel tonight, and maybe the captain will come ashore, and maybe he won't. But that won't make much difference to my life in the long run. I'm lost myself, and here I am looking for someone else in the night who might be lost. It's absurd. Does any of this make sense?"

"That depends," said Abigail. "Perhaps each person we help, or help find, may prove to be a vital step towards finding ourselves."

"You sound like you feel sorry for yourself," came a gentle voice from behind him. Feruka spoke for the first time since they'd set sail, and James had nearly forgotten her presence.

"Maybe you should think less about yourself and focus more on the task at hand," said Feruka.

"Which is?" asked James, feeling irritated.

Feruka said, "To find our sisters, to assure ourselves that Rachel and Jana are safe, and to see if we can establish harmony with Captain Oxford."

"What Feruka is saying is essentially true," said Abigail. "Although harmony is already established through spiritual law. We need only to realize its perfection more fully. The Bible says we are to love one another and serve others."

Feruka added, "If you truly wish to find yourself, direction as you call it, then you are welcome at Angel's Lake for as long as you desire. That is true for all of *Midnight*'s passengers, and that is why most of them have come to this haven."

"What about my real home? I've got to get back there if I can."
His tone softened to more closely match the composed voices of
the two women.

"It's been your decision from the beginning," said Abigail.
"We can talk more about this after our immediate task is accomplished. In the morning, perhaps."

"Perhaps."

The sailboat picked up speed with an increase of wind, skim-
ming across the center of the lake, and soon the north shore was
close at hand. James saw they were heading for the small outlet
stream the ran from the lake to the river's bay. Elegant, long-leg-
ged white birds that had begun night feeding along that stream
stirred and ruffled their wings as the sleek sailboat approached.

James felt certain they could sail right down the stream to
the barge, but at the last minute Abigail shifted the rudder, purposely running the craft aground on the sandy north beach.
Feruka folded the lowered sail, and James waited in puzzlement,
realizing the two women had worked out a plan of which he was
unaware.

"There's a small canoe by the stream's edge," said Abigail.
She spoke in a lowered voice as they stepped out of the sailboat.
"It will move you quietly to the river's bay, and from there you
may easily dock at the pier."

"You're not coming?" asked James.

"Feruka will go with you. I will remain here at the north shore,
doing some work, until one or both of you return. If you decide
to stay on board the barge tonight, James, that is your privilege.
It's late, and you could join the other passengers in the morning. That is," she emphasized, "if Jana and Rachel have already
returned by the bluff trail."

"I don't understand," said James.

"Feruka will brief you as you paddle. If the women are still at
the barge, return with them by the woods trail, as we discussed,
Feruka. Life is ever present. All is good. Go in peace."

. . .

Later, from their canoe, James saw Captain Oxford come on deck as the moon was partially obscured by dark clouds that seemed to have appeared from nowhere.

Something is wrong up there, James thought as he scanned the deck. No sign of Rachel or Jana. Oxford also seemed to search the pier and darkened shoreline with quick, nervous glances while making his way to *Midnight*'s stern. Blackie was gone, which happened from time to time, and everything was too quiet.

"Jana, you still here?" Oxford called out. Hushed silence. "Hello! Anybody on board but me?"

"Hi! Hi!" came Blackie's staccato call as he flew up from the direction of the darkened woods. He flew at once to Oxford's shoulder.

"Yeah, yeah. I don't mean you bird. What about this here sandal? It wasn't here before. Ain't you keeping lookout? Off chasing mice in the woods? Not a single peep out of you, and Jana comes below deck like a skulking pirate. It ain't right and you know it. I ought to roast your black carcass for snacks."

James could only faintly hear part of Oxford's rambling as he and Feruka bent to their paddles. Then, at the same moment, James and Oxford saw the fishing boat bobbing behind *Midnight*.

It took some moments for its significance to register with James. A shiver of recognition went up and down his spine. His heart froze for an instant, but was quickly thawed by the heat of anger.

"Snyder!" Oxford knew what James knew, too. "If you're lurking on or around my ship you'd better—"

James heard Oxford stop in mid-sentence and saw him climb down into the small boat. Blackie posted himself at the stern. After a moment's hesitation, Oxford scrambled back on board *Midnight*. From his approaching canoe, James saw Oxford squinting in his direction, looking past the barge's dim night lights.

James and Feruka paddled closer to the barge, and for some reason he felt the muscles of his back and neck tighten.

CHAPTER FIFTEEN

Thoughts are the real things
From whence all joy, from
whence all sorrow springs.

-Rev. Thomas Traherne

James and Feruka glided silently on the dark water as they eased back on their paddles, straining to see. He spoke in a hushed tone, saying, "I still wonder exactly why Abigail couldn't have come. Is she afraid or something?" He dug his paddle into quiet water, and the canoe veered left towards the barge.

"That would be the last reason," said Feruka. "She knows her presence antagonizes the captain. He doesn't understand our way of life, and she more than anyone sets an example for—"

"Wait! Look at the cabin roof, above Oxie!" said James.

The moon was momentarily free of drifting clouds, and they were close enough that both saw the crouching figure of a man atop the roof of the women's cabin.

"Captain Oxford!" yelled James, forgetting caution. "Look out above you, Captain, on the roof!"

As they pulled closer, they heard a woman yell from the cabin. "That sounds like Jana," said Feruka. Captain Oxford jumped out from the cabin's shadow, looking up at the roof. At that moment Snyder also rose into plain view, lighting his cigar.

"Go back the way you came, James! You and whoever that is with you. I've got some unfinished business with Oxford, and I don't want anyone's interference. The captain is finally thinking about selling his barge to me."

"The hell I am!" thundered Oxford. "You get your fat can off my cabin roof and tell me why—"

"I'm prepared to negotiate from a position of more power this time," said Snyder. Oxford went silent, and James could see why. Snyder brandished a stick of explosive for all to see. He lit the fuse, which hissed like a snake. He appeared not to be taking deadly aim, but rather flipped the stick in the general direction of the approaching canoe.

"Look out!" screamed Oxford.

The explosion, along with James's own frantic movements, capsized the canoe, throwing himself and Feruka into the cool night water of the bay.

"You okay?" he called to her, both treading water.

"I'm fine. Can you get back in?" The night air was even more cool than the water against their wet skin, and Feruka's teeth chattered.

"Nope. But I'm all right. Listen, he might throw another stick for all we know. You get back to Abigail and tell her what's happened." He paused, still treading water. "I'll stay and see what can be done here, okay? And hurry!"

She did exactly that, swimming to shore, and quickly disappeared into the shadowy cover of the woods. James watched her progress, then took several deep breaths before submerging underwater in search of a safer place. He soon surfaced under the pier, close to midship of the docked barge.

Well, he thought, at least we know where Snyder stands.

With Feruka gone, he began to figure out how he might get on board *Midnight* without being seen by the completely unpredictable Snyder. He mentally reviewed all he knew of the man, and he concluded the arrogant salesman was capable of lethal violence.

• • •

After James had stealthily pulled himself out of the bay into the barge through a large galley porthole, he'd immediately hurried on deck. Crouching in the front cabin doorway he could clearly hear Snyder and Oxford going at it.

"You ain't taking over my ship!" yelled Captain Oxford. "You couldn't buy it from me, and you can't steal it from me either. You might just as well come down from up there and take your medicine like a man. Get some sense, Snyder, before somebody around here gets themselves hurt bad."

"Begging your pardon, Captain, if anyone gets hurt, it's not going to be me." Snyder's voice oozed with sarcasm. "I've got all the cards in case you're not bright enough to notice. See this?" he asked, brandishing another stick of explosive.

"I ain't blind," said Oxford. "But what good is it going to do you? Let's say you blow up *Midnight* or blow me up—what happens? I'll tell you. If you take me out, you take yourself out, because I'm this close to you. And if you blow up my ship, then you get nothing left but a wrecked boat."

"You bluff like an amateur," said Snyder. "I still hold the aces. Make one wrong move, and you get one of these a lot closer to you than to me. I'll survive. I also have your lovely daughter as my hostage. That's right—Rachel. She's tied up below the very roof on which I stand. All I have to do is turn around, bend down, and flip a stick into the cabin."

"Sounds to me like you're bluffing yourself," said Oxford.

"I'm not bluffing, Captain. You'd better put down that oar and give up your foolish notion of knocking me off this roof. You have far more to lose than I do, and your voice tells me you realize that."

Oxford gave up the oar, tossing it alongside the railing, just as people were coming out of the dark woods. They paused at the trellis, then came forward to the foot of the pier.

"Hold it right there!" said Snyder. "Captain Oxford and I are bargaining for his barge. No one will interfere with my negotiations. Is that clearly understood? Don't come any closer."

Still intently watching, James then noticed Jana and Rachel appear in the doorway of the women's cabin. Obviously Snyder doesn't know Rachel got free—Jana must have rescued her! he thought.

Meanwhile, Snyder hastily lit a fuse and threw another stick out into the open water. Again, the aim was not really that close to anyone else. It was as if the violent explosion that rocked the night was merely to punctuate Snyder's demands.

. . .

James put a finger to his lips, and when the next explosion sounded he urgently beckoned the two women to hurry across the deck to his own forward cabin position, away from Snyder. James welcomed Rachel into his arms, while Jana spoke hurriedly, yet with exceptional calm. She quickly explained how she also had been tied up by Snyder, but worked herself free.

"That must be Feruka or Abigail or both by the pier," Jana said to James in a whisper. "Who is that beastly man?"

"His name is Snyder," James whispered back. "He's no good and he's up to no good as you can hear for yourself. I only hope the people out there have enough sense to stay out of his way. He really has a vicious streak."

"Abigail and Feruka know how to take care of themselves, as well as this Snyder person." She smiled.

James couldn't help thinking this woman was overprotected in her isolated river valley, and most likely somewhat naive. But she had rescued Rachel, if Snyder's claim was true about taking her hostage. His thoughts raced, considering whether to try and attack Snyder, or retreat for the time being and get the women to safety.

"We could go below deck," said James. "I came in through a porthole, and you two could get out that same way. But I'd like to get Snyder, or see if I can help Oxie."

"Please wait, James," said Jana. "First I have to see what Abigail does. Maybe we can help you and Oxford if we stay here and keep out of Snyder's sight. There's really nothing to fear."

James shivered in his wet clothes and wondered how it was all going to end. He knew very well how stubborn both Oxford and Snyder could be. He also realized that Jana barely knew the captain, and didn't know Snyder at all.

James kept the women behind cover, and he inched closer to the action to hear what Snyder was yelling to the group on shore.

"I told you people that was close enough," said Snyder. "Stay off the pier! Is that you, Dennis? I told you before, you should have teamed up with me when you had the chance. Instead it appears you've hooked up with a herd of sheep. Stay where you are and state your business, if you have any."

James saw the tall man on shore step forward. He paused at the edge of the pier and began speaking in his resonant voice.

"Yes," he said, "this is Reverend Dennis. I'm here with Rusty, and these good women are not sheep. This is Abigail, handmaiden of Jossandra, leader of the lake people that live here and serve others. And this is Feruka, the woman who was sent along with James to find Rachel and Jana. We'd like to talk with you."

When he turned towards shore to get a better view, James shifted his position slightly beyond the main cabin doorway, and evidently that movement caught Snyder's attention.

"All right, is that you on deck, James? Come out, or there will be hell to pay!"

His voice had a fanatical quality that hadn't been there before. James motioned the two women behind him to stay back in the shadows, and then he stepped boldly forward into the ship's dim light.

"Ah ha! A large rat prowling my little ship!"

"It still ain't your ship," said Captain Oxford in protest from the deck below Snyder's perch on the rear cabin roof.

Then, to the complete amazement of James, Jana stepped out beside him, and she turned to call out Rachel as well. He heard her say, "Have no fear. He's not going to harm anyone."

"That's right, lady," said Snyder. "I don't know how you and Rachel got free, and right now I don't care. I want all of you on the pier directly in front of me, where I can see every last one of you in the light. It's time for everyone to decide who wants to sail with Admiral Snyder, and who wants to crawl back into those woods." Snyder appeared confident, and his voice grew louder.

"I told you I was going to be in charge when I escaped from Devil's Canyon in the rowboat. My time to command a larger vessel has arrived, and my proposition remains the same. I will be in absolute control."

James, Jana, and Rachel gathered at the barge's railing nearest the huge pier. Captain Oxford joined them, hugging his daughter and kissing her on the cheek. Meanwhile, Rev. Dennis, Rusty, Abigail, and Feruka lined up on the pier, facing *Midnight* and Snyder. James thought the latter seemed quite pleased with himself, as if everyone had finally been coerced or intimidated into recognizing his newfound position of authority.

"Listen very closely, people. This is simply how it's going to be. You four on the deck join your four friends on the pier. I'll take any of you back on board this ship if and when you have the correct answers."

James could barely believe Snyder was serious, and that this was actually happening. It had taken place so fast, and Snyder did seem to have the complete control he craved so badly. James felt Oxford tensing at his side, and then Snyder's voice rang out again.

"Oxford, you drop that other oar, or I'll drop you! Try to remember in your feeble brain that one stick of this stuff can blow you and your whole bunch to kingdom come. You try to be a hero and you'll have a dead daughter, too!"

Oxford reluctantly dropped the oar with a dull thud and was the last person to leave *Midnight*. James saw how slowly the captain left his ship and felt sorry for him. Even his mascot crow, Blackie, had abandoned its place on the railing, flying to a post that supported the Port of Jossandra's only pier.

· · ·

James listened with the others to Snyder's ultimatum. It gave eight of them thirty minutes to decide who would sail with Snyder, who would recognize him as *Midnight*'s new skipper, and who would remain behind. Half of the allotted time had already passed. Snyder sat atop the cabin roof, silent as stone, while the small group on the pier furtively talked among themselves. He clutched the explosives that gave him the upper hand.

"Well, he ain't going to stay in charge very long," said Captain Oxford. "Once we get underway I'll bash him in his watermelon head."

Abigail countered, "Anyone who goes aboard *Midnight* anticipating violent overthrow should be prepared for deadly consequences."

"I ain't exactly sure what she means," said Oxford in his own defense, "but the rest of you know I'm a fair man." He glared at Abigail. "I don't plan to kill even a thieving crook like Snyder, unless I'm forced to."

"That's not the point," said Abigail. "You may not intend to kill, yet your heart has embraced the possibility. You have already taken an irrational stance, which offers mindless passion an opportunity."

"Can't you say it simple? That's part of what I don't like about you women and your Port. Fancy words, nice smiles, and more fancy words. You're a sight worse than Reverend Dennis here, and he makes his living at preaching. Why can't you let people live their lives the way they want to?"

"Because you endanger innocent people," said Abigail. "Your daughter and our guests have been brought to the brink of disaster because you have broken laws of life. Pleading ignorance, as someone like Snyder might do, will not change that. Fearful and hate-filled minds invite violent acts that seek to disrupt natural harmony."

"Ah hell. More fancy words," said Oxford.

She continued, undaunted. "If you would allow that man to take your barge, for example, everyone left behind could remain in our valley. We welcome lovers of peace, and we have a vast supply of everything needed for a fulfilled life."

"No, and I'll tell you why. I make my living with that boat," said Oxford. "It's not your boat and it's not been in your family for years, so it's easy for you to stand there and preach."

While the captain argued, James grew more and more uncomfortable. He realized his own decision would have to be made quickly, and it wasn't an easy one. He took Rev. Dennis to one side, hoping to clarify his alternatives.

"We haven't got much time left," whispered James. "What are you and Rusty going to do?"

"I shouldn't speak for Rusty, but I'd guess he's going to stick with the captain come hell or high water."

"Say, how did you guys get over here anyway? I thought you'd gone to sleep for the night." James's curiosity allowed him to use precious time on that question.

"Well, I'd gone to bed immediately, but Rusty saw your sailboat going out across the lake. He got me from my room, and we decided our help might be needed at the barge. Call it a hunch. We stumbled along that Rock-Dell path all the way to the north-shore. The moon helped some, but it was slow going. I expected to find a mess here when we heard the explosion from the rocks. When we got to the north beach we saw Abigail, and then Feruka came running to her from the woods path. They filled us in while we all hurried over here, and that's about it. I just thank heaven no one's been harmed."

"Yeah, I know, but it doesn't look good." James continued to whisper. "Did you hear Oxie? He wants us to take Snyder out from the sound of it. So I'm thinking of going on the barge with him. He's going to need help, and—"

They ceased talking as Snyder rose to face the small group from atop the cabin roof.

"You people have precisely seven minutes more to make a final decision. Remember, I'll listen to all points of view, and we'll charge a fair price to take people where they want to go."

James felt as if that was addressed to him.

"But as I stated before, I will have complete authority as befits the captain of a ship. I'm ready to forget any past disagreements. Even you are welcome as second-in-command, Oxford. Think about it. Isn't that better than having no ship at all? You'll make more money with me in charge than you did before. That's a promise. All I ask in return is an honest day's labor, and respect for my decisions."

Snyder paused, and then added, "You now have five minutes to make up your minds."

CHAPTER SIXTEEN

*One learns that the only way to escape
the abyss is to look at it, measure it,
sound its depths, and go down into it.*

-Cesare Pavese

Darkening clouds continued to gather across a once star-bright sky. Blackie flew back to the barge railing and paraded back and forth like a nervous admiral. More than five minutes had passed, and still Snyder waited. Finally, when lightning was beginning to flicker behind the mountains across the river, Snyder spoke.

"All right, Oxford. You're the first one that needs to decide. The rest of you listen carefully because I'm not open to further debate. We're sailing the instant I've got my crew assembled."

"That just goes to show you ain't got too much sense," said Oxford. "It's the dead of night, there's a storm brewing yonder, and you're thinking of leaving a safe port. I may not take to these here women and their weird lake ways, but I got to admit there ain't a better place to ride out a storm than the Port of Jossandra."

"Nice try," said Snyder. "But I'm not about to wait for daylight or the fainthearted. You either show me you've got nerve to handle a rough river passage, or you stay undecided and snivel your opportunity away."

"I ain't scared or undecided," said Oxford. "Just so you know how I see things, you better know this. You get yourself in trouble on that river, and you'll be glad enough to have me on board."

Snyder grinned. "That's one. Come on board, Oxford, and make ready to ship out. Why are you women standing there with your eyes shut? Are you sleeping on your feet or something?"

James looked, and it was true. Abigail, Feruka, and Jana stood as serenely as the statues he thought he saw when *Midnight* docked that afternoon. He thought he understood, although Rev. Dennis was the one who spoke.

"They're praying, Snyder. It doesn't take much intelligence to see that's their way. May I suggest we give them a few minutes more?"

"Negative. They're stalling, and that's a fact. I've never encountered such a pack of sheep. Rachel, where do you think you're going?" said Snyder.

James stepped forward to help her back onto the deck of the barge. "It's obvious, isn't it?" said James. "She goes where her dad goes. Captain Oxford is her only family." Once he helped her over the railing, James stepped back onto the pier.

"He's not Captain Oxford anymore," said Snyder with a tone of derision. "Just plain Oxford. All right, that's two. Rusty, are you coming along?"

"Yep. I like this port's food, but I'll stick with Oxie, unless you got some objections."

"No. Come on board, matey. That makes three."

James saw the women's eyes were now open, although their composed expressions hadn't changed. It was clear Snyder was baffled by their behavior, and he waited to see if they were going to speak. Abigail stepped forward.

"We do not have a place prepared for you, Snyder," she began in a clear, patient tone. Her unusual deep blue eyes did not waiver under his critical gaze. "But if you should wait out tonight on Captain Oxford's barge, leaving your weapons behind in the morning, we would welcome you to come in peace at daylight as our brother."

"Too little, too late," said Snyder. "A barge in hand is worth more than sheep in the bush. I'm going back the way we came. This ship will turn profits for me Oxford's never even dreamed of. With my contacts up and down the river, the sky itself is no limit. After I've amassed another fortune, I might take you up on your offer. Right now you've got nothing I want. Do you understand? I've heard some things about the great Port of Jossandra, but I've got to say this crummy pier in the middle of uncharted wilderness greatly disappoints me. This place is fit for nothing but fishermen, shepherds, and farmers. Isn't that right, Oxford?"

"You ain't far off there," said Oxford. He stood mute then, the old fire gone from his voice.

James felt a wave of pity for him, and at that moment he made his own choice.

"I happen to like this valley, Snyder. We could all learn something here. But I've got to get back to home and family." James thought Rachel looked startled when he spoke, as if she never realized he had a family of his own. I guess I never told her, he admitted to himself. "So like Rusty says, if you've got no objections, I'll come along for the ride and work my way back."

"Splendid," said Snyder, sounding pleased to have things going his way. "The tide has turned." He chuckled aloud.

With the rapid change in mood by Snyder, James wondered for the first time about the man's sanity. As he stood next to Rachel and Oxford, this thought came to him. How else can one explain Snyder threatening to kill us one minute, then turn around and take us on as crew and passengers? His second-guessing was interrupted by Snyder's voice.

"Dennis, that leaves only you. I suppose you'd like to stay with these good ladies at the Port of Jossandra?"

Rev. Dennis looked uncertain, and James knew him well enough to realize he was still wrestling over the choices involved. Finally, he spoke.

"This valley seems to be what I've been searching for all my life. But all of my adult life I've been asking myself, where am I most needed? So I ask myself now, who needs me more? These women who have everything, or my friends who—"

"We haven't got all night, Dennis. I want to find my own port on the other side of the river yet tonight, so you'd better decide fast. Let me tell you I plan to make a man out of you once we're on the river. I've got no tolerance for do-gooder weakness, and there are times when you—"

"Save your breath," said Rev. Dennis, who interrupted Snyder with more confidence than James had heard before. "We don't see many things the same way, Snyder, that's true. But maybe if I come along we can be of mutual help—all of us help one another. Abigail and her friends, her sisters and brothers if you will, have taught me that much."

"Save your breath, preacher! Come aboard. That makes it a clean sweep."

Everyone present was now on board *Midnight* except the three women. James felt badly that Snyder offered Abigail, Jana, and Feruka nothing but his contempt. The big man called down from the cabin roof, "Maybe next time I pass this way, you Jossandra gals will mind your own business."

Abigail smiled, looking calmly radiant in the gathering gloom. "This is our business," she said, "and there will not be a next time."

Snyder appeared not to hear. Abigail and James exchanged a lingering look. For an uncertain moment James again had serious doubts about leaving the Port of Jossandra in this manner, with a possible madman in charge of his destiny. He yelled at Snyder, "What about Sylvia and Evelyn and Jesse?" He suddenly realized they were leaving those women and the kid behind.

"We sure don't need old women and a young brat when we're building a new crew for my ship," said Snyder.

Abigail ended the issue. "Do not concern yourselves about those former *Midnight* passengers. Let me assure all of you, they have found their reward."

Her cryptic message baffled James, but Rev. Dennis smiled warmly, seeming very satisfied with that esoteric response.

"Cast off!" yelled Snyder.

Oxford and Rusty dutifully began removing heavy mooring lines from the pier, ignoring the three motionless guardians who silently watched. Rachel took the hands of James and Dennis, who stood on either side of her, as *Midnight* began drifting away from the pier.

Perhaps on reckless impulse, perhaps from sheer madness, Snyder lit a fuse and threw one stick, then another, towards the pier. He threw a third explosive. All three sputtered in the night air and dropped impotently into the bay. James attributed that to the increased wind swirling about them.

Rev. Dennis appeared appalled as he removed his glasses and whispered to the other two companions, "I don't know what in the world we're in for, but I've got a pessimistic feeling it's going to get worse before it gets better."

James forced a laugh, and said, "I think you're right." Rachel nodded agreement, as the three friends at *Midnight*'s railing waved farewell to the three stalwart women on the pier. He wondered to himself if they would ever meet again.

• • •

When they exited the bay and reached the river proper, leaving behind the Port of Jossandra's great natural harbor, it was as if Gargol had been waiting for them. James saw the huge beast emerge from shadows at the very moment it surfaced near mid-river.

"Oxford!" screamed Snyder. "Oxford, the Gargol's after us! Turn this damned tub around and head back to port!"

All passengers ran towards the wheel area as each spotted the creature within moments of Snyder's reaction to the new threat. For whatever reason, Oxford continued to steer *Midnight* directly towards the beast before them. James wondered if Oxie was looking for an opportunity to recover his ship by way of this unexpected confrontation. He was at the wheel, yet he took no evasive action.

"Too late, Snyder!" yelled Oxford. "We're going to have to ride this one out. Better keep your powder dry!" Oxford's old familiar laughter pealed defiantly in the semi-darkness.

Storm winds increased and lightning flashes vividly outlined Gargol, who rose higher above the rough waves.

"My gawd, Rusty!" yelled Oxford, obviously taken aback. "The damned Gargol keeps getting bigger. It's huge!"

"Look at the reddish color this time!" yelled Rusty. "It's not natural!"

And indeed, an eerie, pulsating glow appeared to fire the monster's bloated inner body. In the turbulent darkness, even its yellowish eyes seemed to be larger, more menacing than before. Still the captain kept *Midnight* on a collision course.

"Captain Oxford is at the helm now you damned beast! We're going to stuff some metal prow down your stinking throat!"

"Hey, Oxie!" yelled James, seeing his intent. "Don't tangle with that thing unless we have to. Veer away!"

"He's right!" yelled Rev. Dennis. "Get *Midnight* back to the Port before—"

An explosion rocketed brilliant light into the darkened sky ahead of them. James turned to see Snyder heaving another stick. He was far off target, and that monstrous flesh-eater of the river was not deterred in the slightest.

Midnight was in fact well under steam and rapidly closing the distance, for as Oxford deliberately steered towards Gargol, the aggressive beast slithered through choppy water for the barge. There was a sinister malevolence about the creature that defied words, yet sent shudders up and down James's spine. He felt powerless to alter what was happening all too fast.

Less than fifty feet now separated them from the monster. Its reeking stench was reaching out, caught up in the night's swirling storm winds. The jaws of Gargol went slack, then closed with an audible snap, then opened again.

Rusty looked beside himself. "Throw more of those blasting sticks, Snyder! Kill that stinking bastard! Get up here on the forward roof. You're too far back."

Rusty was literally hopping up and down. For the first time James thought of getting Rachel and the others away from what looked like an inevitable head-on crash.

Snyder made one last throw from his poor position, but a crash of thunder drowned out its sound, if it went off at all. The large man clambered down onto the deck to improve his accuracy. His eyes were glazed, his mouth set and determined, as he ran past a retreating James, Rachel, and Dennis. James turned in time to see Snyder scale the forward cabin with his small bag of explosives, evidently heeding Rusty's advice. Rusty stayed close to the captain, who grimly held the wheel, fixed on his target.

The foul beast lay dead ahead. It rose higher than the barge's railing, then higher than the forward cabin's roof. A putrid drool oozed from the creature's gaping jaws as its gaze was fixed upon the onrushing *Midnight*.

"You want to play tough guy?" screamed Snyder down at the white-faced Captain Oxford. He hastily lit another stick as the barge closed for the inevitable crash, but grew even more furious when the fuse wouldn't stay lit in the howling wind.

James could see a glowing fuse tip remained at the end of the stick Snyder grasped in his right hand. It merely glowed and didn't burn. Rather than make an attempt to re-light it, an angry Snyder began to wave it furiously in the rushing air, apparently trying to fan the ember into flame once more.

"Don't!" screamed James.

Oxford locked the wheel into position, then he and Rusty turned and fled. In growing horror, James knew that between the beast, Snyder, and Oxford, little hope remained except for a tragic ending. He wondered if Oxie realized yet that the attempt to match Snyder's recklessness was a horrible blunder.

"Take cover, everybody!" yelled Oxford as loud as he could. He ran, belly-flopped on *Midnight's* slippery deck, sliding and crawling for the rear cabin's protection. Rusty was on Oxford's heels like a frightened cur who hung onto his master's shoes.

James held his gaze long enough to see Snyder overshadowed by Gargol's immense size. The would-be captain continued to wave the deadly stick whose fuse still would not burn for him.

Oh no! James groaned to himself. It's every bit of twenty feet high, and more! It must weigh tons!

Seconds, fleeting seconds before *Midnight* rammed the savage creature's midsection, Snyder waved the wayward fuse too hard. An errant spark of fire ignited the stick in Snyder's outstretched hand.

A sickening crunch of the barge's prow and the accidental explosion were nearly simultaneous. Then the wounded beast forged its way over the disintegrating forward cabin onto an even more violent explosion.

In a barge-rending, blinding flash Snyder and the forward cabin were blown away. Debris scattered on the river and littered the entire deck, while the horrified passengers were sent tumbling and sprawling.

Gargol rumbled and shrieked in the night storm, maddened with pain. It towered above all, snorting unholy wrath. It was an ancient, gargantuan reptile in the midst of frail humans. The adults were transformed into mindless children as the monstrosity swung its great webbed fore-claws and methodically crushed what remained of the shattered wheelhouse and forward area.

The beast seemed to calculate. It struggled towards the cargo of human flesh that survived. Yet an enormous lower girth prevented it from getting a solid position aboard *Midnight.*

Then, tiny tongues of flame found more explosives that Snyder had evidently held in reserve below deck. While Gargol inched its way aboard, towards the survivors, and extended its sinuous body through molten wreckage in swollen anger, a deep explosion belched flame on all sides of the gruesome attacker.

The great beast's bearable pain became instantly unbearable. It had been rammed by a rugged barge under full steam, it had sustained grave injury by Snyder's fatal miscalculation, and now its exposed underbelly took a full, explosive force. Finally came the flames to roast what remained of the beast.

Whether the creature was living or dying was not within the power of the survivors to determine. They clung to whatever seemed solid, and prayed.

Gargol rolled its fearsome head from side to side, expelling rancid odors of death. Beyond all that was imaginable, the final howls of the ancient reptilian beast pierced the night with withering agony. If die Gargol must, it was seemingly an endless death.

James and the rest of the passengers endured the most horrendous moments of their lives, while indifferent currents grasped a ravaged *Midnight* amid thunder and wind. Lightning and flames stabbed the darkness, while those passengers who were still conscious, struggled to see if there would be any victors in this terrible last battle of a war that unfolded around them like a living nightmare.

Putrid air wafted into the nostrils of James, and drifting smoke blinded his eyes. The thunder finally rumbled into the distance, and the rain gradually dissolved into drizzle. In place of the storm, patchy fog was mixing with smoky darkness that enveloped the badly crippled barge.

James stood in the flickering light of dying flames, next to Rachel, with a fire ax in his hands, and looked at the dreaded head of Gargol. Rusty lay unconscious nearby, his shirt in tatters, his right arm bleeding. Rachel looked dazed and unsteady on her feet.

James listened again to a rumbling noise that sent a chill through his heart. No, it was not the beast. It was something in the dark distance coming closer.

Rachel looked for other survivors, and James turned to see her approach him again across *Midnight's* broken deck through swirling gray smoke that drifted from the burning remains of the charred forward cabin. Her face was smudged, and he saw bruises on her upper arms and shoulders, but she didn't appear seriously hurt. Uttering a strange cry of fear mingled with joy, she came into his arms.

"Careful, Rachel. I think it's dead, but look at those eyes. Maybe they never close. It's like it could rear up again at any moment. I can't be certain until I do what must be done." He took a deep breath.

"Look away."

He raised the ax above his head, and when he began to swing downward she turned and covered her face. He swung and connected a second time.

The beast's eyes will see no more, he thought.

A sidelong glance at the flow of fluid from gaping sockets proved his aim had been true. In disgust, James flung the ax aside, while a spasmodic ripple moved along the length of the enormous mutilated corpse, and then it moved no more.

• • •

"Your dad is up front, Rachel. He's physically all right, I think. He's poking around where the wheelhouse used to be. We'd better tend to Rusty, wrap his arm, and see if we can find Dennis."

Rachel knelt down beside the fallen Rusty, who already tried to get up, groaning as he did. James left him to Rachel's care, so that he could check through the rubble for Rev. Dennis. James caught sight of some white cloth under debris along the stern, when Captain Oxford walked slowly in his direction.

"It's no use," said Oxford. "Hopeless. The fire's going out, but it sure looks like *Midnight*'s had her last cruise. I'm sorry, Pa. That crazy bastard Snyder went and wrecked your barge. Damn the luck."

"Oxie! Get back here! I think Dennis is under this pile of junk. Hey, Captain, are you deaf? Give me some help."

"It don't hardly make no difference now, James."

"The heck it doesn't!"

"It's not what you think," said Oxford. "You hear that low, roaring sound, like far-off thunder? That's no storm thunder. That there's the roar of Great Falls, and we got nothing left to get us out of this strong current."

He spoke soberly, drained of any trace of excitement, and James recognized an element of stoic finality in Oxie's few words of utter discouragement.

"James. Ohh . . . get me out!"

"Oxie! That's Dennis under there! C'mon, we've got to get all this stuff off of him!"

He began to pull up loose boards, bits and pieces of everything imaginable, from the forward cabin to railing fragments. Rusty staggered over and wordlessly yanked on things with his one good hand. When Rachel pitched in as well, the disconsolate Oxie finally tried to help them.

"Look at this," said James. "The rowboat must have flipped right up out of the water and over the top of him. Lift this up and I'll pull him out. Rachel, get his legs."

With an effort from all of them, Rev. Dennis was pulled free from underneath the protective hull of the fishing boat. He appeared only semi-coherent as he struggled to speak.

"Got to get back," he murmured. "Got to get back to the Port, Captain."

"He's got himself banged on the head like me in Devil's Canyon," said Oxford. "But I'm trying to tell you all, we got far worse coming right at us, and I can't do nothing. The Great Falls. You hear me, Rusty? *Midnight*'s all busted up and drifting in a real strong current right into them damn falls, and there ain't nobody here, not one of us getting over them alive."

He paused and uttered a long, mournful sigh, looking at his only child. "Unless," he added, "someone here knows something about miracles."

James looked down at the fallen Rev. Dennis and over at the completely ruined foredeck with its smoldering corpse. He read the utter disgust in Oxford's face as they stood before the continuing cremation of the beast's carcass.

"I'd almost go happy to a watery grave if I could get that stinking, blood-rotted Gargol off of my poor old *Midnight.* Oh Lord, what an awful end for the barge and Rachel and me."

It was the first time James had ever seen tears in Captain Oxford's eyes. They trickled sparingly down into the smudges on his lined, weary face.

Great Falls, mused James, with curiosity greater than fear. What in hell could be worse than what we've just been through?

CHAPTER SEVENTEEN

Upon the flood's black waste
upon the waters of the end
upon the sea of death, where still we sail
darkly, for we cannot steer, and have no port.

-D. H. Lawrence

The men stood staring, fascinated by Gargol's corpse. Its immense midsection was badly charred and had gradually sunk into a pit where the forward cabin once existed. The entire section had collapsed into the rooms below deck, but water was buoying up the nauseating remains. The beast's entire tail section, including rear webbed feet, hung over the ship's prow, trailing in the water as the disabled *Midnight* temporarily drifted backwards in the swift current.

"Lord, I wish we could get that filthy hunk of stinking meat off my barge," Captain Oxford said again. "But we can throw this other crap overboard. Let's go! We ain't going to have nothing left but the clothes on our backs and James's old fishing boat. Who knows, that might come in handy again if anyone's alive after we go over the falls."

He gave a modest effort at laughing, but it rang hollow.

"Then you think we might survive going over the falls?" asked Rev. Dennis, who moved like Rusty, at about half-speed.

Oxford appeared to try and laugh his question off, and again the laugh died in his throat. James studied the captain's face as he grimaced and wiped his furrowed brow with a dirty handkerchief for the tenth time.

"Reverend," said Oxford, "for once you're better off just praying. I've seen them falls at a distance from shore, and trust me, it ain't really something you want to hear about. Least not just yet. I reckon it's about ten to fifteen minutes off, at best, so you'll see for yourself soon enough."

There were so many things to throw overboard that they finally gave up on getting it all. For awhile though, it gave them something to do with a newfound nervous energy.

"That's quite a roar already," said James, who kept calm by throwing useless things overboard as Oxford had suggested.

"It gets a lot worse, believe me," said Oxford. "Look at the power of that current! Man, even if I still had an engine I'd never pull *Midnight* out of this. Nope, we got to say our good-byes, maybe do some praying, or hum a few tunes. Damned if I know just what to say or do for once. I ain't never took no suicide cruise before."

This time his laughter came more easily, and James welcomed it as a release from the building nervous strain and tension.

James walked to where Rachel stood apart from the men, who worked at debris removal. He turned her away and pointed out a lone star winking far above them. She nodded and smiled, and soon all of them halted work and lifted their gaze skyward. James nodded his approval when she tapped Rev. Dennis on his chest and formed her hands in a gesture of prayer.

Rev. Dennis inhaled deeply, nodded in return, and got down on his knees. Rachel did the same, and although he felt awkward, James followed suit.

Oxford and Rusty moved about fifteen feet away from the kneeling threesome, talking between themselves with quiet intensity. "That ain't really a bad idea, ya know, Rusty. Rachel's got more sense than me. She takes after her good-hearted ma. Well, at least *Midnight* finally got her ma's killer."

"If praying is such a good idea, Oxie, then why aren't you doing what they're doing? I don't see you down on your knees."

"Hell, man, it's kind of late for the likes of me to try changing my ways all at once.

Like I said before, it's all mostly a case of luck, good or bad."

They stood beside the smoking pit that was slowly filling with water. The monster's mutilated head was still visible among the ruins. *Midnight* herself rode ever lower in the powerful current, as most assuredly she was slowly sinking.

"You feeling lucky, Oxie?" said Rusty in a weak voice.

"Can't really say yet. Ask me when we hit the edge of Great Falls. Better yet, ask me again when we hit the bottom of the gorge."

· · ·

The foul creature that lay dead before them once took Oxford's wife to her death. The beast's head testified to all that even worldly cunning and power could quickly be destroyed.

"Wasn't that something, Oxie?" said Rusty, as he broke the silence. "I mean the way Snyder blew himself up. I wonder what killed old Gargol? The way you plowed *Midnight* into his guts, or those explosives that tore everything apart? One thing's sure, Snyder blasted himself into nothing but bits and pieces."

"Stop your babbling, Rusty. You're just making folks nervous. But I guess you could say Gargol killed itself, if you want my opinion."

"Why do you say that, Oxie?"

"Because the damned thing came right at us. He sure didn't have to aim right direct at *Midnight*. Aw, hell, who cares now? But it sure was something to see, Rusty, you're right about that. I just wish it had a better ending for us."

The three others joined them, and all were silent. Rusty held his injured arm and finally said, "I was thinking of swimming for it, but my shoulder hurts like the devil."

"Don't be a darned fool, Rusty. Anybody would drown before getting halfway to shore in a current that strong, or get swept over Great Falls with no protection at all."

"But I'll drown anyway, won't I?"

"You're darned right," said Oxford with a grin. "But there's a right way and a wrong way to go about drowning. You follow what I say, Rusty, and I'll show you how to hold on till the last minute, so you got a chance. Then you go down with the ship. So if we got to drown because there ain't no other way, I'll see you drown good and proper."

Rusty bowed his head, put his right hand to his temple, and wagged his head from side to side. Together, the two friends shared a wry moment.

"We might sink before the falls—water's coming in pretty steady up front!" yelled James over the growing roar of Great Falls.

"Don't you think I know!" yelled Oxie. "Old *Midnight*'s sailed her last, boys! All right, get those mattresses over the steps there. We'll all ride it over from back here. Forget the forward stuff, Rusty! We ain't steering or stopping!"

"Captain! What about the rowboat? Can't we use that somehow?" Rev. Dennis yelled to make himself heard, while the noise increased with every precious second.

"No way!" bellowed Oxie. "Maybe *Midnight* will get hung up on the brink right before we go over. That's the only hope left. But try riding a small boat, like Snyder done in Devil's Canyon, and you'd be dead before you knew it!"

Water that rose from below sloshed across the remnant deck. It was clear to all that the battered barge was close to sinking, even without the falls. Now it was merely a question of getting the remaining few hundred yards to an ultimate destination.

Rev. Dennis and James braced themselves at the lower steps of the rear cabin close to the rising waterline. Rachel was positioned slightly above and between them. Just above her on either side were Oxie and Rusty. Suddenly Rusty could not bear to wait another minute. He crawled out onto the ravaged deck, got up and slipped on grimy water, then rose again to make his way forward.

"Come back here, you darned fool!" shouted Oxie. "You want to get yourself killed? Get back here and do things shipshape proper, like I tell you."

Oxie shook his hatless head and yelled to the others. "Just a few more minutes, folks! Rachel, girl, I love ya!" He turned away as if to try and spot Rusty in the darkness.

"Oxie, I saw it coming! There's no more fog! Oh God! Let's get out of here!"

James and Oxie yanked the trembling man down against the soggy mattress, then they resumed their positions, bracing for whatever awaited them.

James could barely hear Oxie yelling over the fall's ferocious volume. "There ain't no place to go, Rusty, unless you crawl into Gargol's burned-out guts and choke on the stink! Just close your eyes and wait!"

"We're almost there!" screamed Rusty.

James saw the impending horror transform Rusty's face. The merchant's eyes bulged like those of a trembling, trapped animal. Oxie slapped him, and that at least stopped his shaking. "Sorry, Rusty," said Oxie. "Rachel, you hang tight to that mattress no matter what! James? Dennis? Hang on!"

The deafening tumult seemed all the more wild in darkness. James thought they might have gone over the edge of a mile-high abyss, yet they had not reached the brink. But it was now upon them, waiting like a monster that dwarfed the once hideous Gargol.

James inched forward and put his right arm around Rachel's back. Dennis did the same from the other side, as they both grasped the mattress that lay across the rear cabin steps. Dennis's left arm crossed Rachel's back and James's arm. Oxie protectively hugged Rusty's inert form, as he had passed out. Then the semiconscious man revived sufficiently to speak.

"What happened? Are we all right?"

"God is with us!" yelled Rev. Dennis as loudly as he could.

We can't die now, James thought. I've got to get back home to Bethany and my family. He tried to shut the horrendous sounds from consciousness, and a vivid flash came of how he'd imagined himself as a boy on Angel Lake's north shore the day they arrived at the Port of Jossandra.

Peace and warmth, he repeated in thought. Warmth and peace.

Then a terrible stillness enveloped him. It felt to James like they were no longer moving. He thought he heard Oxie scream, "The brink! The brink!" But the words sounded far away, unreal.

He squeezed his own arm and felt Rachel's warm body close beside him. He wondered if they were falling.

. . .

James thought he saw Oxie and Rusty slide out across *Midnight*'s deck, clinging to their single mattress. And then he was twisted sideways. Water engulfed him, washing over him.

He let go of Rachel as their bodies banged back and forth between the stairwell walls, and then he was floating in a weightless world of sound. His breath was crushed away as he slammed back and forth, and somehow he managed a painful, deeper breath that tasted so good. He braced again and felt a body collide with him which could have been either Rachel or Dennis.

I can't see!

Blinding wetness and darkness intertwined. He felt almost exhilarated. James heard screaming and did not recognize its source. It might have been his own voice, but he was uncertain.

He swore the barge was turning over, upside down and breaking up, except it never seemed to end. James only knew he was caught up in a wet vortex of utter confusion.

The others were gone. Was he imagining *Midnight*'s disintegration all around him?

"Rachel! Dennis! Oxford!"

It was no use. He thought he was screaming their names, but he couldn't hear his own voice. It was not a nightmare. The cold water and the smell of the dead beast told him he was awake. And he thought there was the cawing of a crow.

I am awake! I am alive! He clung to those thoughts.

Or was the sensory information only in his thoughts, like in a sleeping dream? His eyes saw nothing and he swore they were wide open. Thinking was everything—thinking and feeling!

He was thinking himself to be larger than Gargol, to be enormous, gigantic. James felt that he was living and Gargol was dead. Where was the little barge and all the tiny people?

Images and sounds flashed and pounded, but they were not of the river or Great Falls. He heard Oxie's ringing laughter, echoing far away. He saw gorgeous Rachel dancing madly to Elf's intoxicating music. He tasted beer and brandy and something bewitching called green death, and he felt he was staggering across emblazoned sky, drunker than anyone had ever been.

There was Bethany, far in the distance on a nameless green hill, walking towards the clouds. She was oblivious to his existence, walking with another man, and their backs were turned to him.

He screamed and could not be heard.

Now they were walking in the clouds. James tried to paddle a boat by hand after the oars turned into snakes and slithered away, overboard.

Then these images rapidly faded, and he sensed himself swimming endlessly underwater. James felt he could breathe underwater, like a fish moving effortlessly, and that pleased him. Only once again he could not see.

He thought of himself as a huge, blind fish that could swim in water, crawl on land, and fly in the heavens. How can I die? James thought.

Thought also informed James that he was tumbling end over end within violent sheets of water, plunging to a pain that was somehow being held at bay.

That body must not be me. I am right here, safe. He was going to survive, he realized, until there was light enough to see again. He was as certain of that as he was of the hope he'd felt anew at the Port of Jossandra. It was something about the allness of life.

James thought the darkness was breaking up. The pink haze had turned red. It ran across the darkness like a river of blood pulsating through a desolate, dark canyon. At some point he recalled Devil's Canyon and how Oxie had been unconscious for hours.

That's it, James thought. I'm unconscious, but then how am I thinking these thoughts?

James had a sensation of floating, and he felt the distant red might be Great Falls. There was flaming red falling and splattering. He yearned for more precious light.

I've forgotten time—how much has passed?

There came a shaking in the darkness, slow at first, then stronger until he gritted his teeth. How long did it last? Everything drifted, and then something solid. Shore? Land?

He rolled off what could have been a mattress, or planks with something on them cushioning his body. James thought he might be bleeding, but he still couldn't see. There was a warm wetness all around, and then he felt the solidness again. Got to get free. Got to get dry.

James tried to crawl, then rolled onto his back and pushed with his feet. He saw another flash of red in the distance. Red sky at night, sailor's delight, he thought. James drifted away into what he hoped was nothing more than harmless sleep.

CHAPTER EIGHTEEN

Time, like an ever-rolling stream,
Bears all its sons away;
They fly forgotten, as a dream
Dies at the opening day.

-Isaac Watts

James felt as though he had been drugged. His body became heavier and heavier, and it weighed him down. There was constant ringing in his ears. He made a semi-conscious effort to breathe, and that hurt.

He felt an oppressive weight on his back as his lungs struggled to function normally. The light he had prayed for was returning, and he thought he heard voices. Someone is pushing on my back!

"That's it, James! Breathe! Come on, James, breathe!"

It was Rev. Dennis in the distance, then Dennis coming closer, and James experienced quiet joy to find himself alive. When he relaxed and stopped struggling the pain lessened, and he was at last able to breathe more easily.

He felt something touching his face, and he thought of a childhood puppy. Then he saw Rachel close to him, her lips nipping his cheeks, forehead, and eyes with a half dozen rapid kisses. She looked wonderful. Her hair was a mess and there were bruises on her face and arms, but that was dwarfed by the fact she was still alive. He fought with all the remaining inner strength he could muster and managed to raise himself partway up.

"Easy, James," said Rev. Dennis. "You've drunk some rather rotten water and gotten pretty well banged up, like the rest of us. Easy there."

James started coughing as the water in his lungs was being expelled. The warm air tasted better and better. Rachel and Dennis knelt beside him, broad grins spreading across their faces.

"Where are the others?" James asked between coughs. "Where's the barge?"

He sat on a rocky shelf of barren land, reddish brown in color, some twenty-five feet from a strange-looking river. It was brown and steaming, and looked inhospitable to say the least. James scanned a scattered pile of debris strewn across the rocky shore.

"That's what's left of *Midnight*," said Rev. Dennis in a low voice. "All that stuff scattered along the bank."

"That's all?" James was incredulous. He simply did not recognize a barge in the shambles of wood and other material.

"I can't believe it," said James. "How did any of us live through that? And why do the falls look so far away? They seem reddish from here. Where's the sun?"

"Whoa, one question at a time," said Rev. Dennis. "God delivered us from death, but none of us got out unscathed. I came to floating on wreckage in the river. I found everyone washed ashore, unconscious. Rusty's in the worst shape. He's down there by your old fishing boat. Somehow it wasn't smashed. But I don't think Rusty . . . can last much longer. We just tried to make him comfortable."

After a minute, Dennis continued, "Rachel and Oxie must have struck shore very hard, too. They came around about half an hour ago. Like me they're battered and bruised, but nothing broken. How about you?"

James stood gingerly, placing weight on first one foot and then the other. "I ache from top to bottom." He laughed. "But I'm darned glad to be alive."

"That's exactly how I feel," said Rev. Dennis, managing a smile. "You'll notice something else. Gargol's corpse is gone. I can't help but wonder if it didn't help cushion our impact, although

I suppose we'll never really know. I blacked out early. When I started looking around this place with Oxie, we had trouble getting our bearings. Take your time, James."

James looked inland and was startled to see openings in the craggy, reddish brown rock. Caves!

Some of the rock was reddish gray, some darker, almost purple, and there was nothing else except rock along this shoreline. Looking even farther up along the rocky slopes and downriver, James did not see even the slightest sign of foliage, not tufts of grass or shrubs!

"Why is there so much red?" James wondered out loud. "The water, the land?"

Rachel stood mutely, shaking her head.

"We don't know," said Dennis. "Oxie went up to that largest cave. He's trying to figure out where we are, and looking for Blackie. By the way, the falls are even farther away than they look. I tried to scout back that way. It's impossible to climb, and there's something else."

"What's that?" asked James, sensing anxiety in Dennis.

"Lava flows. It's true. See how the water's steaming? It comes in through rocky gulches and fissures. I couldn't get anywhere. Now! Feel that?"

The ground began to tremble while Dennis talked, and Rachel moved closer to James. The shaking quickly subsided, but strewn boulders left little doubt this had happened before, and with greater intensity.

"Every so often, without warning, it's been doing that," said Dennis. "I'd have warned you, but you kept asking other questions."

"That's all right," said a baffled James. He tried to laugh it off. "I've felt shaky even before the tremor." He shook his head. "I've heard of earthquakes in other places, but how can it happen here?"

"Where's here?" asked Rev. Dennis. He also shook his head in wonder and added, "I've lost my glasses, too. What I can see is a bit fuzzy. From this distance I can barely see Great Falls."

"Well, they're none too clear to me either," said James. "In fact, nothing's clear," he said with a feeling of bitterness. "It's like when I was rescued from the river that first time. There's an awful sense of here I go again. Why do these things happen?"

No one attempted to answer him. Through the steaming haze he watched the dimly flowing reddish waters. The river itself looked hot, while the rocky ground was almost as warm as the muggy, oppressive air.

Dennis turned and walked back towards Rusty, who lay on makeshift bedding near the barge's mangled wreckage. James stared incredulously at the caves, wondered where Oxie had gone, and then he remembered what Dennis had said about Rusty. He moved gingerly towards him, following Dennis and Rachel, and noticed an ugly scrape on the back of her right thigh.

Rusty's upper body was propped against the partial remains of a tattered mattress. At first glance his face shocked James. Is Rusty dying? He couldn't accept his own thought.

· · ·

An hour passed under tan-gray clouds which were tinged with reddish hues. The survivors decided that somewhere beyond their sight was a volcano that must have been blowing ash skyward.

Rusty was blindly trying to yank clothing from his body while muttering unconsciously from a feverish coma. "It's like he's trying to communicate something, but has lost the power to talk," said Dennis. "Can you make it out?"

"No, it's like 'he says, she says,' over and over. And his expression never changes," said James.

"He says, she says," said Dennis. "Does that mean anything? I keep thinking he'll open his eyes, but I'm afraid he never will."

"Why?"

"His pulse is extremely weak. I'm afraid he could slip away from us at any minute."

"Where in the heck has Oxie gone off to?" asked James in angry frustration. "His friend is dying and he runs off somewhere." He stopped talking as soon as he saw Rachel walking away, up towards the largest cave.

"Rachel, wait!"

"You'd better get her, James. I'll look after Rusty the best I can. Give a yell up there and see if you can make contact with Oxie. He should have been back by now. And don't let Rachel get lost. We've got to stick together. Okay?"

"Right. So where did you see Oxie last?" asked James, already moving after Rachel, who was halfway to the caves.

"Exactly where Rachel's heading. It was that cave, the largest one. Oxie said he wouldn't go too far inside, but you know Oxie."

James tried to run, but his legs still felt rubbery. He settled for a rapid walk, which was closing the distance on Rachel who had paused at the jagged cave's entrance. She looked back at him, and he looked back at the river for a moment. She waited for him to catch up to her. As tired and worn as he felt, James knew that with Oxie missing there was no time for them to rest.

From the higher ground James again looked out across the river where Rachel had been raptly gazing. He thought he glimpsed a generous patch of green on the far side and that made him feel somewhat better.

That must be what Rachel is trying to see more clearly, he thought. Thank heaven there's green somewhere in this godforsaken gorge.

Pausing at the entrance of the large cavern, James also looked again towards Great Falls, but he could no longer see it. Reddish brown and gray cliffs blocked his view.

"Rachel, before we go any farther, let me yell and see if your dad can hear me."

"Maybe if we both yelled together," said Rachel with a shy smile, "Oxie would be more apt to hear us."

"My God! Rachel! You're talking!" James felt like an idiot, realizing his mouth was hanging open in disbelief.

"Of course I am. It's about time, don't you think?" She giggled at his bewilderment.

"But when? How long have you been able to talk?"

"I'm not sure exactly," she said with a laugh. "I think when Gargol died, something happened to my thinking. And when we went over Great Falls, I heard myself screaming out names over and over. Didn't you hear me? Anyway, when I came to on the rocky shore, I was pretty certain I could speak again."

"But then why didn't you, I mean, right away?" asked James.

"I don't know. I was kind of scared. When Oxie went off I waited for him to return. I wanted him to be the first one to hear me speak. Then, just now, I was looking at the river, almost afraid of seeing Gargol rise up again. But my heart sings, telling me he never will again. He's dead, dead, dead!" She paused, and smiled at James. "When you said, 'let me yell,' I thought why not yell together, and then I just started talking to you. I guess you're special, too, and so you are the first to hear me instead of my dad. Okay?"

"Okay? It's great!" He gave her a big hug. "Now, let's try yelling together, like you said, and see what happens."

For a full minute they both yelled together into the cave. Then James called for a short while longer, and when he stopped, Rachel resumed calling out on her own. Nothing answered but reverberating echoes.

At last there came a faint sound that was not an echo. At least James didn't think it was his own voice. It certainly wasn't Rachel's. She was excited by it, and she tugged at his torn sleeve.

"Did you hear that, James?"

"Yeah, but I can't quite figure it out."

She urged him forward, and with a last glance at Rev. Dennis, who was kneeling by Rusty, James followed her into the darkness of the cave.

• • •

It was yet another world. Well after his eyes adjusted to the darkness, he felt different.

Was it partly because Rachel could finally speak? He didn't know. Perhaps it was the numerous artifacts they found discarded alongside a main path inside the shadowy cavern. Most of all it felt to him like they had stepped back in time. The first man and woman? In bare feet he felt primitive, like early man seeking to survive in a hostile domain.

Where is the dim light coming from? he wondered.

Rachel picked up a drinking cup and several small bowls to examine. It was not possible to know for certain how recently others had been there, and perhaps they had merely passed by and sought temporary shelter.

Coupled with Oxie's disappearance, however, these findings increased curiosity and caution in both of them. James risked yelling again. They waited, listening.

He pointed back the way they'd come in the dim light. "We've already lost sight of the entrance. It veers to the left up ahead, and I think it's going downward. That's where the light seems to come from, too."

"I think it is," she said. "Why doesn't he answer again, if that was him we heard before?"

"I don't like the feel of this," he said to her in a whisper. "Oxie's gone too far. And I've seen pieces of hammers and spears. We could run into—"

They tensed together as a tremor ran through the cavern. The faint light from ahead of them flickered. Their section of the cave was twenty or more feet across, and fully ten feet high. It appeared solid enough to James, but falling pebbles and rocks could be heard farther ahead.

Without warning, a figure from the shadows leaped between them. James was sent reeling from a violent shove, and Rachel screamed. He rolled to his knees and whirled to face their unknown adversary. The attacker quickly grabbed Rachel with a hairy forearm around her throat, and although she struggled, his strength was too great.

"You move bad, I hurt woman."

The low, powerful voice echoed along the rough walls. James froze, stunned as the savage-looking man positioned Rachel in front of himself, like a shield.

"Let me go!"

The man looped a rusty chain over Rachel's head and across her neck. It looked so tight now James doubted she could speak. The savage lowered one arm to her waist, and for the moment she was powerless.

Her captor was no taller than she, but broadly built and scarred from many wounds, most of them healed over. Darker hair covered much of his body, yet his head was capped by wild, tumbling blond locks that were matted with what looked like dried blood.

Some cuts on his head appeared to be recent, and a crude animal skin covered one eye. The other eye stared in blatant antagonism at James. Only a twisted skin belt and loincloth adorned the stranger's well-developed body.

"We won't hurt you," said James, trying to show no fear. "Let us go, and we'll leave."

"No."

He showed his teeth and tightened the chain which was now obviously hurting Rachel. Then James noticed that the chain also ran through a heavy shackle at one of his ankles. The savage was trapped.

James moved one step forward, and the man retreated one step. James held his position and tried to calculate what actual danger Rachel faced if he attacked the stranger.

"Rachel, he's chained to the cave floor!"

"Me chained, but your woman die! You loose me, or she die!"

As he flexed a muscular right arm, Rachel slammed an elbow into his stomach. James leaped for her hands, and as the savage opened his mouth in surprise, she stamped on his foot. At that precise moment James yanked her free, but only for a second.

Rachel fell backwards, partly atop the savage, as the chain pulled her before it dropped. When the chained man attempted to hold her by the hair, James drove his fist into the captor's jaw. The shocked savage collapsed, and James finally pulled Rachel to a space beyond her tormentor's limited reach. They stood panting, watching their assailant stagger to his feet, turn away, and fall with a thud.

"Let's get the heck back to the river," said James. He grabbed Rachel's hand.

"What about Dad? Oxie? I can't leave without him. And look at this poor thing. He's covered with cuts and scrapes as bad as ours. Someone's chained him here to die."

She said the last in undisguised pity.

"Maybe he deserves it. He just threatened to kill you, Rachel. Don't forget that for a second."

"You'd say the same thing if you were in his place. Do you think he's hurt my dad?"

"Well, there aren't any signs of that. And look here. He's got a bit of crust and water. Rachel! Maybe someone brings him stuff. We have no weapons. I say we get Dennis and arm ourselves before we go any farther."

He awaited her reaction, but Rachel stared down the passageway. "Oxie!" she suddenly screamed. "Where are you, Dad?"

James clamped a hand over her mouth, and she bit his hand.

"Darn it! Do you have to tell everyone where we are?"

"I'm going to find Dad, and then we get out of here, but not before!" There wasn't a trace of doubt in Rachel's voice.

"I think I liked you better when you couldn't talk," he said loud enough for her to hear. "Tell me again how it happened."

She laughed, but a puzzled look came over her face when she tried to answer his question. The stranger crouched in semi-darkness while she hurriedly spoke to James.

"It's mostly like I told you when we were about to enter the cave, but something may have begun when Jana rescued me on the barge. At the Port of Jossandra, for the first time, I wanted to speak but couldn't. Then when Gargol was killed, it was like Ma was avenged or something like that. I really don't understand it myself. I'm sorry if it sounds confused, but that's all I know."

"It makes some sense, I guess." He gave her a gentle hug, and for a moment she clung to him.

"Listen," he said, feeling flustered to be so close to her in the semi-darkness. "Go to Dennis. Please. At least let him know about this character and the problem we've got finding Oxie. I'll watch from here, and in the meantime, maybe I can talk some sense to this guy and get some information about your dad."

"You won't hurt him will you? If you plan to strike him or kill him I'm not leaving." Rachel's great eyes seemed larger than usual. They looked like luminous black pools to James, who admired her mysterious qualities.

"No, I won't. That would be stupid. If he sees we mean no harm, I think he might talk. He certainly knows more about this place than we do. Now get going. Wait! If Rusty's still alive, you watch him and send Dennis in here with some clubs."

"No. Then I'm not going."

James cringed when her tone reminded him of Oxie's, and her stubbornness irritated him. "Why not, Rachel? I need someone stronger until we find out exactly what we're up against."

"No, you don't. You need me, and I've got to find my dad. That's my business."

"All right. Just tell Dennis what's happened, and one of you get back here as quick as you can,"

"What about you?" she asked, her worried expression barely visible in the poor light.

"I'll be okay. If it gets too much to handle, I'm a darn fast runner." They exchanged smiles. "Rachel, I'm really glad that you can talk again."

She stared at him like he'd just said something remarkably stupid, but there was no reply. Rachel glanced at the savage-looking man on the chain, and once again at James. Without another word she started back for daylight.

Geez, I wish Rusty would get better fast, James thought. We sure could use him.

As soon as Rachel was gone, James began to study the walls, floors, and nearby rocky corridors. He was amazed to find burning torches for light, without venturing too far from the wild man. At last he returned to the pitiful creature, hoping to gain some badly needed answers.

Who chained this poor devil? Who left the lights burning, and when will they return?

CHAPTER NINETEEN

I've known rivers:
Ancient, dusky rivers.
My soul has grown deep
like the rivers.

-Langston Hughes

"Hey, fella! Let's talk. Yeah, you. I'm not going to hurt you." James spoke with bold, now-or-never confidence.

The stranger stirred and retreated as far as the twelve-foot chain would allow him to move. In return, James himself backed off somewhat. The chained man dropped to his haunches, bowed his head, and then raised it to look directly into the eyes of James. There was a puzzled, half-frightened look on his face.

"You kill Bear Man?" He waited, as if resigned to that fate.

"No. We really mean you no harm. Is your name Bear Man?"

"Yes, Bear Man," he said again, striking his chest. "Flesh eaters. They call me wild man. My people, they call me Bear."

James dropped to his haunches, still looking the chained man in the eye. "Who are the flesh eaters, Bear, and where are your people?"

The wild man studied James, then pointed and said, "Flesh eaters that way, down in mountain belly. Chain Bear for bait near their light. My people good. Fish people of river. River hot when mountain shake. I get in big fight. Flesh eaters catch me."

James tried to figure out exactly what Bear Man was saying. "Listen, do you mean these flesh eaters are some tribe who caught you to bait a trap? I don't understand."

"They afraid wild beasts. I bait. Beasts come, eat me and go away. Not go to flesh eater's dark world." Again he pointed down the passageway. "Down there they safe. No wild beasts get them."

"So if wild beasts come into this cave, they will feed on you? Eat you? That's why they staked you here?" It seemed more unreal to James than anything he'd yet encountered on his bizarre journey. He thought of the nightmarish visions he'd had while plunging over Great Falls, but this time he was fully conscious.

How can such things be? He repeated his question to Bear Man. "That is why you are staked here?"

"Me chained. Yes. You more smart." He gave a weak smile. "You make Bear loose?"

"Maybe. But we would have to help each other."

"Bear help fish people. They my people."

James smiled. "Would you help us if we set you free?"

He watched the man's single, unblinking eye, and wondered if cooperation was possible in this world of shadows. James sensed Bear's primitive cunning and was also wary of his strength. He took Bear Man's hesitation to be a negative sign. He tried another line of questions, hoping to learn something about the fate of Captain Oxford.

"Did you see another man like me? A short time ago. Not flesh eater, not fish people, not wild man, looking more like me?"

Bear Man grinned. "Not like you. Him too fat, small, but smell like you. Small, fat, smelly man."

"All right! Listen, this is important. Ah, big news. He is my friend. He is of my tribe. We floated downriver on a big boat."

"Ah, boat people. I like you sometime yes, sometime no. You good people?"

"We try to be good," said James. "If you help me find the little fat man, I will help you get loose. We will break your chain, Bear Man. Do you understand?"

"Iron rope? You help me," he said, then paused. "Me help you. Flesh eaters take little man down by pit fires. Bad place. Let Bear loose. I show where."

James thought they appeared to have reached an agreement. He now felt certain Oxie had blundered into whoever had chained Bear Man. The next move might prove more difficult, but he was satisfied to know Rachel or Dennis would return soon to help him decide their next course of action.

• • •

Finally, after what seemed to be an hour, James heard voices and cautiously called out, "Rachel?"

"Yes, James. It's Rachel and Dennis." It was Rev. Dennis who spoke as they emerged from the shadows. "Sorry we took so long, but I'm afraid we have brought some bad news for you."

"Rusty?" James awaited the dreaded answer, and it came from Rachel's lowered voice. She spoke so softly he could barely hear.

"He's dead, James. I found the Reverend burying him. Then he said some holy words, and we prayed."

James said nothing for a minute. Oxie is gone. Rusty is gone. He felt empty. He then heard his own quiet voice sounding composed, but asked what he knew was a stupid question.

"How could you bury him, Dennis? The ground is so hard. There's no soil . . . ."

His voice drifted away in the gloomy tunnel.

"I took his body to a small ravine and piled rocks over him. I'd have waited for you, too, except for the heat. It's so warm I thought . . . I thought I'd better get it done. Rusty went quietly as could be. He just stopped breathing."

The sound of Bear Man's chain rattled in the shadows, and Dennis stepped backwards so fast he nearly lost his balance. Then he said, "Rachel told me about him. He certainly does look savage."

"He's okay for now," said James. "But I think I'm going to hack that chain off for him, and he might lead us to Oxie. It definitely sounds like he saw him."

"Is that right? He saw my dad? James, what did he say? Tell me."

"It's a simple story," said James. "His name is Bear Man, or just Bear. Bear said he saw a man smaller and fatter than me who smells like us—or me—come into this cave, and I guess get grabbed by some people he calls flesh eaters."

"Who the devil are the flesh eaters?" said Rev. Dennis.

"Again, and I'm partly guessing, he says they're a tribe that lives mostly underground, deep in the caverns. His own people are fisherman, 'fish people' he calls them. I think he got left behind after a fight and was captured, or the other way around. It seems his people are following the river in search of the sea, where they hope to find a better food supply."

"We brought the ship's ax that Dennis found in the wreckage," said Rachel. "I say we get the chain off him and get going. Oxie needs our help."

"She's probably right," said Rev. Dennis. "I don't like the sound of flesh eaters at all.

What kind of flesh do you suppose he means?" He visibly shuddered. "All flesh," was the wild man's eerie reply from the shadows of the silent cave.

While they contemplated his answer, James took the ax and placed the chain over a rock. The only sound in the cave was the striking of metal against metal, and metal against rock.

• • •

After James showed them the torches for light, the small band stayed close together through a meagerly lit section of cave. Bear Man led the way, followed by Rachel and James, while Rev. Dennis stayed close behind. They passed through cavernous rooms where additional light filtered through, and to their bafflement they occasionally encountered small bowls of burning oil that helped them to get their bearings.

"How much farther?" asked James when they entered a rocky enclosure with a shaft of murky light coming from somewhere above sheer, gray walls.

"Not far," said Bear. "See, they stop, eat, rest. Smoke from fire."

Before them were small stones that formed a rough circle several feet in diameter. Wisps of gray smoke disappeared into the heavy air. Bear squatted and poked among the remains.

Small bones, seeds, and hard crusts were scattered on the rocky floor.

Passageways beckoned in several directions from the dismal room. For the first time, James was afraid it was possible they were already irrevocably lost in the winding maze of caves.

Rev. Dennis must have had similar thoughts when he said, "Rachel, perhaps we've done as much as we can. We can't continue going deeper without risking grave danger to everyone. At times back there I couldn't see any of you, and I didn't have the slightest idea of where I was."

James sat quietly watching Bear, who appeared less menacing with more light in the cave, and then he looked at Rachel.

She sighed deeply. "Don't you guys think I know that? What do you think, James? We can't give up, can we?"

He stared grimly up at the opening in the jagged gray stone at least thirty-five feet above them. "No, I suppose not. What concerns me, too, is what happens if and when we do catch up with these people. All we have is an ax and some pieces of chain. We know they see Bear as an enemy, and that probably doesn't help us if we're caught. From what he told me, they're rough people who don't mind killing. But it's still possible we might rescue Oxie and not be captured by them or the mountain. So I think saving Oxie's life is worth the risk."

Bear Man took the opportunity to grab James by the hands, saying, "You my brother." He moved towards Dennis, who retreated a step, and again Bear took both hands in his own, saying, "You my brother." Bear's eye fairly shone in the modest light.

When the wild man stepped back and regarded them with a smile, James realized Bear was thanking them for his freedom. Then he stepped forward again and clasped Rachel's hands, and said, with gratitude reflected in his rugged features, "You my sister."

The small party saw this gesture as genuine. With the reference to sister, James thought back to the warmth of Abigail, Feruka, and Jana, and thought how good that brief time with them at Angel's Lake had been.

"You trust Bear. Bear trust you. Fish people and boat people go good."

The three boat people exchanged smiles at this welcome silver lining, until another shudder shook the vast labyrinth. This time the shaking continued for several agonizing minutes. A brief shower of stones forced them to hug the slanted walls, until all was quiet once again.

"That does it!" said Dennis. "We've got to get out of here before we're buried alive!"

"It go away," said Bear Man with surprising calm, helping a shaken Rachel to her feet. "It always come, it always go."

They stood poised for action after the shaking subsided and listened as the rumbling seemed to pervade the very heart of the mountain. When Bear did not panic and retreat, however, the others tried to follow his example.

James watched as Bear studied the openings in the rock that faced them, and at last the wild man made a choice. "That tunnel go no place," he said, pointing to the opening on their far right. "These go to far place very bad, much fire."

He paused and appeared to watch Rachel's pretty face with fascination. "One cave go to rock house of flesh eaters. Big, big circle room. Firewater never stop. Come there, maybe find small fat man friend."

James also watched Rachel's face and knew they could not abandon the search for Oxie. He realized, and hoped Dennis would too, that there was an inevitable choice. Oxie had led them on the river, and inadvertently he led them on once again.

"You come?" asked Bear when the distant noise did not return.

"Yes." James answered for them all, reading their mood and voicing the group's resolve and final decision.

Dennis carried the longest length of chain, and James the ax. Bear held out a three-foot chain that Rachel used to be guided behind him. And then, in a nearly silent procession, the wild man led them deeper into the bowels of that uncertain mountain.

"God be with us," murmured Rev. Dennis.

Hang on Oxie, thought James. We're coming to the rescue. I hope!

CHAPTER TWENTY

When joys have lost their bloom and breath,
And life itself is vapid,
Why, as we reach to falls of death,
Feel we its tide more rapid?

-Thomas Campbell

James began to realize that their journey to find Oxie and the flesh eaters was taking much longer than Bear had first predicted. The wild man simply did not measure time and distance as did the three searchers. When they paused at a dimly lit hollow in the rock, James knew they had to rest.

"We've got to sleep before we can go any farther," said James.

Rev. Dennis and Rachel looked as exhausted as James felt, and immediately the young woman curled up against a rock and fell asleep. Dennis stretched out nearby, looked up at James, and said, "Sorry James, I can't keep my eyes open any longer." And soon he too had drifted into sleep.

James felt the sting of his own resentment as he turned to face Bear. The wild man did not appear the least bit tired from their walking and crawling through the endless darkened maze of tunnels. Since James had already decided they were lost, he felt doubly frustrated.

"You lied to us, Bear. Why did you say the flesh eaters were not far away?"

"I not lie. You come see."

"I can't, you darned fool. Look at them. They can't travel another step, and I've also got to sleep. Now. I can't even stand guard while they're sleeping, because I'd fall asleep myself."

"You trust Bear. He watch. First you come see," persisted the wild man. There was an eagerness in his voice that fanned a small flame of curiosity in James. Bear pointed down the tunnel.

"See light down there? You smell stink? I show. Come back for friends. See where little fat man went. Then I go free."

James watched the savage stare at him with a single, unblinking brown eye, and he knew there was no choice but to trust Bear again. Perhaps it was the tiredness that weighed on him, but he couldn't think of anything except to continue what they'd begun.

"How far away is that light?" James peered into a narrow passageway and thought the distance might prove to be deceptive.

"You come. I show."

Bear took several steps, but James remained rooted at the place where his comrades had fallen asleep.

"You smell stink. Not far."

"No, I don't smell—wait a minute! What is that?" A stench came to his nostrils, and there was something quite familiar about it. For a moment James wondered if the wild man had defecated, but the smell was too strong.

"All right, friend. But let's go there fast. I don't want to leave Rachel and Dennis unguarded for more than a few minutes."

Bear nodded and moved forward in the darkness towards the dim light ahead. James followed quickly, for he now sensed something different loomed before them. He mentally vowed to enter no side passages, or new tunnels of any kind. He'd made that mistake before, when they had first blindly followed Bear.

What he planned for at this point involved just a few hundred yards. He wanted to know if what he saw and smelled represented an end to their unproductive journey.

When they came to the end of the narrow tunnel, James felt his heart pounding.

It smelled like the farm of his grandparents. As unpleasant as the odor was, he began to fondly remember cows and pigs and horses. It reminded him of the many times as a boy he and his younger brother had shoveled manure, a part of their daily chores.

"You see down. Look out flesh eaters. They take you like little fat man. Maybe chain you like Bear Man."

James scrambled forward on his hands and knees, oblivious to the rocky floor, imitating Bear, who then stopped and crouched in the shadows ahead of him. He crawled up beside Bear and looked out into empty space. He wondered if they'd come out on the other side of the mountain.

"It's huge, Bear. What is it?"

"Place of flesh eaters. Bear Man not stay. You look. Go back to others."

James wriggled forward on his stomach to get a better view, then looked down into an enclosed valley of rock and stone. It was staggering. Enormous, he thought.

Trails and ledges cut into rock ran along the walls, but it was the sheer enormity of the scene below that baffled and amazed James. Everything seemed out of place, or at least like no place he'd ever dreamed existed. The cavern walls rose several hundred feet skyward, but there was no sky.

Sixty feet down he saw pens of animals through a smoky haze—cattle, sheep, and pigs. There was also a large graveyard to the right, conventional in every detail. To the far left, beyond the animal pens, James saw a junkyard containing every type of refuse imaginable.

For some moments James considered the possibility that he might be hallucinating or dreaming. In fact, those were the explanations he most desired. Then he heard the muffled laughter of Bear behind him.

"Awful stink. You leave?"

"No! Bear, that's a town across the river, built on the floor! Is that an underground river?" His voice shook with excitement.

James strained to see more clearly, and suddenly he wished Rachel and Dennis were there to see what he saw, or thought he saw. He rubbed his smarting eyes and wished only to know what was real. A reddish brown river moved almost imperceptibly from right to left. How could it be?

It's lava!

He thought he saw figures walking on the other side of the flow, along a variety of storefronts: a grocery store, taverns, and more he couldn't identify. Down the valley of stone, to the right on the river's other side, there appeared to be factories.

And a church!

He turned and glared at Bear. Did he know before that there was an underground town?

The wild man seemed pleased that James was so impressed with what had been found. But Bear hung back, as if he feared contamination. James moved back into the shadows, next to Bear, and sat stunned.

When James was drawn forward again, he watched the murky river flow through what appeared to be a mighty stone aqueduct. It was also apparently the only bridge to the town, or at least the only one visible. There were two figures there, one on either side of the bridge.

Where the flow actually began and ended was as yet unseen. James surmised it must originate from some kind of active volcanic activity. But where? He had never even heard of this kind of internal lava flow and never imagined such a place existed.

To his sense of reason, it was unlike any volcano, active or dormant, could possibly be. It doesn't make sense, he thought. Then James considered all the facts once more. He saw nothing growing except very sparse vegetation. Far above, there was light coming from around a deep, black circle. It looked like a distorted, or inverted, sun. Upon study, he felt the light was artificial.

A volcanic cone?

While trying to decipher more of the riddle, James knew he had to rouse Rachel and Dennis at once. Without speaking to Bear, he turned and shook like someone in shock, and headed back down the tunnel the way they'd come.

Bear didn't speak either. He mutely followed the boat man to his sleeping friends, who were only several hundred yards back.

James wondered, Is that where they've taken Oxie? What in heck do we do now?

His intentions were all for immediate action, but when he reached Rachel and Dennis, the desire for sleep had become too powerful to fight any longer. He felt paralyzed with drowsiness. He lay down beside Rachel, not far from Rev. Dennis.

James had not had a good night's sleep since coming to the Port of Jossandra, and he had lost track of days and nights while underground. Images of Angel's Lake, Great Falls, the caverns, and lava flows all swam together in his mind. It was too much to handle, and his body begged him into sleep. While the trio slept, Bear Man stole away, finally free to conduct his own search for the fish people, true brothers and sisters of the river, enemies of the flesh eaters.

• • •

James and his girlfriend, Bethany, lay beneath a splendid tree, enjoying the warmth of very late summer. They watched the green, gold, and red of ripening fruit and changing leaves. She rose up, laughing, and he was entranced by her fresh beauty. Now sitting on his lap, Bethany threw back her chestnut hair and arched her back in carefree abandonment.

When he caressed her with eagerness, she suddenly began to resist his advances. James felt stabs of pain along his ribs and that began to draw him away from his dream.

"James! Wake up! You're dreaming. Let go." Her sharp knuckles hit his side again.

He sat bolt upright, pushing her aside. It seemed to him that he'd been out drinking again, because he knew Bethany was angry.

No, not Bethany! It's Rachel!

"It's all right, James," she whispered. "You can kiss me if you want to."

"I'm sorry, Rachel, believe me I'm awful sorry. Listen, I thought I was back in Riverton and—"

"Shh. Hold me."

James held her in the dim light. He wondered if it were day or night, and it felt as though he'd been asleep for quite some time. There was no way to know. Rachel was so close to him that she blocked his view, and when their lips brushed he hungrily responded.

"James, what's that awful smell?" asked Rev. Dennis in a sleepy voice.

Instantly James pulled away from Rachel. And then he began to remember the vast volcanic enclosure, the bizarre stone valley with people and livestock.

Was I dreaming that, too?

Rachel had turned away from the men, pulling her T-shirt into place and smoothing her sleep-tangled hair. James was pleased with her open naturalness and by the fact she was not flustered by the untimely interruption of Dennis.

Rev. Dennis had risen to his knees, and called out again. "Rachel, can't you smell that ghastly odor?"

She came back towards them, composed, looking refreshed, and smiling. "Your darned right it smells. James, what is that, and what's happened to Bear?"

"Get over here," said James. "Sit. I want both of you to hear this together." He ran his fingers through a stubble of beard. "I hardly know where to start, but I'll bet our wild man is gone for good. Probably to catch up with his people, or just to get out of these godforsaken holes in the rock, now that he's helped us get where we wanted. All right. That stink is exactly what it smells like. But I'm not going to try and describe all that I saw with Bear before I conked out. Down that tunnel, right there. C'mon."

They rose up together and brushed themselves off. "How far is it?" asked Rev. Dennis, who also looked better with rest.

"Not much over a few hundred yards, through there," said James. "The more I think about it, the more I wonder if maybe I wasn't dreaming. Let's find out. Follow me."

James led the way, with Rachel and Dennis close behind. Although the tunnel kept getting smaller, they covered the distance at double their usual speed. The acrid smell of manure increased, and all three were holding their breath or their nose when they could.

"That's it!" said James. He beckoned them to the outer rim of the tunnel. "Take a look at that, Reverend Dennis, and tell me we're not having a nightmare."

"It . . . it can't be!" said Rev. Dennis.

"I don't believe it," said Rachel, staring in awe. "But they look like civilized people. Can't we hurry down and get over there? Look, the trail on this side of the slope is wide enough. Let's follow it down."

"Wait a minute," said James. "First let's be certain we're agreed on what's the best thing to do."

"He's right, Rachel," said Rev. Dennis. "I think I see—God in heaven, I think I see people across that river. Walking! Oh, if only I had my glasses."

"They are people," said Rachel. "I'm sure of it—just like us!"

"They can't be like us," said James. "Who in their right minds would live in such a hole? And remember they're the ones Bear said took Oxie. They left Bear on that chain to die. We should go slow and suspicious. I don't want anyone to see us until it can't be helped."

"I agree," said Rev. Dennis. His voice was steady again after recovering from the initial shock. "But what in the world can this be, or mean?"

"A waking nightmare?" James gave a nervous laugh. "And Dennis, that is not a river. It's tons of moving lava inside of what looks like an otherwise dormant volcano. Look at the sheer size of it. I can't begin to guess how or why they built all of this. Or why they choose to live inside a mountain. None of it seems right. Wouldn't you say something smells rotten here?" He laughed once again, as if it was the only thing that offered relief. Rachel and Dennis did not laugh with him.

James continued, "My guess is we're going to have to find Oxie somewhere down there. Then we all try to get out of here the fastest way possible. Can either of you imagine actually living in a hellhole like this place?"

"I think I finally see where the smell is coming from," said Rachel. She grinned and pointed down to the pens of animals.

"What is it?" asked Rev. Dennis, rubbing his eyes.

"Pigs and cows. And I see some sheep, too. That must be why Bear called them flesh eaters," said Rachel. "They farm with animals the way we do."

"Well," said James, "they've got animals all right, but they sure don't farm like Turf would."

"I just hope that's all there is to their flesh eating," said Rev. Dennis. "I didn't like the way that Bear sounded when he talked about it. But hopefully we've found some friendly people who are willing to—"

"Still, it doesn't make sense, does it?" said James.

"No," said Rev. Dennis, abandoning his mite of optimism. "It sure as heck doesn't make sense to me, either."

CHAPTER
TWENTY-ONE

The Stars, Sun, Moon, all shrink away,
A desert vast without a bound,
And nothing left to eat or drink,
And a dark desert all around.

-William Blake

Their descent within the crater was not difficult. The ledges averaged three or four feet in width, and sometimes more, with porous rock giving way to grottos, shelves with bushes, and even rock benches to rest upon. When they had nearly reached the bottom of the ledges that ran down to the great crater's floor, Rachel breathlessly caught up with her two companions.

"You know what? I found a few bushes and a small tree beyond those boulders. And guess what?" she said.

"What?" The two men responded in unison.

"They're not real. And neither is that bit of grass over there against the wall. Nothing is real except the rocks!"

"You know, it figures," said James. "Most of this stuff doesn't follow the true pattern of nature, like the artificial lighting, and even where these people choose to live. That thing we keep calling a river sure isn't a real river, either."

"Well those animals sound real, and they certainly smell real," said Rev. Dennis. "Let's check them out."

The three of them moved quietly down the remaining incline, single file, with James leading the way. Within a short time they reached the crater floor and examined a dreary-looking pen of sheep—a dozen scrawny animals bleating piteously. Manure was piled several feet high inside the pen, and foul juices trickled in rivulets across the surrounding rock floor.

"At least they're real," said James after he reached through gray meshed wire and stroked an ewe's bony head. "But this stuff they've got to eat looks more like green sawdust than forage. And there sure isn't anything around here for grazing."

The terrain on their side of the continuous lava flow was indeed desolate. Smoke or steam arose from numerous potholes or fissures in the rocky floor, and the flat ground was strewn with bones and other refuse. Except for the sporadic bleating of the sheep and nervous milling by cattle scrawnier than the sheep, the area was eerily silent. Pigs in a nearby pen lay dozing.

James looked back the way they had descended, and he mentally charted their exit route. It was almost impossible to see the small opening from which they had recently emerged. As he calculated the distance, Rachel pulled up beside him.

"Those two men on the stone bridge are looking over this way, James," she said in a husky voice, not sounding like herself.

"Then we might as well get the suspense over with," said James. "They've probably seen us anyway. Are you two ready?"

For half a minute they gathered their courage, realizing they had to go forward before they could retreat. To travel this far without making contact was out of the question. They had not forgotten that Oxie was probably being held captive by the strange people beyond the lava flow. But whatever their customs, these people still seemed to be humans like themselves.

"Halt!" came a distant, masculine voice.

"Come out and identify!" a second harsh voice commanded from the viaduct-bridge, perhaps seventy-five yards away.

"At least they speak our language. Stay calm and cool," whispered James. But perspiration flowed as the nervous trio of friends moved through the oppressive heat and dull light towards the guardian strangers.

. . .

Far down in the cratered stone valley, Oxford thought he saw a familiar threesome approaching the huge concrete culverts that formed twin circles through which molten lava oozed. He hardly trusted his own eyes after the dreams and hallucinations which had haunted him ever since Great Falls.

His prison cell was built into a recessed rock wall. The only hope he now entertained was that his faithful mascot, Blackie, who had been pacing for nearly an hour outside of his master's cell, would somehow get help.

He thought, I've got to get out of here before them bastards get my poor Rachel, and the others, and Blackie, too!

The stone floor trembled for at least the tenth time since his captivity. Again Oxie wondered if the quake might loosen the metal bonds from the solid rock, but once more the cage's reinforced construction proved too strong. He could hear other prisoners muttering down the line from nearby cells, some in alien languages, and Oxie was curious about them. He wondered how many of them had also refused to become slave-workers, and if that was why they too were locked up.

Gradually Oxie became fairly sure that this latest vision through the smoldering haze was real. It had to be. When he felt sure it was Rachel, he yelled a warning, even though he risked death from the guards.

"Rachel!" he screamed repeatedly. "Go back! Run!"

No one seemed to hear him. No guards came, and Rachel was much too far away. His own voice didn't carry as it should. He felt weak, and his once powerful voice—used to barking orders—was no exception.

Then he saw it—a small, gaping hole some six inches across near the bottom, on the right front corner of his cage. The quake had jarred loose several bits of stone to reveal a small opening. Falling to his sore knees, Oxie began to claw at the brittle, red-brown fragments.

Finally Blackie came to life. First he hopped excitedly, watching his master stab at the rock inside his cell. Just outside the cage, Blackie pulled and pecked at small bits of rock, too. Then he stopped, cocking his head. A frantic Oxie stared at the bird's beady eyes, and he also stopped his work.

"It's no damned use," he said to himself, his fingers bleeding from the effort.

"Blackie, fly to Rachel! Warn her!"

Oxford watched as the bird kept staring at him. It hopped closer to the hole. "Bye-bye!" cawed the jet-black mascot, who squeezed himself down and thrust his way into the cage, flapping and cawing.

"Hi! Hi!" his shrill voice sounded, while Oxie glared into its gleaming eyes.

"You dumb bird! You're going the wrong way! Get out! Rachel! Go to Rachel!"

Oxie pushed Blackie out through the small hole in the rock, then shook his fist at the bird, who appeared puzzled. "Tell them Oxie is alive and kicking! That's it. C'mon, fella. Warn them, but tell them Daddy ain't dead yet. Go, baby, go!"

Oxie knew he must look a sight, racing back and forth like a caged monkey, flapping his arms. Blackie appeared to enjoy the show, but didn't seem to understand his master's odd antics.

"All gone! Bye-bye!" chirped the bird, still an audience of one for Oxie's performance.

"Don't just stand there, you dumb overgrown starling!" cried Oxford in despair.

· · ·

There were more strong earth tremors as the trio walked through the filth of ashes, bones, and small pools of brackish liquid towards the two hulking men who guarded the passage into town. Then James heard words coming from Rev. Dennis that he himself had nearly forgotten. They touched his heart and quickened his courage. Rachel managed a half smile.

"I will fear no evil," continued Rev. Dennis, "for thou art with me, thy rod and thy staff they comfort me . . ."

Each in turn was amazed to see men in contemporary military uniforms carrying spears. Although guns were strapped to their waists in leather holsters, it was the spears that were brandished as the three approached the bridge.

"Halt and identify!" ordered the larger man when they were within twenty feet of the odd bridge.

"We are survivors from a boat crash on the river," James heard himself explaining.

"We've come looking for someone, a man called Captain Oxford. We have reason to believe he came this way."

"Ah," said the smaller guard, who stood taller than James and Dennis by half a head. "You have come at a good time. We need more workers in town. Are you ready to serve the town?"

"The captain is . . . is part of my family," said Rachel with a slight stammer. Then more boldly, "Do you know him? Has he come here? That's all we want to find out."

James noticed that the men's expressions didn't change and that their hardened features were like masks of gray. Their eyes were piercing, like creatures of the night, but everything else about them was as drab as the immense concrete monument they patrolled. Across the lava flow, he observed that the buildings were in flagrant disrepair. From that distance the town looked bleak and unpromising. It seemed to be getting darker, and there were no longer people on the walks and streets.

"We accept no strange names here," said the larger guard, who stood nearly seven feet tall. "What is his number?"

Now it was Rev. Dennis who attempted civil communication. "None of us has a number. Our friend Oxford has no number. We are survivors, as my friend James has said. This young woman is Rachel. It's her father, Captain Oxford, that we seek. My name is Reverend Dennis. We have all journeyed a great distance together. We come from a world far from here, and we would appreciate—"

"That is enough talk," said the guard. "You must enter the town and report to number 427. Or else you spend a rest period over in the cages. It's your choice."

The three companions backed off and began whispering among themselves. The guards stood at attention, with spears ready. They were not overtly hostile, yet it was very clear they would not acknowledge Oxford's existence. At that precise moment, however, someone else did.

"Hi! Hi! Welcome aboard!" came the staccato outburst from down the valley of stone, approaching on the same side of the lava bridge as that of the three searchers. There was a shock of joyful recognition that instantly informed them they were on the right trail in their quest to find Oxie.

"I've got to go over that way!" said Rachel in a wildly excited voice. "To those lights along the steep walls of rock. What are those lights? Please help us!"

"There are bad fissures that way," said the smaller guard, positioning his spear. "One wrong step in the dark and we lose another worker. Come with me, into town to get your exam and numbers. When you rise from rest—"

"No!" screamed Rachel. "You don't understand! I know that bird—it's Oxie's bird! They travel together, always!"

Rachel backed farther away from the heated glow of the lava flow. James and Dennis stood their ground, hoping to cover her retreat. The huge guard poised to throw his spear, and James grabbed the ax at his belt. Dennis loosed the length of chain wrapped around his waist.

When Rachel hesitated at the edge of darkness, the towering guard threw his weapon while James and Dennis were retreating. Rachel screamed. James leaped and swung at the flying spear with his ax. He slowed and deflected its flight, but it struck him in the side. He felt the hot, cutting edge, and with a groan fell to his knees.

Dennis swung his chain at the advancing smaller guard and pulled the man's booted feet out from under him. The guard lay stunned, but Dennis was forced to drop the chain when the other giant guard advanced on them.

The guard drew his gun and fired just as Dennis spun sideways. James was fast losing consciousness when he saw Dennis clutch at his chest. He saw Dennis struggle to raise himself, and watched in helpless horror as the attacking guard brought down the gun barrel against the side of Dennis's head.

Unable to move himself, James saw Rachel trying to run away. He was struck in the head from behind, and darkness enlarged to envelop him completely.

• • •

Double flames of flickering light merged into a single glow, and James started to remember the flight of the spear. Rachel's sympathetic smile helped put things back into focus. When he clutched at his burning side, he suddenly saw Captain Oxford near them.

"You sure don't know much about how to rescue a guy," said Oxie. "You walked right into their arms like a bunch of hicks on a Sunday stroll. The only good news I got is to have my little girl talking again. That does my old heart good." Oxie sighed. "And I'm darn glad to see you two lads are still breathing. It looks like your heads was knocked like me that time back on the river. Must be yours are harder than mine." His laugh was half-hearted.

James groaned, trying again to ease the spear point from his burning flesh. They had succeeded in removing the wooden shaft, but the pointed blade was another matter. When Dennis pulled again, James gave a muffled cry of pain as the bloody point at last came free.

Rachel dropped down beside James, helping to staunch the fresh flow of blood. Oxie offered what was left of his shirt. Dennis gently restrained James, who insisted on rising to his knees.

"Lie flat," said Rev. Dennis. "We've got to stop the bleeding." After seeing what he wanted to see, James eased back into Rachel's soft lap.

"We're caged," he said. "Like those poor dumb animals." Then he lay quietly, and tried to think more clearly.

While he attempted to clear his thoughts, James watched Dennis take the medium-sized spear point and hold it broadside in the flame of a small fire at the edge of their cage. James looked up at Rachel, who was trying to soothe him, or herself, by humming a soft melody. Then James realized what Dennis was doing and nodded his agreement when Dennis stared questioningly at him. After the metal became nearly too hot to hold, even with a protecting cloth, he approached James, who grimaced but again nodded his approval to Dennis.

James watched the faces of Rachel and Oxie turn away from him. Dennis pushed the red-hot flat side of the blade against the open wound. James screamed and at once slumped into unconsciousness. The cauterized wound looked ugly, but the bleeding had been stopped.

• • •

In the wee hours of an artificial rest period for the prisoners, Rachel continued to cradle James's head, while he stared at the metal barrier fixed in solid rock and concrete. His spirit sank.

It was now a fully darkened valley, with shimmering lava slicing the night like an elongated, red-gold Gargol. It appeared to be white-hot in places and seemed to move without a stop. Hundreds of feet overhead, a flaming ring of fire—perhaps oil or pitch burning from bowls or poles—circled the teeth of the jagged cone. A black hole encircled with flickering yellow tongues suggested a bizarrely inverted moon.

No one spoke for many minutes. James felt his aching head and scanned the torso of Dennis. A savage red crease ran across the preacher's chest, from right to left.

James shuddered to think how close he and Rev. Dennis had come to instant death.

CHAPTER
TWENTY-TWO

Try no more. Where we are
Never can be sky or star
From prison, in a prison, we fly;
There's no way into the sky.

-C. S. Lewis

"It ain't no normal town, and these ain't no normal folks. Them buildings, for instance," said Oxford. "They ain't got much to them except the outsides. Real screwy. And the people must live mostly up in those caves on the other side of the lava river, because I didn't see nobody look like they was living in them shabby houses."

James listened to the familiar sound of Oxie's rasping voice.

"Why were you over there?" asked Rev. Dennis, who was resting with his back against the metal bands that imprisoned them all.

"They forced me into their town," said Oxie. "Them guards and some others. They took me to their hospital, and some big shots and doctors gaped at me, asking real dumb questions. They wanted me to work for nothing fixing up their walks and streets. Well, it was crazy. They got slaves, and the slaves got themselves slaves. I couldn't explain it straight in a year! Like I said before, we got to get out of here. I can't stand the dreams, neither. I swear I don't rightly know half the time if I've been sleeping or awake. I can't seem to stop the dreams."

"What do you mean, Pa?" asked Rachel. "You've never been much of a dreamer."

"Oh, hell. I can't hardly say it, but like the last time I was trying to sleep. Them people came across that bridge from their town, all dressed up fancy, and then they grabbed two men and two women out of their cages farther down. They was fighting with them. I think maybe I was dreaming, but there's no way I could really tell. That's what scares me."

"I still don't get it," said James. "What are you trying to say?"

"I mean I can't tell you if I was dreaming, or not," said Oxie. "Maybe it was real and maybe it wasn't. Like I say, maybe it was all a nightmare. Can't you hear?" Oxie bowed his head, took a deep breath, and kept on talking, staring past Dennis at the endless lava flowing in the night.

"They got the man fighting the man, you see, not against the town folks. And the woman fighting with the other woman till there was killing. The winners got stuck back in their cages."

"They actually let people murder each other?" asked Rev. Dennis, his voice almost inaudible.

"That ain't the half of it, and that's why I think dreaming done it to me." Oxie shuddered.

"What is it, Pa? If it was a nightmare it's better to say it right out to us and then try to forget about it."

"Yeah, maybe. They took these here long knives and carved up them losers, like dead meat. And they brought over sheep and pigs and they got everything there butchered up bloody. Half-drunk or all drunk, I think they was, and half-naked. It was the worst dream I ever seen. I keep hoping to hell it was just a bad nightmare because I'd rather go over the Great Falls in a canoe than be part of this, this—whatever it is."

"Flesh eaters," said Rev. Dennis. "I had an odd, creepy feeling in my bones when Bear Man said those words to us."

Oxie acted like he didn't hear Dennis. "It was over the lava, on screens of some kind, like what covers this cage." His voice trailed off. "They went and roasted everything they cut up, and they . . . ain't no way I can say it." He pounded a raw fist against the cage screen and bars. "These here folks are animals, and they treat us like animals."

"What happened?" asked Rev. Dennis in a whisper.

"They kept chanting and dancing and screaming and they kept laughing, like savages out of their holes in the rock. Eating like pigs," he said in disgust. Oxie covered his face. His shoulders began to shake, and he wept like a little boy while Rachel moved to his side to comfort him.

"You woke up then, Pa, right?"

Oxie soon regained control, and he walked back to the farthest wall of solid rock. "I don't know," he said in a muted voice to the captive audience. "I don't really know if I'm awake right now."

• • •

The subterranean night seemed endless. Everyone made attempts to sleep, but the periodic tremors made that next to impossible. James noticed that Rev. Dennis was withdrawing more and more into a prayer-like state, until he wondered if the preacher was slipping in and out of consciousness.

While James investigated every square inch of their communal prison cell, Rachel and Oxie spent their time quietly talking together when they could not sleep.

"I can't find one darned thing, except for that small hole Blackie squeezed through," James reported to Oxie, who again appeared not to hear him. James gripped the metal bands, timing his pushes and pulls with another earth tremor.

"Give it up, James," said Rev. Dennis. "Don't get yourself bleeding again. Listen, the bars may look hopeless, but I can assure you that our situation is not."

James felt indignant towards what seemed to be surface optimism on the part of Rev. Dennis.

"I know," said Rev. Dennis smiling, "I sound like a foolish man caught up in feverish delusions. Come here, James, and give me the benefit of the doubt for a few minutes. That's all I'm asking of you."

James responded to the request, leaning with a sigh against the bars.

"I'm beginning to see more clearly," said Rev. Dennis. "Really. Just think back, James, and perhaps you'll see what I mean." Something in his confident manner drew the attention of both James and Rachel, and then Oxie followed his daughter so that all them were gathered together to listen to what the preacher had to say.

"Doesn't it strike you," he continued, "that we managed to survive Great Falls? We were relatively unscathed."

"Except for poor old Rusty," said Oxie, who had learned of his friend's death from Rachel.

"That I don't pretend to understand, or be able to explain," said Rev. Dennis. "But *Midnight* was in complete ruin, right Oxie? There was nothing left intact except your fishing boat, right James? Now what does that suggest?"

"That four of us was damned lucky?" said Oxie.

"Perhaps," said an undaunted Rev. Dennis, "but something else came to me tonight. I can't explain it as precisely as I'd like to, except to say the definite feeling exists that we are being watched over, or protected. Don't you feel it? James? Rachel?"

"I believe in God, if that's what you mean," said Rachel. "I was very angry for a long time because of what happened to my mom, but I never stopped believing in God."

"It's more than mere belief that I'm talking about," said Rev. Dennis with an understanding softness in his voice. "All my life I've searched for something deeper than blind belief. What about you, James? Have you felt anything special?"

James shrugged. "Ever since Riverton I've felt more like what Oxie was saying earlier, about dreams. It still doesn't seem like all these things could have happened, or can still be happening. And since we went over Great Falls it's gotten even more weird. Really strange and bizarre. The quaking goes on and on, and then we've got these animals who only look like people! It seems to me God wouldn't be here, in a place like this. If God was with us before, okay. Maybe that got us over Great Falls in one piece, because we were praying hard back on the river after Gargol and *Midnight* getting wrecked. But this is . . . this is—"

"This is hell," said Oxie. "Where's your God when things get this bad, Reverend?"

"Don't you suppose that if we prayed before and were answered, we ought to pray some more?" James felt his stare before the preacher smiled once more. It was a smile that suddenly froze.

"I'll tell you this," said Rev. Dennis, "it's the only thing that's going to help us now. Look over towards the town."

"They're coming again! God help us, Dennis," said Oxie, who embraced Rachel, and hugged her tightly. "Don't let them take my baby girl!"

. . .

Somewhat later, Rev. Dennis opened his eyes and said, "You know, I just had the most remarkable feeling, maybe a prayer insight, that none of this is real—so if it isn't real, it can't harm us. Right?"

"But them savages is coming again, just like they done before. I can see them starting to gather at the bridge!" said Oxie, his voice shaking.

"Then look away!" said Rev. Dennis. "Turn away from evil, Oxie. Once a child has been burned, doesn't it turn away from fire?"

At that moment James felt his knees trembling, and then he realized a more powerful quake was opening crevices and new fissures in the crater's floor. The lava river surged in slow-motion, shooting scattered red-gold arrows of fire into the stifling, darkened air.

They heard the flesh eaters chanting. James pulled Rachel to her feet, and they strained to see what was happening. The distant words, chanted in rhythmic unison, were undecipherable, reverberating like tribal drums.

James and his friends all pushed against the cage's barrier gate, like a group reflex action. It seemed certain the lava river now overflowed its normal channel.

A small cheer went up from the prisoners when the torches of the advancing townspeople were being dropped and abandoned in obvious panic. Small chunks of debris fell from above. Some were afire.

James saw one guard running in acute anguish, his uniform burning. "It's raining hot ash!" he screamed, as he raced blindly past their cage.

"Maybe it's finally going to shake this damned gate out of the stone!" yelled Oxie. "Keep us in them prayers, Reverend!"

But Dennis had joined the others in shoving their combined weight against the stubborn cage restraints, while together they watched molten lava shooting skyward.

It happened. A huge rock, one of a series from above, bounced wildly into the metal cage that heretofore had barred them from freedom. It split the barrier with a grinding crash and came to a stop just inside the gate's entranceway.

"Stay back!" said James. "The entire top of the mountain may be shaking loose!"

"The heat's getting bad!" said Oxie. "We've got to get out of here or get fried or buried alive!"

James saw that the lava river was gradually being transformed into a molten lake, and that the lake's edge was slowly advancing on their position, although it was still some fifty yards away.

James and Oxie pushed the top half of the split gate skyward while Dennis and Rachel shoved remnants of the bottom half down against the floor of rock. The huge boulder filled over half of the opening, but there remained enough room for them to squeeze out separately if and when they chose to do so.

"What are we going to do?" said Rachel. "Like Pa says, we can't just wait!"

"We've got to wait at least until those rocks stop falling," said James. Dennis quickly agreed with him.

"How long?" said Oxie. "It's better to try getting out than to sit here like a bunch of sheep, ain't it?"

He nervously edged around the hot boulder, pushing more of the split gate upwards. With James's help, Oxie pushed the upper part of the dangling metal bars from the ceiling, and managed to squeeze through the opening.

"I'm going to check and see if we can still get up the wall trail!" he shouted over the din. "Rachel, you stay with these guys till I get back. If anything happens to me, they'll get you out! James! Dennis! Wish me luck and pray! Take care of my little girl and I'll be back quick as I can!"

And he was gone.

"He's braver than most, you've got to admit that," James said to Dennis, pointing to the chaos Oxie had rashly entered.

"Sometimes," said Rev. Dennis, "it takes more courage to wait. Let's pray his courage comes from God and not from fear."

The quaking seemed to diminish, but a low rumble could be heard from deep within the earth. James wondered how fast they would die if it all let loose at once. Maybe Oxie's right, he thought.

Within minutes of Oxie's departure, Rachel pleaded for someone to go after him. "If you guys don't have the nerve, I'm going after him myself."

James restrained her while giving her a hasty reassurance. "Listen, I'm going after him, Rachel, and don't worry, he's a tough old bird." When he tried to laugh, he found he couldn't, then squeezed around the boulder after releasing her.

"Dennis," he called back, "there are still some rocks falling, but it's getting better. The place looks like a black hailstorm hit with all the damned cinders. If I'm not back soon, forget it. You two stay put till all this stops completely."

Alone outside the cell, James looked up and down the desolated valley. Dimly he saw dozens of people sprawled on the stone bridge viaduct. It was now totally surrounded by bubbling, molten lava. They appeared to be dead, or without hope.

Across the way, the town site was obscured except for shadowy figures, people frantically carrying their torches along the side of the crater's unstable far wall. To James they looked for all the world like erratic lightning bugs with no place to go.

Then from far above, James heard cawing. Almost invisible, then gliding across his field of vision, sailed a singed but intact bird. "Blackie! Where've you been? Come here!"

The bold bird hopped onto a nearby boulder. He flapped his wings, cawing loudly. "Oxie! Come and get it! Oxie! Hi there!"

"Oxie's gone!" James shouted, "Help me find Oxie!" He felt frustrated as he tried to communicate with the mascot. "Come here! What's that on your leg?"

At first he thought it was a bandage, but it turned out to be a tiny, white case attached to Blackie's right leg. With shaking fingers James carefully extracted a bit of paper that had been folded several times.

Stay put! Help on the way. Abigail.

Signed by Abigail!

James darted back a short distance to the semi-blocked cage, quickly informed Dennis and Rachel, then set off with Blackie in search of the wayward Oxie.

As he ran in the direction he thought Oxie had taken, James sighed to himself, "At least now we have hope!"

CHAPTER
TWENTY-THREE

The untold want by life and land ne'er granted
Now voyager sail thou forth to seek and find.

-Walt Whitman

James ran quickly while he dodged debris, with Blackie flying overhead. He hoped that somehow the mascot understood their mission to locate Oxie. Although he had to dodge stones from above, the larger rocks no longer fell. Still, he found himself in a state of controlled panic. Looking ahead, James saw livestock running in every direction. One maddened cow lumbered bawling into the rising lava flow and was swiftly incinerated.

Near those dismal pens, which now lay in ruins, he spotted Blackie circling over the body of Oxie. His master lay facedown in the place where the trail began to climb along the rocky wall. At least half of the trail was gone. By the time James reached Oxie's side, he had to gasp for breath in the hot, sulfuric air. He gently rolled the captain over.

"Oxie! Wake up! C'mon! Help is on the way, but you've got to get on your feet." Oxie stirred and groaned, but did not speak. He gave a weak smile and gazed raptly at the faithful Blackie.

"Oxie, I can't carry you all that way. We've got to get back to the others at the cage for some shelter!"

Oxie struggled to rise, but collapsed again. A shower of rocks and stones fell, and one struck James on his right shoulder while he used his body to protect Oxie. With renewed effort, James labored to lift the captain over his good shoulder and staggered in retreat, heading for the shelter of their cell in the rock. It was the only thing he could think to do, and it was based on the hope that things would get better before they got any worse.

If it does get worse, James thought, we'll be dead!

Three-fourths of the way back, a large steaming rock struck the ground directly in front of the two men and caused James and Oxie to go sprawling towards a zigzag fissure filled with gurgling red lava. At that moment, amid sulfurous fumes, James felt himself being lifted by strong hands. He looked up and saw that Rev. Dennis had pulled himself and Oxie away from the brink of fire.

"Don't be afraid, men, we're going to make it." Dennis smiled as he spoke, which amazed James.

He sure must know something I don't, thought James. The world has gone chaotic and he tells us not to worry! James winced in pain as he brought his aching, bruised body into a standing position. Oxie did not rise as easily, but together the two men managed to bear him onward.

"He's barely conscious," said James. "I think he's been pummeled by stones or rocks. Thank God you came along."

"Now you're getting the right idea," said Rev. Dennis.

"Any sign of Abigail yet, like Blackie's note said?" asked James. "Here, lift him over these rocks—I think the cage is just around that corner."

"No, she's not here in person," said Rev. Dennis, still smiling, "but something is happening. And the cage is covered. That's why I'm here."

"I don't get it," said James, stopping for a breather. "What's happened?"

"With the last rumbling, Rachel bolted out, and minutes later while we were outside of the cage, the wall crashed down. All the cages are buried. Rachel is waiting there for us, under a ledge."

"What else? You said something was happening. Or is that what you meant, that you and Rachel were protected again? You know, like you said before?"

"You can see for yourself, James, just around that huge pile of rocks. I just hope it lasts for awhile longer."

Now James was intrigued, although he couldn't see what bright note could possibly be sounded amidst the fiery chaos going on around them. Maybe Dennis has finally lost it, he thought.

. . .

From a new position, a spellbound James watched crater walls crumble and sink bit by bit into a growing devil's lake of lava. He could think of no way Abigail could find them, but did not want to dwell on that negative thought. Instead, the fascinating spectacle of physical destruction held his rapt attention. Then it came again, a strange hissing noise that seemed to be getting louder. He strained to see through the clouds of smoke and steam, and thought he saw the figure of a woman.

"Rachel? We're coming! Rachel?"

"Over here! Higher! Up here!" She evidently was afraid they wouldn't locate her in the steam and smoke.

"We have Oxie," yelled James. "Hang on, we'll be there in a few minutes."

Along the far end of the crater, clouds of steam billowed, and as soon as James and Dennis had pulled Oxie up to a flat slab of rock near Rachel, James focused his sight on the steam clouds.

"Look up there!" Rev. Dennis said to James. "No, not that high! About halfway up where the caves and—"

"I see it! That's water coming in—lots of it!"

"That's right, and more is coming in now than when I left to find you and Oxie."

"But so what? I don't see what's so great about that," said James. "We're still trapped. It's a question of time, and we've about run out."

"It's a sign," said Rev. Dennis. "It's got to be. The quaking has stopped, too."

"For how long? And we can't get back the way we came, through the caves."

"For crying out loud," said Rachel. "My Dad's half-dead and you two guys stand there rapping. Let's get him out of here."

She knelt between James and Dennis, beside Oxie, and wiped his face. His eyes were open, but glazed, and James could detect no indication that the captain recognized his own daughter. It was obvious Oxie couldn't be moved very far, to say nothing of trying to navigate any cavern mazes in his condition. Still, James sensed Rachel did not want to acknowledge that Oxie represented an insurmountable burden.

"Let's stop talking and get him out of here," she said again.

"Rachel," said Rev. Dennis, "remember Blackie's note?"

"Where's Blackie?" said James. "He was with me when we started back with Oxie."

"Just a minute, James," said Rev. Dennis. "We've got to get this settled with Rachel."

"I don't need more talk," said Rachel. "I want to get moving. You guys carry Oxie. I'll help. Back the way we came, right?"

"Wrong." Rev. Dennis sounded deadly serious, and James wondered how the preacher could be so sure of himself. Dennis placed a firm hand on Rachel's shoulder, and only then did James notice how troubled her eyes were. He knew that Dennis was trying to get her to face difficult but irrevocable facts.

"Rachel," said Rev. Dennis, "please listen very carefully to what I have to say. Even if Oxie were able to walk, we'd be trapped here. James saw that our trail is gone, we don't have a guide like Bear, and I doubt that many of the passages are even open after the quake. Fortunately, we don't have to risk that danger because there is no way in heaven or earth we could carry Oxie so far."

"No," she said with tears welling up. "You guys want to leave him behind?"

Rev. Dennis said with a gentle smile, "No, Rachel, no way. We're all staying together. Now listen. The one thing we could do is send someone for help. But that would be senseless, right? Don't you see? Blackie already went for us. The note he brought back to James about help on the way is from Abigail herself."

"Yeah, Dennis, but be realistic, too," said James. "I'm for high hopes and all that, but what's Abigail going to do? Throw down rope ladders from the smoking crater that's coming apart? Or from the high caves? And now look at that!" He pointed to the avalanche of water spilling out from the caves.

"You know what that really means?" said James. "Two things. One, lots of the caves somehow got flooded from the river, or some underground reservoir busted up in the quakes. And two, the thing you don't seem to have thought of is that if water keeps pouring in here, we're most likely going to get another chance to drown. If, and this is the big if, that molten lava doesn't rise fast enough to fry us first. So how is it you're all smiles?" he asked, with a trace of bitterness impossible to mask.

"Patience. A grain of faith. Both of you. Weren't we saved from certain death at Great Falls? Do you remember how the three of us prayed together before *Midnight* went over the falls? Jossandra wrote that there is an unseen spiritual law of good, and we simply have to awaken to it. Let's pray to see the good that's at hand, right now. I think that is what Abigail would say to us if she were here."

"You still think she's coming, don't you?" asked James.

"I know it, with all my heart," said Rev. Dennis.

• • •

Pieces from the crater's inner walls continued to slide and crash to the valley's molten floor. There were pools of lava everywhere, but now they were competing with the water for territory. And there was something else new. It was raining.

"It's not as dark, is it?" whispered Rachel to anyone who might answer.

"I noticed that when we first saw the water falling from the caves," said Rev. Dennis. "I just wish we could see the lava flow and the far wall better. Can you see them, James? It's tough to see without my glasses, too."

"No, but I hear water gushing. Let's see if we can get Oxie up to that higher rock," said James.

The struggle to reach the higher ledge was not an easy one. Some rocks were sharp, some were hot, and Oxie in his unconscious state was a dead weight.

"Hold his wrists, Rachel," said James. "Dennis and I will push him upward from down here. Take care with your footing, Dennis."

James glanced down to watch the steady rise of the molten lake, which now reached the foot of the jumbled rocks below their perch. In the dim light it was difficult to tell whether it was lava, water, or most likely a mixture of both. Steam billowed everywhere.

A slip now is disaster, thought James.

"Just a little more," said Rev. Dennis. "Pull, Rachel, as hard as you can!"

Finally, with all three sweating profusely, their task was accomplished. They were as high as they could climb, cut off from other ledges, the valley floor, and the caves.

"Well," said James, gasping for air, "we need another miracle, Dennis. It looks like we've painted ourselves into a corner. To tell you the truth, I don't see any way out, unless we want to try to swim in hot, watered-down lava."

"But it is getting lighter, above, where the cone top was," said Rev. Dennis. "The opening up there is larger, or—"

"Look out from above!" screamed Rachel.

Several large rock slabs whistled past their heads before anyone but Rachel could duck. James and Dennis shoved Oxie as close to the sloping wall as possible, and all of them hugged that area of minimal protection.

No one spoke. The waiting was unbearable. A steaming cauldron waited for them with impersonal patience. James realized each of them, except for Oxie, must know another quake would spell their doom. And even without a quake, the steaming liquid was steadily creeping towards their isolated perch.

Oxie groaned. "Drop anchor, men. Let's ride out this here storm." His eyes were open, unseeing, or as James felt, perhaps he saw what no one else could see. Rachel kissed her dad's cheek and wept.

James and Dennis stared at one another, then James spoke. "I figure we've got fifteen feet to spare. If it keeps rising at this rate, I think maybe we've got about an hour left."

"Have you heard the splashes though?" asked Rev. Dennis "I think the water might be overtaking the lava. This may be a blessing in disguise."

"It's darned well disguised, Dennis. Unless maybe you think we can spend a few days floating in boiling liquid, until we float up over the top of the crater and maybe fly down the mountain with angel wings."

"Let's be thankful we're still alive," said Rev. Dennis.

Oxie closed his eyes and seemed to be asleep. Rachel followed suit. Weariness and hunger and thirst began to take their toll on James and Dennis, too. In fact James was unable to tell where hunger pangs stopped and exhaustion began. His senses drifted with little hope except to escape conscious suffering. And finally, he also slept, as did Dennis.

• • •

James didn't think he'd slept long, and when he awakened he watched the distant water pour forth from the caves. His tired eyes searched between steam clouds, and his wonderment grew. It no longer looked like the same cratered valley of stone.

If only I could see more clearly, he thought. He could make out that the giant stone bridge was completely covered. People, livestock, and town were gone, vanished as if they had never existed. Nothing looked familiar through the steam clouds except light itself. He tried to visualize the golden sunlight of Angel's Lake, and his eyelids still felt heavy. His neck and shoulder muscles began to relax, although his side still ached.

When the light grew brighter still, he thought he might be dreaming once again. An immense, white butterfly floated atop the liquid lake, and he watched its progress with fascination. His heart beat faster, and he reached across the narrow ledge to wake Rev. Dennis.

"Dennis! Wake up! I want you to see something. What does that look like to you?"

Rev. Dennis sat upright so quickly he nearly slipped over the precarious edge. "What's wrong with you, James? I almost fell—"

"Dennis! I think it's a sailboat!" For James it was almost too clear, like a rich portrait of Bethany in a painted dream of all he wanted to see. This new picture of a transformed butterfly was like a mirage come to life that threatened to vanish if he so much as blinked. His greatest fear was that the vision wasn't real. So it was that James dared not blink or breathe. He whispered a wonderful revelation, "It's the sailboat." He paused. "Dennis, Rachel, do you see it? It's Abigail's sailboat!"

CHAPTER
TWENTY-FOUR

*And the waters returned, and covered
the chariots, and the horsemen, and all
the host of Pharaoh that came into the
sea after them.*

-Exodus 14:28

Ominous darkness and rumbling now challenged the growing light. At first James thought the quake had resumed, so loudly did the thunder reverberate through the crater.

Rain was falling, and as lightning flashed above the crater remnants, the graceful outline of a white sailboat was seen silently moving ever closer, with Abigail at the helm. Blackie was perched above the twenty-foot mast.

"Over here!" the companions shouted in unison, their voices harmonizing as one.

James tore off what was left of his shirt and waved it in the steady downpour. When it became thoroughly soaked, he pressed it to his face, then down his neck, arms, and chest. It felt deliciously cool. Hope sang in his heart, but there was also a vestige of fear.

So close and yet so far! he thought.

Rachel jumped with such fervor he had to hold her steady on their precarious rock.

"You'll knock this hunk of rock loose," said Rev. Dennis. With a grin, he added, "I told you, James! Here comes our miracle!"

"We're not out of here yet, not by a long shot," said James. "Hey, look, what's that she's dragging behind the sailboat?"

Within minutes, Abigail had skillfully guided her sailboat to a point just under the isolated ledge. James marveled that she seemed so serene, just as he remembered her at Angel's Lake. Her light hair remained in place, and her white tunic was wet but unruffled,

"There's nothing to be afraid of," said Abigail in a clear, calm voice. "I'm so happy to locate you this quickly. From Blackie's appearance there was little doubt of your predicament."

"How in the world did you do it?" asked James. He did not mean just the rescue effort alone. "I mean . . . I mean . . . ," he stammered, became speechless, and then pointed behind the sailboat.

"I think he means the old fishing boat," said Rev. Dennis.

"Feruka and Jana found it when they discovered the wreckage of your barge. That's where Blackie took them first. The rest we pieced together."

My fishing boat! James was dumbfounded, struck as mute as Rachel had once been. He also began to see Abigail in a new light, with a touch of awe. To say the least, he felt profound respect and admiration for her.

The storm had nearly dissipated when they boarded the rescue boats. There remained light rainfall and a refreshing breeze. Abigail commented as they found their places, "The elements of destructiveness war on each other and themselves. There is nothing to them, nothing to fear."

Rev. Dennis sat at the sailboat's mast, with Abigail at the tiller. Oxie was stretched out in James's fishing boat in which the cross-sectioned seats were long since gone. Rachel cradled his head in her lap, while James knelt at the rear of the old, durable rowboat.

It grew brighter again, and for the first time James was struck by the relative quiet. The tumult of quaking earth, violent thunder, and choking fumes was gone, erased like a bad nightmare in the morning when terror subsides. Only flowing water and the rising steam it caused remained. They sailed over the bridge, the bones, the town, buoyed up not only by the boats, but also by feelings of blissful relief and gratitude.

We're alive! thought James, as waves of indescribable joy overwhelmed all other thought. He simply basked in feelings of pure joyfulness.

• • •

Water continued to gush into the crater causing slabs of its walls to crumble inwards, revealing more and more sky. "Is that sunlight?" asked Rachel, indicating brighter vistas straight ahead.

Abigail smiled and pointed. "We're going through there," she said for all to hear. "The collapsed cave on the right is deep enough to sail. On the other side of these walls a brief portage is required to reach the lower basin of Lost Lake. The crossing there presents no problem for us. When we get to that lake's far shore, you'll see the outer boundaries of Jossandra's domain. I thought you might welcome the good news."

"Oh!" said Rachel. "Look at the crater coming apart!"

"Don't look back!" said Abigail. "All of you, our new work is before us. All that was evil or error is now behind you. The captain, as well as each one of you, need nothing except the healing good the Port of Jossandra has prepared for you."

James obeyed her request with no regret and strained to look ahead through the steam clouds. The sides of a rock canal lay in jagged ruin, but the boats, bound together by a steel chain, glided forward as if impelled by unseen power.

There is more to this woman than meets the eye, thought James. It's as if this is all routine, and here four people have just been saved from certain death.

He closed his weary eyes and remembered again the tranquil beauty of Angel's Lake.

How he longed for the comfort it promised.

James was nudged by Rachel, who pushed a small basket of fresh oranges against his chin. He looked up and saw the others laughing at what must have been his surprised expression. The fruit tasted as good as it looked, its fresh flavor eliciting memories of golden sunlight and happier times.

"Our portage is directly ahead," said Abigail. "We can slide the boats over the rocks if we are unable to lift them. There is no cause for alarm."

It's not so much what she says, thought James, but the way it sounds. I just wish poor Rusty could be with us.

Through the rocky openings, their lead craft pierced the murky water with precision. Dead ahead, however, they found themselves at the lower end of a series of newly formed rapids. The rocks abruptly changed from reddish brown to gray-purple, and the predicted portage was at hand.

"I don't understand," said Rev. Dennis. "We seem to have sailed right out of the crater."

Abigail smiled, looking radiant. "There is much that you don't yet understand—all of you. Perhaps when we return to the Port of Jossandra you may wish to join our classes. It's never too late to learn more about Life." She lowered the sail and prepared them for the portage.

. . .

They were now completely clear of the crater. That much was very evident to James.

He and Dennis managed to slide the fishing boat, with Oxie in it, upward over numerous rocks, from the improvised canal to Lost Lake. James had no true sense of where they were. Only his growing trust and respect for Abigail made the labor easier, and doubt yielded to hopeful expectancy. They were in good hands.

At the rim of Lost Lake's lower basin, Abigail offered everyone water from a large, silver flask. It was fresh, cool, and clear.

"Oh, man, does that taste good," said James with a deep sigh.

"It's from one of our springs," said Abigail. "We will continue due east." She pointed across the lake. "The far shore is on the westernmost part of our immediate domain. One day all this will be cultivated and green, but for now it's barren as you can see."

"Nothing seems to grow here except rocks," said Rev. Dennis. "Say, these rocks have been moved, and recently."

"That's right," said Abigail. "It was not our usual method, but we blasted." A bubbling, melodic laugh James had not heard before came easily from her. Suddenly he realized the flooding water had not been entirely a chance occurrence.

"You made the water flow into the crater?" asked James.

"The quakes started our work for us. Let's say an inclination in that direction was revealed to us. We saw the idea develop, and then gave it all the help we could."

"We?"

"Jana and Feruka were also here. They have gone back to Angel's Lake. In fact, it was Feruka who salvaged several of Snyder's explosive sticks. Charges placed here, and over there, completed what the quakes had already started in Lost Lake's lower basin."

"I'm beginning to get the picture," said Rev. Dennis. "But I'd thought it was an out-and-out miracle." He laughed.

"It was," said Rachel. "I never was so happy to see anyone in my entire life."

Abigail smiled. "It was natural enough. So-called miracles are spiritually natural. We were led to the right place, and of course were delighted to be of service. The right ideas were provided. Now, let's see how quickly we can get these boats back to more pleasant water."

As they glided along the still water of Lost Lake, James was struck by its lowered level, revealed by new waterline marks on rock walls, and by its inky blackness. The shores were barren, gray-purple rocks, and the sunlight was filtered by thin clouds. Even so, they were bathed in light compared to the death valley from which they had just narrowly escaped.

• • •

When green trees appeared James felt another surge of reassurance, and it surpassed that provided earlier by Abigail's optimistic words. His tiredness receded to a not unpleasant ache, and even his side felt much better. Abigail offered them the water flask again as the sun's rays pierced the clouds.

"It feels good to be alive, doesn't it?" said Rev. Dennis, speaking to no one in particular.

"What the hell's going on here?" said Oxie, sitting upright with a sudden start.

"You've been sleeping on the job, Captain," said James. "You're not going to believe half of what's happened."

"Try me," said Oxie, rubbing his eyes, unaccustomed to the sunlight.

"Later," said Abigail. "We have a hike ahead of us, and I want all of you to deal with that first. You will all enjoy supper at Angel's Lake with your friends before too long, if you follow some simple directions."

"Ain't I the captain?" asked a dazed Oxford, scanning the unfamiliar waters.

"Not now, Dad," said Rachel.

"She rescued us, Oxie. Remember the crater and your prison cage?" asked James.

"Geez, don't remind me," Oxford lapsed into silence.

They pulled the boats ashore among a clump of mighty oak trees, where a mother raccoon and her squirming offspring were frisking at the water's edge. Their mask-like eyes studied the humans out of curiosity, not fear. James found himself delighted by their simple antics.

Oxie evidently couldn't restrain himself. "Where's this here lake located?"

"We are now on the eastern shore of the upper basin of Lost Lake," said Abigail, countering the captain's gruff tone with patience. "This is the westernmost border of the Port of Jossandra. We'll beach the boats here and return for them later. James, please help Reverend Dennis with the sailboat."

James responded, pulling on the prow. He noticed the sides of the boat were scorched, but there was no serious damage. His own curiosity settled on something Abigail had said earlier, and he looked at her inquisitively.

"What is it, James?"

"Why didn't Jana and Feruka stay to help you with your rescue?"

"They had their own work to accomplish, getting Rusty back safely to Angel's Lake. He couldn't very well navigate on his own."

"That's not very funny. He's . . . he was—," Rev. Dennis was interrupted.

"I know what you're thinking," she said with a radiant smile. "You are wrong."

Rachel appeared too busy fussing with Oxie to hear, but James and Dennis stared at Abigail with open mouths. James watched her bend over to pet a baby raccoon that came forward to nibble at her sandals, fluffing its black-ringed tail.

"He's no doubt having lunch this very moment at Angel's Lake," she continued, and then turned her attention to Oxie, who struggled to keep from falling. He tried to regain his land legs. James felt totally baffled.

"You have a pleasant hike ahead of you, Captain Oxford. Rachel, stay close to steady him if he needs it, but he is able to do just fine."

Oxie grinned his appreciation, and he surprised James by not breaking into his characteristic laugh.

Rev. Dennis had noticeably paled. He whispered to a confused James, "I know he was dead. Listen, really, I would never bury someone if . . . if . . ."

"There's so much more to these people than meets the eye," James whispered to Dennis. "We'll find out about Rusty soon enough." Secretly, James wondered what to believe, considering that Rev. Dennis had been under a great deal of strain, as had they all. A final verdict would have to wait.

Rolling hills and woodlands beckoned from the east, and the trail looked inviting. Abigail hoisted the water flask to her back and headed east by northeast with two firm words.

"Follow me."

CHAPTER
TWENTY-FIVE

From sense to Soul my pathway lies before me,
From mist and shadow into Truth's clear day;
The dawn of all things real is breaking o'er me,
My heart is singing: I have found the way.

-Violet Hay

The wiry man worked efficiently in the early morning light, carefully positioning a huge oak table on the south shore beach of Angel's Lake. A short distance from the mansion, two women helped him place chairs so that they all faced the lake, upon which the rays of the risen sun danced and sparkled.

"Now you know, too," Evelyn was saying to the man as she and Sylvia spread out an immense, green tablecloth with matching green napkins. "It's heaven on earth."

"Well, if it's not," said Rusty, who watched waves lap against the pure, white sand, "then it's sure the closest I've ever come. I wish my family could be here."

Sylvia smiled. "Abigail says that with the right kind of thinking, we can eliminate the frustrations of merely wishing for things."

"I suppose it might be possible," said Rusty. "Look, here comes the kid."

Jesse ran up with baskets of fruit, bread, and jam. "We heard James and Reverend Dennis and Captain Oxford upstairs. They're getting dressed," said Jesse. "Everyone's coming!" He was unable to conceal his excitement. "I'll go back for the milk and juice. And I can swim after breakfast. Look! Not a single cloud in the sky."

Soon the newly arrived guests began exchanging heartfelt greetings on the beach.

"Rusty! You old son of a sea cook! You had me plenty worried," said Captain Oxford. His laugh spilled forth without restraint. Rusty and Oxford embraced without further words between them.

James, Rev. Dennis, and Rachel mingled with the others, basking in the warm feelings of a restful reunion of good friends.

"I don't believe my eyes," said Rev. Dennis. "But I guess I shouldn't have believed them the last time I saw you, Rusty, when we parted company."

Rusty wiped an eye and regained his composure. "Listen, Reverend Dennis, we all make mistakes. If it makes you feel any better, I would have done the exact same thing you did. I mean, if our positions had been reversed. Now, let's all sit down to some breakfast, and we can talk about our adventures awhile."

"Okay! Everybody sit!" said Oxford, who sounded like he was giving orders aboard *Midnight*. "Jesse, get that stuff on the table, and then how about you say the prayer? That's right, unless you want to Reverend Dennis."

"Nope. Jesse, go ahead."

A hushed silence came over the grateful gathering of friends. Only the sound of gentle waves lapping on the beach and birds singing in the background disturbed the stillness. Then came Jesse's words, more deeply felt than when he'd learned them from Sylvia, and heard them spoken by Rev. Dennis, aboard *Midnight*:

"We thank thee, God, for these thy gifts of food and fellowship; Be in our midst to bless and strengthen us with thy spirit. Amen."

Everyone, even Oxford, added, "Amen." Then all of them were quiet. Finally, Evelyn rose, speaking with deep feeling, and said, "I am very pleased for my newfound health, for Rachel being able to talk again, for everyone back to Port safe and sound—and to be feeling whole again." As soon as she sat down, Sylvia got up to speak.

"I am so thankful to God for the Port of Jossandra and for a new sense of home and belonging." She also sat down.

From his chair at the end of the table, Rusty said, "I'm happy to be alive and among such good company and friends again."

"Hear, hear!" said Oxie, his voice booming like old times. "Me too!"

"And me," said James, rising to his feet. "We owe these people a debt of gratitude we can never repay."

"I would like to stay here and work to better understand your teaching and your ways," said Rev. Dennis, addressing Abigail, Feruka, and Jana, who once again came forth to serve their guests.

"I want to stay, too," said Rachel. Her radiant smile was rivaled by the three women hosts.

"Each of you are welcome, of course, to stay here as long as you wish," said Abigail. "Your words of gratitude this morning are most appropriate. We all rejoice with you. Let us give thanks to our Father-Mother, God, to Life itself." All nodded their agreement. Then no one seemed to have more to say, and everyone lapsed into reflective silence.

Finally, a request came from Jesse. "Please pass the biscuits and strawberry jam." Then the laughter and eating and conversation among friends began in earnest.

There were eggs, scrambled and fried; biscuits, toast, and lots of fresh butter; cow's and goat's milk, with three kinds of fruit juice. As the food began to disappear, Feruka and Jana reappeared with pancakes and homemade maple syrup. Honey, and more fresh fruit arrived, too.

Conversation was freely flowing, and the cares of the previous days and weeks could now be made light of, and they were. Rusty continued to be the center of attention, and he warmed to his fellow passengers as never before.

"I can't tell you what it means to me to be here with all of you today," he said, beaming. "I don't think I'll ever be afraid again, because I can now see there's more to this life than flesh and blood." He paused, and looked searchingly at the others. "My only concern is that if I keep talking I'll sound more like

Reverend Dennis than he does." Whatever tension might have existed was broken by torrents of the group's laughter.

Rev. Dennis raised his right hand and defended himself with a disarming grin. "It's all right. Let it out, folks. Rusty, you do the talking for a change. How did it happen?"

Everyone awaited a profound reply, but none was forthcoming. Rusty shrugged. "Listen, I remember the hike back here to the Port better than the rest."

"But," interrupted Rev. Dennis, "how did you get free of the rocks? You've at least got to tell me that."

"Not if he doesn't want to," said Jana.

"It's okay," said Rusty. "I saw you putting the rocks on top of my body, Dennis, but I wasn't in my flesh body. I was higher up, floating within or near a warm, bright light. After you'd gone, I don't know how long it was, I heard Blackie cawing away and then came these two women, Feruka and Jana. They got quiet, and then spoke directly to me. Before, Reverend Dennis couldn't hear me, so I felt real good when these two could speak to me. Does that make sense?"

"Yes, go on," said Rev. Dennis, all ears along with James and the other companions.

"That's about it. They freed my body from the rocks while I watched from above them, and then somehow I came back into my regular body again. They calmed me down, cleaned me up, gave me fresh water, and got me on my feet. We dragged that rowboat for a long ways—and I felt as good as I ever have—to this Lost Lake. Even my arm was okay. We met Abigail there briefly, but it was these two who brought me back here. That's really all I think I know for sure. Even though I admit I looked dead, I was thinking and feeling all the time, so I don't think I actually was dead. Oh, yeah—I guess I went back into my body because I have more to learn and to do in this world." He paused, as if reflecting on the import of what he had tried to put into words.

"Then last night I heard Oxie and all the rest of you coming in," said Rusty, "but I thought I'd wait until this morning, when everyone was rested, and I'm glad I did."

"So am I," said Rachel, brushing her dark hair out of her eyes. "That was wonderful, Rusty, and this is the loveliest picnic I have ever been on in my life. Although I don't think I've ever been to a breakfast picnic before."

James laughed. "Haven't you ever been camping? Bethany, my girlfriend, and I went camping last summer. Would I ever love to bring her here."

"That's just what I've been thinking about," said Rusty. "If this isn't the best place I've ever seen for a family vacation, I'd like to know what beats it. Evelyn, isn't that just what I was saying?"

"Yes, you were, and I agree. What about you, Captain Oxford? You travel up and down the river. What do you think?"

Oxie finished a mouthful of pancake, as Sylvia said, "This is the quietest the captain has ever been since I've known him, except when he was unconscious on the river. Are you certain you brought back the right man, James?"

Everyone laughed again.

"He slept through most of our rescue, so he can't be too tired," said James, giving Oxie a pat on the back.

"Okay. Okay. Let's not spoil the good eats by too much blabbing. Listen, this here place is all new to me. I mean it. Give me some time to get used to it. All I know is I should have come ashore a long time ago." He sighed, and went back to eating.

• • •

The following morning, James, Captain Oxford, and Rusty found themselves sailing upriver, bound for Riverton by way of Cool Water. Somehow everyone's plans had solidified. Oxie was the only one of the three to have part of his wishes immediately satisfied—once more he was the skipper of a sailing craft.

It only mattered slightly that it was Abigail's modest sailboat, still towing the old fishing boat, this time loaded with travel supplies. A small armada of Jossandrian vessels followed them, stretched out on either side, escorting the three companions through the beautiful valley at the start of their return voyage.

"Ain't it a pretty sight?" said Oxie. "And I got to admit, Abigail done me more good turns than one. I owe that woman, like James said at breakfast yesterday."

"We all owe her, and the rest of them, more than we can ever repay," said James again. "Things have really turned around for all of us. Last night I told Abigail about my drinking problem, and about a recurring dream I have of drinking at Riverton with Elf. Maybe Elf holds a key for finding Riverton and my getting things resolved. And I guess we'd all like to check on Turf, right Captain?"

"Right you are, lad. I don't think Elf's ever been to Riverton though. You're probably just having some screwy nightmares, like we all had back there in that awful crater where we almost got ourselves killed. Speaking of weird, I still don't exactly know how to get to this here town of yours myself."

"If we make Cool Water by dark like they say we can, I don't think Riverton's going to be that difficult to find. We simply back-track," said James. "I think I'll just feel the place in my gut when we get there."

"C'mon, Rusty," said the captain. "Sit down in your seat before you tip this thing over. I still ain't real checked out on sailboats, you know. Not that I can't sail anything that floats, boys, but I need a few more hours to get the hang of this baby."

Rusty sat down, looking somewhat foolish. The three friends shared a laugh, and James pointed to several figures along the shoreline.

"That's Rachel and Dennis. Wave Oxie! It's your last chance."

"Aw, shoot. We said our goodbyes last night. Rachel said flat out we'd get too choked up today. Darned if she ain't right, like usual."

James marveled at this new evidence of Oxie's inner feelings, which had been masked so well before Great Falls. Now the gruffness was gone. He was waving to Rachel like a little kid starting out for his first day of school.

James felt a twinge of something similar himself. Abigail had given her blessing for their departure, but the threesome left the Port of Jossandra with mixed emotions. Then finally, home and beautiful Bethany were all that James could think about, and fortunately Oxie's longing to sail again fit into the scheme of things.

Foremost for Oxie was the desire to build *Midnight II*. Although the Port of Jossandra provided sanctuary as well as lumber, James informed Oxie that Riverton could supply more expertise and skilled labor in barge-building. More than once James assured Oxie of this—provided the captain had the necessary funds. And Oxie said he had the insurance policy on the old barge to provide the money. There was even a policy Snyder had sold him, although he doubted its validity.

At quite some distance, James saw Rachel and Dennis embracing on the green shore, by the great pine trees, after all the waving was done. He half imagined they kissed, and with a bittersweet stab he found himself thinking, They might not make a bad couple!

Then the other boats were falling back, like so many butterflies in the sun. The three men grew quiet, having waved their last farewells. There remained too many memories, good and bad, to let go quickly. But for the most part, if one could judge by their conversation, they chose to dwell on the positive outcome of their adventures.

After some time had passed, James gathered that Rusty was enthusiastic about getting back into what he called the real world. The mission of James and Oxie provided him with that opportunity. Riverton sounded like his cup of tea, another opportunity to buy and sell. He craved necessary work and to earn his own money again. All his savings had been lost in the crash that destroyed *Midnight*.

"When we get to Backwater Bend, see here," said Oxie, looking at the map for the third time, "then we're on our own. That's what I like best, and it's sure going to beat that hell-raising trip we took down Devil's Canyon."

• • •

They arrived at Cool Water at sunset, their trip so far unmarred by negative incidents. All was going according to Abigail's charted map, which directed them only as far as Cool Water, but proved to be a model of accuracy.

"Hey, look at the seedlings," said Oxie in a booming voice. "Elf sure ain't been sitting and playing his fiddle all day."

"That's nothing," said Rusty. "Look at what Turf's been up to!"

It was a spectacle only half-appreciated from their docking point on the bank. Newly planted fields of tender corn shoots, grain, and other crops were already in evidence. As soon as they got ashore, the irrigation ditches—crude as they were—showed what had required days of labor.

"I can't figure out how they've done all this," said James.

Rusty's response was almost cryptic. "I figure," he said, "you don't reckon where we've been by just days and nights, or even weeks and months."

James smiled. "Then you've felt it, too? I never said a word, but I've sure had some odd feelings about the passage of time. Abigail never clarified any of that for me. Maybe if we'd stayed longer I'd have learned more about it. She just laughed her merry laugh and said spiritual reality has no time. Anyway, here comes Elf. Elf, how goes it?"

"Ah, lads, you're a fine sight for my weary eyes. This forest growing doesn't go like lightning." He paused, taking in the sailboat and fishing boat. His curiosity was as apparent as a child's.

"I'll go fetch Turf from his cultivating. We've got some comparing and telling of tales to do from the looks of it. You lost old *Midnight*, did you?"

• • •

Work precluded an immediate answer to Elf's question, but soon a campfire provided the five men with heat and light for their evening meal in the cool night air. Flapjacks, beans, and biscuits tasted good to James, but Elf had obviously wearied of such repetition as he shoved his plate away with a shudder.

"I'm not much for Turf's cooking, or even my own if I tell the truth," said Elf. "So, you plan to rebuild *Midnight* at Jamie's Riverton. When do you wish to depart?"

"In the morning, first light," said Oxie. "Abigail wanted to welcome both of you, by the way, to the Port of Jossandra. She wanted you told you're always welcome there. And like I said, they got forests and fields to your heart's content, for both you guys."

"I'm not leaving this new farm of mine for nothing," said Turf with a touch of defiance. "I've worked too hard to get all of this started," he added with a sweep of his work-toughened hands. "These fields are small yet, and the water ditches are rough around the edges, but I got good crops already pushing through my irrigated soil. And Elf has been a fine worker."

Elf briefly lit up with a smile, as if it was the very first praise for all of his work, and James thought, given Turf's nature, that was probably the case.

"You'd best stick here then and make us both some money, Turf," said Oxie. "At least till we come back on our return trip to the Port of Jossandra to visit Rachel on my new *Midnight II.*"

"Not till you finish your new barge? I don't think I could wait that long," said Elf. "I could come and build on that barge with you, and see the wooded hills around Jamie's town. Please, lads, I'm feeling like I need another change of scene."

"How do you know about the hills around my town? I've been wanting to ask you for a long time, Elf, if you've ever been there. Somehow I've been thinking lately we met before I ever got on Oxie's barge."

"I believe we did meet once before, Jamie, and perhaps we shared a drink or two. But you don't remember that, do you?"

"I knew it!" James saw at once that he had startled his companions by the intensity of his response. "Sorry, guys, but I've been working out whether some of my heavy drinking was in this world or another one." Elf's statement, which meant so much to James, seemed to have no meaning whatsoever for the others.

They had so many other things to talk about, and the tales went late into the night. Then it was unanimously agreed that Turf would hold the Cool Water fort, so to speak, at least until Oxie returned. And Elf was welcomed aboard the Riverton expedition as a guide of undetermined ability.

Sometime after midnight, James rolled up in his blanket gazing overhead at the distant stars. Now he had newfound hope that these same stars were shining on Bethany and his family in Riverton. He closed his tired eyes. Images from everywhere danced and paraded in his thought, but mostly there were remembered scenes of home and family and Bethany.

How I love them, he thought. They're precious.

It was something like Abigail had said to him about home being more than a place and special people. Love itself, perhaps, was the key to ending the waking nightmare that began with his heavy drinking and an encounter with Elf and his green death.

CHAPTER
TWENTY-SIX

The sober comfort, all the peace which springs
From the large aggregate of little things;
On these small cares of daughters, wife, or friend,
The almost sacred joys of home depend.

-Hannah More

As the companions were approaching what they thought to be the approximate location of Riverton, James felt certain he would begin to see familiar surroundings, but all he could see was the unfamiliar landscape of Oxford's world. Elf seemed to be of little help and in fact was getting as moody and restless as James himself.

In vain James searched for a friendly town, pasture, or woods, and for some unknown reason Elf was nipping at the green jug again. The thought of joining him in that activity was repulsive. Instead, he sipped water from the silver flask Abigail had provided for his long journey.

At nightfall they pushed on, for James insisted the lights from Riverton would guide them to their destination long before dawn. It didn't happen. They drifted, and the old fishing boat was taking on water. Finally, Elf was forced to move forward into Abigail's sailboat with Oxford and Rusty, while James stayed where he was, bailing river water from the rowboat.

"You're not keeping up with it, lad. Pitch some of them supplies. Like you say, we're almost there," said Oxie, with what sounded to James like strained optimism. However, he followed Oxie's suggestion. Elf lit a candle to aid him as supplies were pitched over the side, into the dark river. Soon James was finished with the task, keeping only his backpack and water flask, and he continued to bail water, but at a faster pace.

"Douse the light," Rusty said to Elf. "All you're doing is drawing bugs. Biggest damn mosquitoes I ever saw. You know something, I never saw one while we were at the Port of Jossandra."

"You ain't never seen this thick a fog, neither," said Oxie. "Fellas, I'm lowering the sail until we can get a better fix on where the heck we're at. That back eddy is carrying the boats forward, but real slow like."

"Can we beach for the night?" asked Rusty.

"Nope. Most times I come through here we slept aboard *Midnight*," said Oxie. "And James ain't about to give up. You ain't seen no sign of this here Riverton though, right?"

"What?"

"I said, you ain't seen no signs of your Riverton, have you?"

"Right."

They took turns dozing as they drifted. Towards dawn, Elf and Rusty were sleeping soundly, while James and Oxie had trouble staying awake themselves.

James struggled with something else he thought he'd heard Abigail say about everything being states and stages of consciousness. He thought she said that, and he wondered how it might apply to this mess. A sudden panic seized him as he moved forward in the leaking rowboat.

I've come loose from the sailboat!

"Oxie! Oxie!"

No answer. They were gone. Then he noticed light off to the left.

Stars?

James knelt and paddled with his hands, silently offering a prayer for help. The water seemed cooler, and his hopes began to rise despite having lost contact with his friends.

. . .

James beached the fishing boat in wet sand as the light of breaking dawn cast red fingers through the lingering night. He pulled the boat into a secure position, then fell back on his butt, trying to orient himself in the dripping fog.

He intended to doze for only a few moments, and then explore, but again found himself in a prayer to find Riverton and for the safety of his friends. He felt responsible for their pushing blindly through the night and thick fog.

If only we'd waited.

James rose up quickly to welcome the dawn and his heart beat faster. The shrouds of darkness had fallen away, and only the fog continued to obscure his sight.

He stumbled waist-deep into the water, lifting handful after handful to his face and body. He swam, daring the capricious river current to catch him. Then something indescribable prompted him to return to shore, and James wondered if he were hallucinating. He heard a woman's voice.

"James! Is that you?"

It's Bethany!

She stood by the battered fishing boat, looking slim and strong. Her thick hair was shining auburn in the morning sunlight.

She's so beautiful!

He approached her gingerly, partly for fear she would disappear, and partly because he felt like a disobedient schoolboy. She broke the tension and restored reality with a shower of kisses across his disbelieving face. He wept.

"Bethany? Tell me, dear God, that I'm not dreaming! Am I?"

"You darned fool! You big, darned, bearded, wonderful fool! I thought you might be, might be . . ."

They wept tears of joy together. There were countless kisses, until they collapsed on the sandy beach, laughing and hugging. As the fog lifted, James finally recognized the very swimming beach from which his long journey had begun.

At last she rose up and said, "Where the devil have you been, Jamie?"

"I was kidnapped."

"Who would do that?" said Bethany.

"My own stupidity. You were right, I was a darned fool. It's a long story, and I've been through hell, but at the end it's somehow worked itself out. There was a taste of heaven, too, and I truly feel like a new man. I just wish my friends were here to tell—"

"You mean your drinking friends?"

"No, of course not."

James then rambled through the events of his bizarre journey. He poured out words that tumbled over one another—strange places and names and people that defied verbal description.

Bethany was quiet for several minutes when he stopped for breath. James carefully studied the beautiful face he'd been so hungry to see again, while she studied him.

"I think something fantastic must have happened to you, Jamie, but it sounds too much like delirium for me to be positive." She made an attempt at an understanding smile. "I warned you something bad might happen to you one day, didn't I?"

"You do believe me, Bethany? You've got to."

"No, I don't have to, but I very much want to, Jamie. I've been coming here at first light every day for weeks, to where I found your shoes, and then today—"

"Weeks? How long have I been gone?"

"Saturday morning will mark six weeks."

"Six weeks!" James shook his head in disbelief. "Now it's my turn to try and believe you. What's today?"

"Why this is Thursday morning. As I was saying, Jamie, if you'll keep quiet and let me finish. I had the strongest feeling this morning. I prayed again, and sensed your presence, although I can't explain it, somewhere out there in the fog."

He took her by the hand, and they walked quickly along the familiar river path. "The people I sailed with might still be somewhere nearby." He stopped to embrace her again.

"Bethany, I absolutely know things are going to be different. I promise you that."

He'd dreamed and wished and prayed for this moment. She's so beautiful, he kept thinking. Bethany's easy litheness reminded him of Rachel, but Bethany had a unique, magical grace all her own.

"Sounds like a typical hangover to me," said Bethany.

"Never again! Not a single drop!" He said this with such force and conviction James hoped she believed him. He knew she wanted to. "No more hangovers—ever!" he added with emphasis.

"It sounds like maybe you've really learned something new, Jamie."

"I really did. Maybe you were scared half to death, but I was afraid I'd actually died, too. Really! It wasn't halfway, or dreaming, that I know. I thought I'd drunk this stuff of Elf's called green death and that I'd gone to hell and that it was some kind of living death, or a different universe altogether."

"Jamie, maybe we're both crazy, but I believe you. Somehow I do believe something bizarre happened, although the mind can play terrible tricks when it's drugged. One thing I don't understand is how in the world you've ended up at the same beach in the very same boat. Old man Smith is going to sue you, or charge you, for taking his fishing boat, I'll promise you that."

James laughed, shaking his head. "I prayed, Bethany. Honest-to-God prayer. And I prayed again this morning, just before you found me, just like you were praying, too."

"You have changed, Jamie."

They hurried along in silence, scanning the broad river. Their thoughts raced faster than their feet. At last they turned the bend in time to glimpse a small figure that climbed the north bank across the river, on its way towards the wooded hills. He appeared to turn and wave to them from that great distance, and then disappeared into the thick, green forest.

A single, black crow lifted from the willow tree behind them, cawing as it flew above the river. James wondered, Can it possibly be Elf headed into the wild bluffs with Blackie in pursuit?

"Go get him, Blackie!" said James. Bethany stared at him, and he tried to explain.

"Elf is supposed to stay and help Oxie build another barge. Blackie, see if you can turn him back!" But the crow just circled, cawing, and for a minute James could almost swear he heard Oxie's raucous laugh blend with his mascot's call.

A rifle shot rang out, seemingly from nowhere. The crow held position in the morning air, then rolled into a banked dive headed towards the water. Small pin feathers flew and drifted, and James screamed his incredulous outrage. The bird struggled to stay aloft.

"Pull up, boy! Blackie! Glide, baby, glide back this way!"

As though responding to his voice, the black crow came sailing in to land on Riverton's shore, collapsing in a tumble of feathers in a clump of dew-soaked, green grass. James and Bethany raced breathlessly to the place of impact.

"Blackie, I thought we'd lost you all on the river! Look what some town fool's gone and done to you." Tears coursed down his cheeks as he gently turned the fluttering bird over for a better look.

Bethany joined him, carefully examining the crow's injured right wing. "I can try to fix this, Jamie. Do you want to look some more for your friends after breakfast, while I patch up this creature? I think the bird will be okay."

They kissed again, and she felt wonderful in his arms. "I've sure got myself a marvelous gal," said James. "You're the best thing that's ever happened to me. With the possible exception of Abigail and the Port of Jossandra," he half-joked.

"I don't know who Abigail is," said Bethany with a radiant smile. "But with a big breakfast I'll coax it out of you, or your friends when you find them. I have heard of Jossandra though. She wrote that book I've been trying to get you to read. Remember, Jamie?"

James experienced an uncanny feeling, and it must have been the surprised expression on his face, he thought, that sent Bethany into peals of laughter. And somewhere, reverberating in his deeper thought, he also imagined Captain Oxford's high-pitched laugh blending with that of angelic Bethany's.

Made in the USA
Lexington, KY
19 February 2018